8/14

Once Upon
a Crime

Once Upon a Crime

An Anthology of Murder, Mayhem, and Suspense

edited by Gary Bush

and Chris Everheart

NODIN PRESS

Our special thanks to: Pat Everheart, Stacey Bush, Vince Flynn, Norton Stillman, John Toren and all the contributors to this anthology. Extra special thanks to our readers, booksellers and librarians everywhere.

ISBN 978-1-932472-71-4

Library of Congress Control Number: 2008925657

Nodin Press, LLC
530 N. Third Street, Suite 120
Minneapolis, MN 55401

To Gary Shultze and Pat Frovarp,
thanks for letting us into the basement.

Preface

Booksellers are the link between author and reader, the first fans and the best advocates of good fiction. So, when Gary Shulze, co-owner with Pat Frovarp of Once Upon a Crime bookstore in Minneapolis, began treatment for leukemia, we wanted to honor our favorite booksellers. What better way than a mystery & suspense anthology entitled *Once Upon A Crime?*

During Gary's treatment and recovery, the community of mystery, suspense and thriller authors they support banded together to highlight the incredible and irreplaceable contribution they've made to the lives of readers and authors in their community and around the nation. This book is an extension of that spirit, an opportunity for authors around the world to say thanks to Gary and Pat.

Yet in a larger sense, bookstores and libraries everywhere deserve praise. The folks who toil there do it for the love of books, just as Gary and Pat do in their store. Most importantly, there are the readers. You deserve to read stories from great writers, and we've collected a few here for you. So read, enjoy and support the booksellers and librarians of the world.

Gary Bush
Chris Everheart
August, 2009

Contents

Contents continued

Introduction

Vince Flynn

I first met Gary Shulze and Pat Frovarp in 1997 when I walked down the short flight of stairs and into their bookstore on West 26th Street in Minneapolis. Frustrated and dismayed by a publishing industry that wouldn't touch my first novel, TERM LIMITS, I had decided to self-publish and was looking for support from booksellers in my backyard. I didn't know what to expect, but I knew that I was hoping to find friendly faces in that tiny basement bookshop.

What I found in that little store full of mysteries and thrillers were two people whose love of books, readers, and authors. It broke all my hard-earned notions about the book world. Pat and Gary welcomed me, introduced me to other writers from the city and from around the country, and took a welcomed interest in my work. We struck up a friendship and a mutual admiration that endures today.

Through all the success I've enjoyed in publishing the last few years, I have never forgotten their kindness and their genuine interest in seeing me do well. Like so many other independent booksellers around the country, these are the people who work the hardest to connect us writers with their customers who become our loyal readers. I owe a debt of gratitude to Pat and Gary that I can't repay, but will honor for years to come.

When Chris Everheart and Gary Bush asked me to write the introduction to the *Once Upon A Crime* anthology, I readily agreed. What could be a better way to pay tribute to Pat and Gary at Once Upon a Crime Bookstore than to create an anthology named after their store?

It was no surprise that so many mystery authors, some who had never even visited the store, were willing to submit a story; a few of them, like Libby Fisher Hellmann, Gary Phillips, Ken Bruen and S. J. Rozan, demanded to be included. You, as the reader are in for a spectacular ride as you read the stories from the world's top mystery and suspense authors.

Michael Stanley's story of a Botswana police detective tracking down a murder suspect combines humor and true police work. Ken Bruen offers a chilling tale of a couple of hard guys going after a child killer. Gary Phillips delights with a story that is Runyonesque in tone, but set in a world not many white Americans are aware of. Anne Frasier's dark little Christmas present is not your usual holiday story. Libby Fischer Hellmann gives us a car thief who finds a surprise in the car he's lifted. S. J. Rozan's story lets you know why she's won the Edgar, Shamus, Anthony, Nero, and Macavity awards. And speaking of award winners, Reed Farrel Coleman's haunting Holocaust story should give you the shivers. C. J. Box's story will send you begging for more. Max Allan Collins and his wife Barbara collaborate on a story right out of *The Twilight Zone*.

Other award-winning authors include William Kent Krueger, Pete Hautman, Sujata Massey, David Housewright, Lois Greiman, and Mary Logue. Neil Anthony Smith's story is as dark as they come. Newcomer Maureen Fischer's story of childhood disappointment takes an unusual twist. Terri Persons story of revenge is a tragic tale, while Lori L. Lake's is a tale of cold revenge. Pat Dennis's story is black humor at its finest. Marilyn Victor delves into the underbelly of carnie life. I'd be remiss if I forgot the editors; Chris Everheart's hardworking P.I. and family man needs all his skills just to survive, and Gary Bush's P.I. satire will leave you laughing.

All the stories are a tribute to Pat and Gary and their wonderful little bookstore called Once Upon A Crime.

Read, enjoy and support your booksellers.

Perfectly Grimm: A Joe Pickett Story

C. J. Box

T HERE WAS A LONE fisherman down there in the small kidney-shaped mountain lake and something about him was wrong.

Wyoming Game Warden Joe Pickett reined to a stop on the summit and and let his horse and pack mule catch their breath from clambering up the mountainside. The late July sun was straight up in the sky—noon—and the only sound was the humming of insects in the wildflowers and the hard breathing of his animals. He shifted in the saddle and got his bearings. He was in the Sierra Madre Mountains of Southern Wyoming and from where he was, he could see into Colorado. The range ran south to north and he was squarely in the middle of it, 18 miles from the trailhead where he'd left his pickup and horse trailer with a local who for thirty dollars would shuttle his vehicle to the other side of the mountains and have it waiting for Joe with the keys hidden up under the front fender. This was day three in the new district he'd been temporarily assigned, and he was trying to get familiar with it, figure out the features and personality of the high country terrain. He'd seen elk, bighorn sheep, mule deer, antelope, bald eagles, empty camps and very few people. The sun was relentless and he welcomed the afternoon thunderstorms that lashed the pine trees and settled the dust and signaled him to stop, pitch his tent, and prepare for nightfall when the temperature would drop forty degrees.

He'd lost radio contact the day before, although prior to his receiver going dead there was a one-hour period in the morning where it would bark and yelp like a kicked puppy, spitting out fragments of inter-agency communication:

"...Couple found dead at the trailhead parking lot..."

"...All points bulletin..."

"...No suspects..."

"...Looks like a car break-in gone bad ... victims may have startled the robber as they came back from hiking the Encampment River Trail..."

No more than that.

He'd tried to raise someone on his satellite phone with no luck. He couldn't determine if it was the phone, the satellite, the batteries, or his own technical ineptness, but he couldn't get the unit to work. There was no way to learn more about the crime or call for help or backup. Being out of radio contact was not unusual in itself, and often he didn't mind it one bit. This time he did.

His imagination arranged and rearranged the sentence fragments to create scenarios, and none of them were good.

He squinted at the fisherman and a new narrative formed.

JOE RAISED his binoculars and focused in, trying to figure out what there was about the man that had struck him as discordant. Several things popped up. The first was although the hundreds of small mountain lakes in Sierra Madres had fish in them, the high country wasn't noted for great angling. Big trout were to be had in the low country, in the legendary blue-ribbon trout waters of the Encampment and North Platte Rivers. Up here, with its long violent winters and achingly short summers, the trout were stunted because the ice-off time was brief. Although today it was a beautiful day, the weather could turn within minutes. Snow was likely any month of the summer. So while hikers might catch a small trout or two for dinner along the trail, the area was not a destination fishing location worth two days hike to access.

Second, the fisherman wasn't dressed or equipped like a modern angler. The man—who at the distance looked very tall and rangy—was wading in filthy denim jeans, a shabby plaid shirt, and a white slouch hat pulled low over his eyes. No wad-ers, no fishing vest, no net. And no horse, tent, or camp, from what Joe could see.

He put away the glasses, clicked his tongue, and started down toward the lake. Leather creaked from his saddles, and horseshoes struck stones. His mule snorted. He was making plenty of noise, but the fisherman appeared not to have seen or heard him. Which, in a place as big and empty and lonely as this, was all wrong.

As he walked his animals down to the lake, Joe untied the leather thong that secured his shotgun in his saddle scabbard, and unbuckled the holster for his departmental .40 Glock semi-auto.

Fat-bodied marmots scattered across the rubble in front of him as he descended toward the lake. They took cover and peeked at him from the gray skree. What did they know that he didn't? Joe wondered.

"Hello," Joe called out as he approached the lake from the other side of the fisherman. "How's the fishing?"

His voice echoed around in the small basin until it dissipated.

"Excuse me, sir. I need to talk to you for a minute and check your fishing license and habitat stamp."

No response.

The fisherman cast, waited a moment for his lure to settle under the surface of the water, then reeled in. The man was a spin-fishing artist, and his lure flicked out like a snake's tongue. Cast. Pause. Reel. Cast. Pause. Reel.

Joe thought, either he's deaf and blind, or has an inhuman power of concentration, or he's ignoring me, pretending I'll just get spooked and give up and go away.

As a courtesy and also for his own protection, Joe never came at a hunter or fisherman head-on. He had learned to skirt them, to approach from an angle. Which he did now, walking his horse and mule around the shore, keeping the fisherman firmly in his peripheral vision. Out of sight from the fisherman, Joe let his right hand slip down along his thigh until it was inches from his shotgun.

Cast. Pause. Reel. Cast. Pause. Reel.

Interaction with others was different in the mountains than it was in town. Where two people may simply pass each other on the street with no more than a glance and a nod, in the wilderness people were drawn to each other the same way animals of the same species instinctively sought each other out. Information was exchanged—weather, trail conditions, hazards ahead. In Joe's experience when a man didn't want to talk something was up and it was rarely good. Joe was obviously a game warden in his red uniform shirt with the pronghorn antelope patch on his shoulder and his weathered gray Stetson. He knew that with each passing minute he and the fishermen were delving further and further into unknown and dangerous territory.

The tip of the fisherman's pole jerked down and the man deftly set the hook and reeled in a feisty twelve-inch rainbow trout. The sun danced off the colors of the trout's belly and back as the fisherman raised it from the water, worked the treble-hook lure out of its mouth, and studied it carefully, turning it over in his hands. Then he bent over and released the fish. He cast again, hooked up just as quickly, and reeled in a trout of the same size and color. After inspecting it, he bit it savagely behind its head to kill it. He spit the mouthful of meat into the water near his feet and slipped the fish into bulging wet fanny pack behind him. Joe looked at the pack—there were a lot of dead fish in it.

"Why did you release the first one and keep the second?" Joe asked. "They looked like the same fish."

The man grunted as if insulted, "Not up close, they didn't. The one I kept had a nick on it's tailfin. The one I threw back was perfect. The perfect ones go free." He spoke in a hard, flat nasal tone.

Joe was puzzled. It made no sense.

"How many imperfect fish do you have there?" Joe asked. He was now around the lake and behind and to the side of the fisherman. "The legal limit is ten. Too many to my mind, but that's the law. It looks like you may have more than that in possession."

The fisherman didn't cast out. He stood silently in the lake, his wide back to Joe. He seemed to be thinking, planning a move or a response. Joe felt the hairs rise on his forearms and on the back of his neck.

It was as if they were the only two humans on earth and something was bound to happen.

"I need to see your license," Joe said.

"Ain't got it on me," the man said, finally, still not turning around, "Might be in my bag."

Joe turned in the saddle and saw a weathered canvas day-pack hung from a broken branch on the side of a pine tree. He'd missed it earlier.

"Mind if I look in it?"

The fisherman shrugged.

"Is that a yes?"

"Yes."

Joe dismounted but never took his eyes off of the fisherman in the water. He led his horse over to the tree, tied her up, and took the bag down. There were very few items in it, and Joe rooted through them looking for a license. In the bag was a knife in a sheath, some string, matches, a box of crackers, a battered journal, an empty water bootle and half a Bible —Old Testament only. It looked as if the New Testament had been torn away.

"I don't see a license," Joe said, stealing a look at the journal while the fisherman kept his back to him. There were hundreds of short entries made in a tiny crimped hand. Joe read a few of them and noted the dates went back to March. He felt a shudder roll through him. Was it possible this man had been in the mountains for five months? A single name was repeated over and over in the entries: Camish.

"Don't be reading my work," the fisherman said.

On the inside cover of the Bible was an inscription: FOR CALEB GRIMM ON HIS 14TH BIRTHDAY FROM AUNT ELAINE.

"Are you Caleb Grimm?" Joe asked.

Pause. "Yup."

"Who is Camish," Joe asked. "I keep seeing that name in in this journal."

"I told you not to read it," Grimm said, angry.

"I was looking for your license," Joe said. "I can't find it. So who is Camish?"

Caleb Grimm sighed, "My brother."

"Where is he? Is he up here with you?"

"None of your business."

"You wrote that he was with you yesterday. It says, 'Camish went down and got some supplies. He ran into some trouble along the way.' What trouble?" Joe asked, his latest scenario hardening in his mind.

Caleb Grimm lowered his fishing rod and slowly turned around. Caleb had close-set dark eyes, a tiny pinched mouth glistening with fish blood and a stubbled chin sequined with scales, and a long thin nose sun-burned so badly that the skin was mottled gray and had peeled away revealing chalk-white bone. Joe's stomach clenched and he felt his toes curl in his boots.

"What trouble?" Joe repeated, trying to keep his voice strong.

"You can ask him yourself."

"He's at your camp?"

"I ain't in charge of his movements, but I think so."

"Where's your camp?"

Grimm chinned to the south but all Joe could see was a wood-studded slope that angled up nearly a thousand feet.

"Up there in the trees?" Joe asked.

"Over the top," the man said. "Down the other side and up and down another mountain."

Joe surveyed the terrain. He estimated the camp to be at least three miles the hard way. Three miles.

"Lead on," Joe said.

"What you gonna' do if I don't?"

Joe thought, there's not much I can do. He said, "We won't

even need to worry about that if you cooperate. You can show me your license, I can have a word with Camish, and if everything's on the level I'll be be on my way. I won't even ask you to show me how many fish you've got there in your bag."

Grimm appeared to be thinking it over although his hard dark eyes never blinked. He raised his rod and hooked the lure on an eyelet so it wouldn't swing around. After a moment, Grimm waded out of the lake. Joe could smell him approaching. Rancid—like rotten animal fat. Without a glance toward Joe, Grimm took the daypack and threw it over his shoulders and started up the mountain. Joe mounted up, breathed in a gulp of clean thin air, and clucked his mare to get her moving.

HALF-WAY UP, Joe prodded on his pack animals. They were laboring on the steep mountainside. Grimm wasn't. The man long-strided up the slope at a pace that was as determined as it was unnatural.

Joe said, "The Brothers Grimm?"

Caleb was obviously annoyed, said, "We prefer the Grimm Brothers."

Later, Joe asked, "Where are you boys from?"

No response.

"How long have you been up here? This is tough country."

Nothing.

"Why just the Old Testament?"

Dismissive grunt.

"What kind of trouble did Camish run into yesterday?"

Silence.

"The Brothers Grimm," Joe said again.

"We prefer the Grimm Brothers, damn you," Caleb spat.

Joe eased his shotgun out of the saddle scabbard, checked his loads, and slid it back in.

THEY WERE in dense timber now, his horse and mule detouring around downed logs while Grimm scrambled over them. Joe thought more than once Grimm was leading him into a trap or trying to lose him and he spurred on his mare harder than he wanted to, working her and not letting her rest, noting the lather creaming out from beneath the saddle and blanket. It was dark and featureless in the timber. Every few minutes Joe would twist in the saddle to look back, to try and find and note a landmark so he could find his way back out. But the lodgepole pine trees all looked the same and the canopy was so thick he couldn't see sky or the horizon.

"Sorry girl," he whispered to her, patting her wet neck, "it can't be much further."

Joe could smell the camp before he could see it. It smelled like rotten garbage and burnt flesh.

FOR A MOMENT, Joe thought he must be hallucinating. How could Caleb Grimm have made it into the camp so much before him that he'd had the time to sit on a log and cross his long legs and read the Bible and wait for him to arrive? Then he realized the man on the log was identical to Caleb in every way including his clothing, slouch hat, and deformed nose, and he was reading the missing half of the book he'd seen in Caleb's daypack earlier—the New Testament.

Caleb Grimm emerged from a stand of trees and tossed his daypack aside and sat down next to his brother. They were identical twins. Joe felt his palms go dry and his heart race.

"Why'd you bring him?" the brother—Joe assumed it was Camish—asked without looking up.

"I didn't," Caleb said. "He followed me."

"I thought we had an agreement about this sort of thing." His voice was nasally as well, but higher pitched. "You know what happened the last time you did this."

"That was different, Camish. I thought you'd like her."

"She was a filthy impure sow."

"I didn't know it at the time."

"You should have known. They're all like that—every damned one of them."

"Even Mom," Caleb said sadly.

"Especially her," Camish said.

They talked to each other as if Joe wasn't there. He tried

to swallow but his mouth was dry. The camp was a shambles. Clothing, wrappers, empty cans and food containers, bones, and bits of hide littered the ground. Their tent was a tiny Boy Scout pup tent and he could see two stained sleeping bags crumpled within it. He wondered how the two tall men managed to sleep there together—and why they'd want to. The bones meant the brothers were poachers because there were no open game seasons in the summer. Joe saw no weapons but assumed they were hidden away. He could arrest them for wanton destruction of game animals, hunting out of season and several other violations on the spot. And then what, he wondered?

"What are we going to do with him, then?" Camish asked Caleb, looking up from his book for the first time. "He can't stay here."

Caleb said, "I know."

"Boys," Joe said, wishing he were anywhere but where he was.

"Get rid of him," Camish said, "I want to take a nap."

"Hold it," Joe said, reaching down for his shotgun.

Without a second of hesitation, Caleb freed the treble-hook lure, whipped the rod back, and fired it through the air so quickly Joe couldn't duck and avoid it. It hit his upper lip and Caleb set the hook with a backward yank of the rod. Electric jolts of pain shot through Joe's face, freezing him in the saddle. Caleb jerked back hard on with his rod and Joe cried out from the pain and felt the barbs of the hooks pop through the flesh of his upper lip but hold fast. Camish moved with lightning speed, launched himself off the log at Joe and pulled him out of the saddle before Joe could pump and raise the shotgun. The game warden was slammed to the ground and he felt his weapon being wrenched away with incredible power.

The mare reared and whinnied and Joe rolled away from her hooves as they sliced back down but Camish stayed with him, clubbing at him with the butt of the shotgun, hitting his shoulders and arms. Caleb walked up reeling the rod, keeping the line tight so Joe couldn't escape. The pain in his face was so sharp Joe's eyes flooded with tears. He reached up and wrapped the line around his hand and pulled back but the line cut into the soft flesh of his palm and sizzled through his fingers as Caleb whipped his rod back to make it tight. Camish finally connected with the shotgun butt that smashed to his face and made him go limp as his eyes rolled up inside his head.

THE STARS were hard and white, pulsing. Their light hurt his head and stabbed him like a million needles. He rolled to his side and grunted. He lay there for a while, picking at the dried blood on his face, chipping it off like paint. They'd cut the line or it had broken but the treble-hook lure hung from his upper lip. He could feel the points of the hook and his entire mouth was swollen and oozing blood and pus.

Joe needed the stability of a trunk of a tree to stand. He swooned as he did, and nearly fell to the ground again. Finally, he was able to take a step, then another. He'd never had a headache so unrelenting, and he tried to see by the moon and starlight through slitted eyes.

He climbed hand-over-hand up the rocky slope where they'd thrown him. Bits of his torn clothing and skin still hung in the brambles from the fall. It took him most of the night to reach the top and when he did he threw himself over the lip of the draw and lay on his back in the bones and garbage of the empty camp, breathing hard. He dreamed of Marybeth and his daughters Sheridan and Lucy, and he was glad they didn't know what had happened to him.

HE EXPLORED what was left of the camp in the golden light of the dawn as the sun filtered through the canopy. He found a cache of elk, deer, and antelope skulls. A few feet away from the cache was a small adult human skull, likely a woman, probably the "filthy impure sow" Camish hadn't liked. There was a hole above the brow the size of a quarter. As Joe stared at it he vaguely remembered an unsuccessful search and rescue for a female hiker in Northern Colorado earlier in the year. She'd gotten into a fight with her companions and left them to walk out alone and was never seen again and her body was never found. He estimated that the location where she'd disappeared was about forty miles to the south, near Steamboat Springs. No doubt that is where Caleb had found her.

Buried under a log were items they'd either forgotten or simply chosen to do without—canned peaches, several novels, articles of clothing, a Palm PDA. He pushed the power button and saw it belonged to Trish Sproul of Boulder, Colorado. She had appointments scheduled for the next week so the Grimm Brothers had obtained it very recently. Joe put the Palm in his pocket. He was sure the PDA belonged to the victim found at the trailhead two days before, the one Camish had surprised while he looted her car for "supplies."

He found his smashed hat where Caleb had clubbed him. He punched the crown back out and clamped it on his head. He sat on the log and used the screen of the PDA for a mirror and clipped the barbs of the hook off. With a roar, he was able to pull the lure free. His eyes filled with tears and it took several moments of moaning and spitting fresh blood before he could stand up.

They'd taken his weapons, equipment, his horse and his mule. He followed their tracks until they turned north toward the jagged sawtooths of the Sierra Madre range. If the brothers stayed up there they could ride the spine of the Rocky Mountains for hundreds of miles before they even saw a road.

They had clubbed him unconscious with his own gun and left him for dead.

Big mistake.

AS HE TREKKED through the timber and at last found the trail that would eventually take him to his pickup and horse trailer, Joe pictured them in a new scenario. Caleb and Camish Grimm, severely damaged and dangerous identical twin brothers from who knows where, riding north on his animals, one brother with the Old Testament and one brother with the New, bickering, on a bloody quest for someone or something clean and pure, but finding that the only people who could satisfy them were themselves.

Merrick

Ken Bruen

Thomas Ryan –

I'd been a year in New York before I ran into Merrick. I'd left Ireland under the fooking proverbial cloud, though cloud is putting it mildly. I've been a Garda siochana.... translate as literally, Guardian of The Peace. Oh yeah. Stationed in Donegal, real close to bandit country, Peace Summit me arse.

The Boyos were still operating in Armagh and that was just a spit from where I was stationed. I was born and reared in Galway and so, I was stationed far from me home.

In jig time, I lost

Me wife

Me career

Me confidence

The scandal surrounding the local Guards and their framing of a local publican had blown up nationwide. Till then, I swear to god, The Guards had a fine rep. Liked by the general populace and how many countries does that occur in? Yeah, count em.

I wasn't great at me job but I liked it a lot. I was young enough then to think I might be effective. Dream on yah ejit. I know about the frame and Hands up, I wasn't actively involved but I did know about it and I did................nothing. That is what they call, silent affirmation.

See the learned vocabulary I have, been poring over the Reader's Digest in an attempt to increase me word power. The only word that describes what went down isn't in the digest—Clusterfuck.

The fall out was biblical. Top officers were up on charges but yeah, they'd get severe reprimands and be allowed to retire with their pensions intact. Us grunts got shafted, big time.

Fired and no pension. One of me mates hanged himself, couldn't take the shame. Me, I legged it to Amer-i-kay. New start.

Lived in a shitty hole in Brooklyn and got a job in construction. Hard graft. But it stopped me thinking and The Mick Mafia got me a Union card.

I was drinking—a lot. Out of self pity, loneliness and rage, the lethal Irish trinity.

I'm not going to suggest that meeting Merrick saved me but it sure changed me life. Thank fook.

I missed me wife, badly. I'd loved her. Oh sweet Jesus, did I ever. She dumped me when I got canned. She re-married a lawyer and has a child on the way. That shrives me heart. Still, and I guess, always will. Mores the frigging Irish-ed pity. Ah fookit.

Moving on. Not 'cos I wanted to but had to. One fierce cold Feb night, I was at a loss as usual and decided to go and sing some jars. Hadn't been out for brews for a time and I'd build up a thirst, headed for a bar in Brooklyn that had a jukebox, played the hit of the eighties. Sounded good.

There was a biting cold and a wind chill factor to freeze your nuts off. The bar was warm, with even a real fire, logs blazing and the place was hopping, Bowie in the juke with *All the Young dudes*. The bar man looked like a real dangerous bollix. Big, with a completely shaved head, arms on him that testified to real graft and he looked mean, he was wearing a T-shirt that read, "Gun Church."

I managed to grab a stool at the counter and he stood before me, wiping down the place in front of me, growled, "Get yah?" Sounded like a grizzly with a bad hangover, I said, "Jameson, Coors back."

He smiled, no warmth in it but a sort of knowing, said, "Mick huh?"

I nodded and he pushed. "You running a tab?"

"Sure."

He brought the drinks and I asked, "Get you one?'

He studied me for a minute then said, "Yeah, I'll join you." To my amazement, he put out a meaty hand, said, "I'm Merrick."

I was surprised, his tone was warmer, I took his grip, and we shook. He said

"Working hands, you on construction?'

"Yeah."

He raised his bottle of Sam Adams, no glass, said, "Mazeltov."

I said, "Slainte."

He leaned over, asked, "Run that by me again."

I did.

He savored the word, like he was tasting it then gave a nigh perfect rendition. He asked "You got a name or I have to like drag every piece of information outa you?'

I said, "Tommy, Tommy Ryan."

He laughed, said, "Well, you ain't Jewish, am I right?'

Before I could respond, he held up his bottle like a hurly, said, "Best warn you buddy, I am.......... so answer real slow."

"Some of me best mates are of that persuasion." Which was a lie but what the fook

It's one of those lines I've always loathed, like, *Gee, what a fookin liberal you are.* Christ on a bike. Lame.

He was massaging his neck, like it hurt, I asked, "That hurt?"

He was taken aback, as if he wasn't even aware he was doing it, said, "I play baskets, did my neck in, that damn S.J.... she gets me every time and Fusilli, never can quite out run him, so today, I got a cortisone shot and lemme tell you buddy, them suckers hurt."

Buddy?

I offered. "Buy you a jar?'

Took him a moment then he smiled. That smile took fifteen years off him, he looked almost like a nice guy. Almost. I didn't think smiling was something he did a whole lot of, he said, "a jar?'

"Yeah, oh sorry, it means a brew."

He reached for a bottle on the shelf, Wild Turkey, poured a shot with a practiced ease, said, "I'm not taking advantage, I'll charge you the price of a bud."

I said, "I got paid yesterday so never no mind."

He clinked my glass to his shot one, said, "L'chaim."

What can you say, I said it, "Back at you."

He let the turkey wield it's magic, said, "Way better than the goddamn cortisone and a damn sight faster."

I sunk my Jay, let it warm my gut. It did. Why I drink it. Without asking he grabbed the Jameson bottle, poured me a lethal dollop, and then looked at me, asked, "You ever in law enforcement?"

He was sharp. I'm Irish, we answer a question with another, keeps them off balance

Why do you ask that?"

He used the cloth to wipe up the spillage from my very full glass, said, "You've got cop eyes." Then added, "Reason I know is, every morning I shave, I see the same eyes."

My shot at a question. "Why'd you quit?"

He let out a long sigh, a sadness flitting across his face and then it was gone, he said,

"My partner got shot, he's in a wheelchair, I lost my taste for the job after that."

The bar got real busy after and I had a few more brews, a nice buzz building.

Thin Lizzy came on the juke box, followed by Rory Gallagher. U2. De Danann. I looked over at Merrick and he gave me the thumbs up. I was warming to the guy. I don't do friends. Not easily or often but this guy, he had some moves.

End of the evening, he was stacking chairs and a heavy guy who'd been acting the bollix all night swayed over towards Merrick, I could see the bottle held down by his side. I moved quickly, took his knees out from behind and for the hell of it, gave him a wallop on the upside of his dumb arse head.

Merrick whirled around, looked at the heap at his feet, saw the bottle and went,

"Phew, the fuck would have cracked my skull."

He gave me an appraising grin, said, "Guess I owe you one buddy."

I went American, badly I'll admit, said, "No biggie."

He laughed, asked, "You wanna go see The Jets choke yet again tomorrow evening, I have some tickets, the way they been playing, you couldn't give the damn things away."

I knew the Yankee's, and that was about it, said, "Sure."

That's how we became friends. He lived on Long Island and I met his wife, two great kids.

The Jets finally won a game and he bought a bottle of Jameson, said. "You and me bro, we're going to get shitfaced."

No argument there. Went to my hole in the wall in Brooklyn. He stared at the 1916 Proclamation on the wall, intoned the lines aloud, he had the perfect voice for it, I put The Pogues on my cheap music set and we got stuck into the Jay.

He looked round the sparse room, said, "Pretty basic buddy."

Got that right.

He was considering something, had been all evening, call it cop instinct and finally he got to it, said, "Time was, I used to work as a P.I.......Me and a buddy named Moe Prager, then I bought the bar and sort of drifted out of the business." He sipped the Jay then, "Moe got hurt a while back and asked me to follow up on a case he was on, a vile nasty piece of work…

He took a deep breath then produced a sheet of paper, handed it over, said, "This is a page from a … well, you'll see."

The very first line chilled me. *I kill children.*

"Fook," I said. Handed it back to him, my stomach in turmoil.

Merrick said, "I'm gonna go after this sick bastard and thing is, I wonder if you'd be willing to tag along?"

Looking back, how easy it would have been to say no, and Jesus, all the carnage that might have been averted.

I said, "Count me in."

Last Laugh

David Housewright

The old man kept repeating himself in different tones of voice and at different volumes, yet still he couldn't make the youngster understand him.

"It's my design," he said.

"It's not," the young man said.

The old man pointed at his photograph. "Look it," he said. "It's the same black marble. It's the same shape and size. It has the same drawing etched into the stone—a pastoral scene with a path leading to a cloud-draped sunset. Here's the plank fence, here's the maple tree; here's the two deer."

"Mr. Garber," the young man said. "I admit the tombstones are similar in appearance. However, if you look closely, you'll see that ours is ten percent larger. As for the etching, in our design we have a road leading to the horizon, not a path, and it follows a picket fence, not a plank fence. We incorporated a fir tree, not a maple, and as for the deer - you have a buck and a doe while we have a buck and a fawn."

"What about the inscription?" Garber said.

"All I seek, the heaven above and the road below me," the young man read. "It's a common slogan. Shakespeare, I believe."

"It's from Robert Louis Stevenson."

Garber felt his granddaughter's hand tighten on his forearm; saw the concern in her face. He had seen the look many times since his last doctor's appointment. He patted Johanna's hand and gave her a smile in return.

"I don't know why I'm upset," he said. "Put the gravestones side-by-side and anyone can see it's like comparing apples to apples."

"Sir," the young man said. "The Studders Monument

Company is not in the habit of pilfering designs. As I explained, our client Mr. Tinklenberg brought a sketch to us and requested that we duplicate it, and so we did…"

"He stole it from me," Garber said.

"Sir, if you believe your copyright has been infringed upon, you have every right to take legal action. I will refer your complaint to our legal department and we will let the courts sort it out."

"How long do you think that'll take? I'd be dead and buried before it went to trial."

The young man leaned back in his chair. "Certainly we would hope not," he said.

ONCE OUTSIDE, JOHANNA gave Garber an arm to lean on as they descended the concrete stairs leading to the mortuary's parking lot. Garber shrugged it off and took her hand, instead.

"Sugar, I'm not an invalid," he said.

"Grandpa, the doctors said - "

"The doctors said…"

Garber sighed like it was a subject he had tired of long ago. Still, he saw the anxiety in Johanna's eyes, so he grinned and rapped his chest with his fist just like Johnny Weissmuller did in all those *Tarzan* movies. It sent a sudden and unexpected shock of pain through his bones; he winced and coughed, and then added a brilliant smile and pretended to stagger so Johanna would think it was a joke.

"I've lived a lot of years," he said. "For the most part I've had a crackerjack of a time. The docs wanna inject me with their drugs and douse me with their radiation but what's that gonna get me? Another year at the most. A bad year. I'd rather take the three months and go out with a little style." He glanced about like he was suddenly afraid the cops were listening and his voice dropped a few octaves. "Especially, if you score some of that medicinal marijuana you promised me."

Johanna chuckled just as he hoped she would. Garber brought Johanna's hand to his lips and kissed her knuckle.

"In the meantime," he said, "I have to figure out what to do about Tinklenberg."

"Who is he?" Johanna said.

"Just a guy from the neighborhood. Vern Tinklenberg. He moved in when we were kids and he didn't know anybody. He wanted to fit in, so he started copying everything I did. I played ball, so he played ball. I played hockey, so he played hockey. I'd get in trouble at school and sure as hell, the next thing he'd be in trouble at school. It got to be a habit with him. I remember the morning after the Japs bombed Pearl Harbor, I was first in line to join the army; didn't even tell my mom until afterward. Vern heard about it so he enlisted the next day; yet he's talked it up ever since like he was the first in line. He'd tell stories about the war, too. Talk about things that happened to me, to others, like they happened to him. I was shelled on, mortared on, rained on, snowed on, strafed, machine-gunned, bombed, and shot at all the way from Normandy to the Rhine. Meanwhile, Vern was in San Antonio eating barbecue. Man didn't even get to Europe until April '45 and by then it was all over but the shouting. Only to hear Vern talk about it, you'd think he was George friggin' Patton and Audie Murphy rolled into one. Didn't stop there, neither. No sir. I'd see him around afterward and it was always how big is your house, mine is bigger; what car do you drive, mine is newer; how much money do you make, I make more; how many kids do you have, three? I got four. Now this. Pretty low, even for him."

"Why would he steal your tombstone?" Johanna said. "Why now? You don't think…?"

Johanna hesitated, frightened by the words that had formed in her head. Garber heard them even though they went unspoken.

"Sugar, only the good die young," he said. "Pricks like Vern Tinklenberg, they live forever. Although…"

Garber halted in the middle of the parking lot; Johanna was three steps past before she realized it and turned to face him.

"If he did die first, people would think I copied his crummy memorial instead of the other way 'round," Garber said.

"Course, if he died soon enough, I'd still have time to build a monument that would make his look like a tar-paper shack on a dirt road."

THEY BLOCKED OFF both ends of the avenue where Garber had grown up with huge sawhorses painted white with orange stripes. There was a sign from the city on the barricades—No Thru Traffic—and another from the neighborhood—Block Party 6-10:30 PM.

Garber sat with Johanna at one of the many picnic tables that had been dragged into the street. He had been drinking ice cold beer and eating flame-grilled chicken and corn-on-the-cob dipped in sweet butter and he thought, if this turned out to be his last meal, it wasn't too shabby. Johanna had tried to dissuade him from coming. She sensed her grandfather's excruciating pain even if he refused to acknowledge it. Yet Garber couldn't resist the chance to see the old neighborhood one last time and those few childhood friends that were still alive and kicking. Besides there was a band and Garber had always loved to dance. Granted, the band wasn't very good and mostly they played Golden Oldies that were nowhere near as aged as the songs that he considered golden, but he could dance to anything.

At first Johanna had refused to dance with him, insisting instead that he sit and rest. She stepped in only after watching Garber shake and shimmy and twist with the forty-year-old babe that was currently living next to the house where he grew up, and then with the thirty-year-old babe who now lived across the street - lately Garber considered nearly every woman he met to be a babe.

"You have moves," Garber told her.

"I inherited them from you," Johanna said.

"Nah, Sugar, you got 'em from your grandmother. My, how that woman could dance. Oww!"

It pleased Johanna that Garber was having fun. Yet at the same time, it distressed her to see him pressing his hand against the small of his back beneath his cotton sports jacket as if there was something there that required constant attention. He had become so old and so thin in just a few weeks. She held him close as the rock band slowed into *Fools Rush In (Where Angeles Fear To Tread)*, a 1940's ballad that Ricky Nelson turned into a Top 40 rock & roll hit twenty-five years later. Garber sang the words sweet and low into her ear. When he stopped abruptly, Johanna looked into his face, expecting the worst. Garber's eyes had narrowed, not with pain, but with anger. She followed his gaze across the makeshift dance floor to where the picnic tables had been set up. A man close to Garber's age was holding court, waving his arms as he told a story.

"Vern Tinklenberg," Garber said. "I knew he'd be here."

"I wish he hadn't come," Johanna said.

"You know what, Sugar? Me, too."

GARBER MOVED UP behind Tinklenberg and listened to him tell his tale. He knew the story well.

"They used to have ski jumping over at Como Park," Tinklenberg said. "This was back in the thirties, early forties. I remember this one time; a guy dared me to go down the jump. Double-dared me. You know how kids are. I couldn't back away from a double-dare. So I climbed the ramp with my toboggan—I had this long, wooden toboggan. I went down the jump, flew off the bottom. Suddenly, I'm airborne. Seemed like I was up there forever, holding on to the toboggan for dear life. It was actually kinda fun for about five seconds. Then I came down, hit the hill. Hard. Next thing I know, I'm spread-eagle over the hood of some guy's car, my toboggan smashed to bits, and the guy's asking if I'm all right. He wanted to take me to the hospital, only I'm more afraid of my mother than I was of being hurt. So I go home, make up a story about the toboggan getting run over by a car, never told my mother anything until three days later when they took me to the hospital cuz I had three broken ribs and one of them punctured my lung. I'll tell you, if I wasn't already in the hospital, that's where she would have put me."

Tinklenberg's audience laughed politely, Garber included. He moved out from behind him.

"That's a good story, Vern," Garber said. "Funny."

Tinklenberg seemed surprised to see his old friend. "Hi, Al," he said cautiously.

"'Cept it didn't happen to you," Garber said. "It happened to Bob Foley. I know cuz I was the one who double-dared him."

"What are you talking about, Al?"

Garber circled Tinklenberg, putting a worn wooden picnic table between them.

"You're a fraud," he said. "A phony. You've never done anything in your life worth talkin' about so you tell other people's stories, pretending they're all about you."

"That's B.S." Tinklenberg turned to his audience. "Al's always been jealous. Ever since we were kids. Cuz I was always better than him."

"Who are you kidding?" Garber said. "You've never been better than me at anything. Ever."

"I hit more home runs than you. I scored more goals, killed more Nazis, made more money; my wife was prettier."

"Lies, lies, lies. Is that how you wanna go out? Rowing across the River Styx in a boat of lies?" Garber found his granddaughter and smiled at her. "Like that, Sugar? River Styx?" He turned back to his adversary. "You were always second best, Vern. At least that's what your wife told me. You know what I'm talking about."

"You sonuvabitch," Tinklenberg said. "Ruth would never have had anything to do with you."

Garber held his hands away from his body, palms up.

"A gentleman never tells," he said.

He found Johanna again and gave her a wink and Johanna wondered if Garber really did sleep with Tinklenberg's wife or if he was just needling him.

"You're a liar," Tinklenberg shouted.

"I'm a liar? Look up the word in the dictionary, pal, and there's your photo, both front and profile like the way the cops take 'em."

Tinklenberg made a move as if he was about to go over the picnic table for Garber. But Garber calmly held his ground. He reached behind him underneath the sports jacket and produced a gun. There was a collected gasp from the neighbors who had gathered round to watch the confrontation; more than one reached for a cell phone. Garber held up the gun for everyone to see.

"Know what this is?" he said.

"It's a Luger," Tinklenberg said.

"That's what we call it. The Krauts call it *Pistolen-08.*"

"Big deal. I have one just like it."

"Except I took mine off a German officer at the Remagen Bridge. You paid fifty bucks for yours in London."

"I got mine off a prisoner."

"You bought it from Jack Finnegan. He told me." Garber smiled some more. "Second best again, Vern."

He leveled the gun on Tinklenberg's chest.

"Grandpa," Johanna called.

Garber waved her away with his free hand.

"Sugar, please," he said. "I'm trying to make a point."

"Don't, Al, please, you can't," Tinklenberg said. "You can't —please—don't shoot me."

"Why not? I won't live long enough to go to trial for it, much less prison."

"Al."

"You stole my tombstone, Vern. Did you think I wouldn't find out? You stole it just like you've stolen my stories and took them for your own, stories about my life and the lives of a lot of other men better than you. Well, why not? Why not steal my tombstone? Your whole life you've been chasing after me - hell, you haven't had a life. You've been too busy living mine. Didn't do nearly as good a job, either. Take the tombstone. What do you think, people are going to point at it and say 'Tinklenberg, what a man, his monument is ten percent bigger than Al Garber's?' That ain't gonna happen. You know what's gonna happen? They're going to point and say, 'It's bigger than Al's monument, but not nearly as good. It's second best.' Just like the life you've lived."

Garber thumbed back the hammer on the Pistolen-08 and

extended his arm.

"No, Al." Tinklenberg brought both his hands up to defend his face. He screamed. "No."

Several neighbors joined in.

"No."

Garber squeezed the trigger.

Click.

There was a moment of perfect silence while dozens of ears strained to hear the sharp snap of a gunshot. When it didn't come, the silence slowly filled with the distant sound of a police siren coming closer, the shouts of neighbors, and with Garber's loud, unrestrained laughter.

"Oh, you should see your face," he said.

Tinklenberg's eyes were wet with tears; a stain spread along his pants from his crotch and down his leg. He cursed Garber but there was no energy in it.

"Hey, I just did you a favor, Vern. Now you have a story to tell that really is your own."

Garber found his granddaughter and smiled.

"Remember, Sugar," he said. "Tombstones, they don't matter all that much. I mean, who gives a crap, really? What matters, is that you live well and have a little fun. Otherwise, what's the point?"

He laughed some more. Laughed as he dropped the unloaded Pistolen-08 into his pocket. Laughed as he made his way back to the dance floor. With a little luck, he figured he could get in a few more dances before it was time to go.

An Issue of Women and Money

Michael Stanley

This one is over a woman, Kubu thought, watching the silent faces around the body.

Whenever Kubu visited his parents and mentioned a case, his mother invariably had a strong opinion. "Remember, David," she would lecture her son, a senior detective in the Botswana police Criminal Investigation Department, "murders are usually over women or money. That is what you need to look for." Kubu had learned not to argue with his mother. "I'm sure you are right as usual, Mother," he would say politely. "May I have another cup of tea? And, perhaps, another biscuit?"

The onlookers kept their distance, perhaps because of the officious constable, or perhaps they awaited action from the senior policeman. Joshua Madi was dead, lying on his back in the street with his fashionable clothes scuffed and torn, blood all over his face, and a knife sticking out of his chest. What would the policeman make of that?

Kubu was not happy. He had just sat down to a stew of young goat prepared with care and fine herbs by his wife, Joy. A bottle of South African shiraz, slightly chilled against the heat of the Botswana summer, was breathing—but not for long, because Kubu joked that the best way to get a wine to breathe was with mouth-to-mouth resuscitation. Now his dinner dried in the oven, and the wine warmed, while he looked down at the unattractive remains of Joshua Madi.

"Where's the pathologist?" he asked the constable, watching the silent crowd.

"He hasn't arrived yet, Assistant Superintendent." The young man was at attention.

"Relax, constable." Kubu sighed. "We may have a long night ahead of us. We'll need to talk to all these witnesses. Get their names."

As though this were a signal, the onlookers all started to speak at once. Kubu held up a hand. "All of your stories will be heard," he told them in Setswana. "All in good time. Thank you." Turning back to the constable he asked, "Where's the culprit?"

"He's in the car with Detective Tau."

Kubu nodded. Going over to the police car, he opened the driver's door, indicated to Tau that he should move to the back, and heaved himself into the seat. He jerked the seat to its most backward position to allow his substantial body to squeeze into the small vehicle. This elicited a yelp from Constable Tau, who had injudiciously chosen to sit behind Kubu rather than behind the prisoner. As he rubbed his bruised knee, Tau speculated on how well the nickname Kubu—Setswana for hippopotamus—fit the large detective, though he would never dare say so.

The remains of a take-away that had been Tau's dinner were now scattered by Kubu's battle with the seat, and the car smelled of fried chicken. Kubu tried to ignore it—it only sharpened his hunger—and concentrated on the man next to him. He, too, completely filled the car seat. A bull of a man, all muscle. His shirt was torn and bloody—whose blood?—and he sported a black eye. The fight had not been entirely one-sided. Kubu nodded. The loser of a fistfight might well resort to upping the stakes.

Kubu addressed the suspect in Setswana. "What is your name?"

"Peter Moroka, Rra."

"Now, Peter, did you kill that other man in the fight?" Kubu held his breath. A quick confession of a punch-up that got out of hand, and the matter could be wrapped up in the morning. Perhaps the goat would still be tender and succulent when he got home. The wine would certainly be fine. His mouth watered.

"No, Rra."

Kubu's heart sank. "Tell me what happened then."

"That man—Madi—he's a pig. He gets money and drink, and he goes looking for a woman." Moroka shrugged indicating that this was a natural way for a Motswana man to behave. "But he looks for someone else's woman! Why does he do that? There are lots of women. Why does he go for my woman?"

Kubu assumed this was rhetorical and nodded sympathetically, encouraging Moroka to embellish his motive.

"I found them together in the shebeen—the bar. He was giving her drink. He had his hand on her leg." He shook his head angrily. "He had it high up her leg! Under her dress!"

"So what did you do?"

"I grabbed the bastard and made him come outside. You don't fight in Mma Toteng's shebeen." He shook his head again. Everyone was scared of the bar owner. Some people said she was a witchdoctor. Moroka didn't believe that, but why take a chance? "He'd already finished several beers. He thought he could fight me. Me!" Moroka made a fist that would shame no man, although it didn't impress Kubu. "So he came with me! Fool!"

"And then?"

"Then I beat the shit out of the bastard!"

"What about your eye?"

"Lucky punch. I was careless. Bastard!"

"Is that when you thought he deserved to be cut a bit? Teach him a lesson?"

Moroka looked very solemn and shook his head. "I don't have a knife. I don't need a knife. A man fights with these." He showed his fists again.

Suddenly there was banging on the car window. A large woman, her head covered in a brightly colored scarf, glared at Kubu. "When will you get this body out of here, hey?" she shouted. "You think I have all night? You think I don't work? That people don't need to drink?"

Kubu sighed and climbed out of the car. "And who are you?" he asked the woman. She had an appealing figure in a generous way and wore a traditional Tswana dress in browns and oranges. A necklace of beads, stones and purple seedpods hung round her neck. Heavy frown lines marred an otherwise open face and belied the generosity of her figure.

"Gracious Toteng. I own the shebeen. What are you going to do with him?" She nodded towards the police car.

Kubu ignored that. "Can you tell me what happened?"

"Moroka came into the bar and found Madi all over his girl, Bongi. She works for me in the bar. He was very angry and told Madi to come outside." She shrugged. "Madi did, the fool."

Kubu wanted more details, but he spotted Ian MacGregor, the police pathologist, examining the body. He headed over to him, dismissing Toteng with a nod.

"Ian! What have you got to tell me?"

"Kubu! They called you out at dinnertime?" The wiry Scot smiled at Kubu's sour look. "Not much as yet. You can see for yourself the cause of death—stabbed in the heart. But there may be several wounds. Not a professional job, obviously."

Kubu grunted. "Stabbed in the fight? Apparently he had a fist fight with the man we're holding."

Ian examined the dead man's knuckles. "Yes, looks like he landed a few good blows." He stood up, looking puzzled. "Not the way you defend yourself against a knife attack though. You would expect gashes on the arms from trying to fend off the attacker. Tell you what, let's get this chap to the morgue and take a proper look at what's under these clothes. I'll get back to you tomorrow. Forensics should be able to pick up fingerprints on the knife, too."

Kubu turned away. There was no option; he'd better start questioning the witnesses. Back to Mma Toteng, he thought without enthusiasm.

The director of the Criminal Investigation Department looked out at Kgale Hill, which overlooked the CID offices in Gaborone. A rumpus of baboons was crashing through the trees, quarreling over marula fruit, and barking loudly. One of the youngsters misjudged a jump, missed the intended branch, and crashed into the lower foliage of the acacia thorn tree with screeches of hurt pride. Director Mabaku laughed. Sometimes he liked the baboons more than people. He turned back to Assistant Superintendent Bengu.

"Kubu, what's the delay here? This man—Moroka?—has a fight with Madi. They've both had a few drinks, it gets out of hand, and one pulls a knife. Charge him with manslaughter."

Kubu hesitated. "Director, there are some very odd aspects to this fight. Moroka denied having a knife, so I thought I'd catch him in a lie. The knife was quite distinctive. Detective Tau traced it to a shop on the Mall. It turns out it was bought there. But not by Moroka. It was bought by Madi."

"So? You say Moroka is a big chap. Probably Madi felt he was losing and pulled the knife. Moroka took it away from him."

"Well, that's possible but it raises more questions. Why did Moroka deny it? He could claim self-defense. And at the autopsy MacGregor found two wounds on the chest at the wrong angle to go between the ribs into the heart. Certainly Madi wasn't fending off the knife with his arms. It was razor sharp, and there were no cuts anywhere except the chest wounds. Also there were no fingerprints on the knife. It'd been wiped clean."

Mabaku chewed his knuckles, watching the baboons move back up the hill to their rocky strongholds. "Perhaps he knocked Madi out and then stabbed him. That would make it murder, of course. But you'll never prove it."

"Well, Ian noted a huge bruise on the side of Madi's head. It certainly could have been a punch that knocked him cold." Kubu looked dissatisfied. "But why stab him? Why not just break his neck? Something that could look like an accident. Stab him with his own knife, leave it in the wound and wipe it clean? Makes no sense."

Mabaku lost patience. "Kubu, we expect people to do stupid things. That's how we catch them. It probably made sense to Moroka at the time."

"There's something else. We interviewed the witnesses, and they agree with the shebeen-owner's description of what happened. But there was much talk of Madi having a big win at the casino. Apparently, he gambled for high stakes. He came straight from the casino and was buying drinks all over the bar. Boasting how clever he was. Telling Moroka's girlfriend how rich he was. Bought her champagne. Well, sparkling wine, really."

"So what?"

"Well, neither Moroka nor Madi had much money on them. Just a few hundred pula."

"Maybe the whole thing was made up to impress the girl."

Kubu shook his head. "The casino confirmed his big win that night. More than twenty thousand pula."

Mabaku whistled. That was a lot of money. Enough for a motive for murder. Why was Kubu always involved in simple cases that became complicated? He threw himself into his chair and thumped his desk with his fist. "All right, Kubu. Keep snooping around on this one."

Kubu smiled, nodded, and left before his boss changed his mind.

◆ ◆ ◆

KUBU FOLLOWED up with Ian MacGregor. The Scot was sitting at his desk, gazing at one of the watercolors he had painted and sucking with gusto on a heavy briar. The tobacco was carefully pressed down; all was ready bar the flame. Ian had given up smoking twenty years earlier.

"Kubu! What can I do for the CID this afternoon? A new body perhaps?"

"Don't get excited, Ian. Nothing like that. I just wanted to go over the Madi case with you."

"Well, I did get more information from forensics. Madi had some fibers in his right hand. Forensics identified them as some sort of dry plant material. Impossible to identify the type, but hardly what you'd expect to find at a casino. And then there was that stuff on his chest."

"What stuff?"

"Some sort of oily material painted criss-cross on his skin.

I guessed it was some sort of potion. Forensics produced an analysis of it, but I'm none the wiser. You'd best consult a witch-doctor!"

Ian had meant it as a joke, but Kubu took it up. While tracing Madi's movements, the police had discovered that he had visited a well-known witchdoctor by the name of Msizi. Kubu was intrigued. First Madi bought a knife, then, no doubt, obtained supernatural help against his opponent. It seemed he was looking for a fight, either with Moroka or with someone else. Kubu decided he should pay Rra Msizi a visit.

Kubu found the witchdoctor sitting at a small table surrounded by an arcane collection of roots, herbs and curiously marked boxes. The grayness of age touched his hair and scraggy beard, but active eyes took in Kubu's size and appraised the quality of his clothes. "What exactly is the problem, Rra?"

Kubu handed over his identification. The witchdoctor stiffened. Much of his business fell close to the line of illegality. "What can I do to help the police," he asked blandly. Without doubt it would be very little.

"Rra Msizi, I wish to hear about one of your…er…patients. Rra Madi."

Msizi handed the identification back. "You must understand, assistant superintendent, that my relationship with patients is confidential."

"Madi is dead. Stabbed. Murdered. I am here to discover if his visit to you was at all related to his death."

The witchdoctor looked shocked. "I will try to help."

"What did Madi want here?"

"It was a woman problem. Most men have problems with money or with women. This was a woman problem."

"A physical problem?"

"No. As far as I know, Madi could sow the mielies. He was in love with a girl who belonged to a bully. So he asked me to help with that. And to encourage the girl's affections for him."

"What did you do?"

The witchdoctor shrugged. "I prescribed a medicine. Something to build confidence and power. That's what was needed."

"How was this medicine applied?"

"Some swallowed, some painted." He gave Kubu a hard look, and added ambiguously, "That is my business."

Kubu had heard enough. Madi had walked out of this office believing himself invincible. And with a razor-sharp hunting knife for insurance. Kubu came up with another question, a typical Kubu question that seemed to come from nowhere but led somewhere.

"Who referred Madi to you, Rra Msizi?"

Msizi looked surprised. "A mutual friend. A colleague in a way. She works sometimes with herbs. Her name is Gracious Toteng."

"Thank you, Rra Msizi. You have been most helpful," said Kubu politely. He didn't believe in the power of witchdoctors, of course, but why annoy one unnecessarily? And the last answer had been very helpful indeed.

◆◆◆

KUBU MADE HIS way to the shebeen. It was on the outskirts of the city, and in the daylight he saw that the area was run down. The bar itself looked well-maintained, although it could use some paint, but the roads were dirt and needed repair. Chickens clucked and fed along the verges. Small houses crowded around. Kubu thought of his own neat house in a better part of town, with its pleasant garden of native plants from his beloved Kalahari. Perhaps Madi's big gambling win was a ladder to a better area and new friends.

He found Toteng in the storeroom behind the bar. She greeted him without enthusiasm.

"Assistant superintendent. What do you want? I'm busy."

Kubu sighed. Her demeanor had not improved in the two days since the murder. Yes, he thought, murder. Not manslaughter. He looked around, deliberately taking his time before he answered. Toteng was working at a table stacked with papers. Cartons of various types of liquor were piled behind her. The opposite wall had a wide door with a heavy security grille on the inside. Kubu realized that it would lead to the alley where

Madi had been killed.

"Is that door always locked?"

Toteng looked at him sharply. "Unless we have a delivery or some other reason to go out the back way."

"Was it open when Madi was killed?"

"No."

Kubu was sure she was lying. "And since then?"

"No."

Kubu collapsed into a plastic chair similar to Mma Toteng's seat. It squealed and bulged warningly. "Why did you send Madi to the witchdoctor?"

Toteng looked surprised. "He was my friend and asked for help with his problem with Moroka and Bongi. I suggested Rra Msize. So what?"

"But you tipped off Moroka when Madi was fondling Bongi."

Toteng shrugged. "Moroka is also my friend. Madi had no right to do that here. In my shebeen. In front of my customers. And flaunting his money."

"Tell me exactly what you did the night of the murder after Madi and Moroka went outside."

"I've told you all that already! You're wasting my time!"

"Tell me again."

Toteng looked as though she would refuse, but saw no way of shifting Kubu's bulk. "Very well. I was helping the customers. They all saw me. Then Moroka came back in and started boasting about beating up Madi. What a superman he was. He was disgusting. I came back here with Bongi to get some more cold beers, and we carried them into the bar. Moroka was buying everyone drinks as though he had lots of money. He was probably just trying to match Madi. Celebrating just after he'd killed him. Pig!"

"Were you and Bongi together the whole time?"

"Yes. She was upset so I kept her with me. Also, I needed her to help me with the beers."

"How long were you back here?"

"Five or ten minutes."

Kubu mulled this over. Five minutes was plenty of time to go through the side door, stab Madi, and get back with the beer. But Toteng's story agreed perfectly with what Bongi had said when he had interviewed her. Too perfectly? Could they have done it together? If so, why? The money was a powerful motive if Madi had it with him. Or was there something else? When women murdered, Kubu wondered, was it always over money or men? He made a mental note to ask his mother.

He wandered around the room, looking behind the stacks of boxes and inside the chest freezer. He started humming a theme from *The Pearl Fishers*, partly because he liked it and partly because he thought it would irritate Toteng.

"Do you have a search warrant?"

"I'm not searching," said Kubu blandly. "Just looking around." He went back to humming Bizet. He then came to the security door. Its lock panel covered the knob of the outer door, protecting it from handling. He turned his back on the bar owner and used his cell phone to call the CID. Finishing, he turned back to Toteng. "I'm getting someone here from forensics. To check this door." He looked at his watch, which agreed with his stomach about it being lunchtime. But he wasn't moving until the fingerprint person arrived. "Do you serve food?" he asked the shebeen owner.

◆◆◆

KUBU'S FISHING expedition turned up a queer fish. One clear print of Bongi's right hand on the inside door-handle and nothing at all on the outside handle. Toteng volunteered that she had cleaned the handles after a grubby delivery man had brought beer the Wednesday before Madi had been killed. No one had touched it since. She had no idea how Bongi's prints came to be on the inside handle. Kubu made a note to trace that delivery man. In the meanwhile, he wanted some straight-talk from the young lady herself.

Seated in the interrogation room, Bongi looked very nervous. Kubu wasn't unhappy about that, and cautioned her as if she was about to be charged. He then went through each step of her story again. At last he leaned back and asked: "If you were always with Mma Toteng, never alone, why did you go out from the storeroom into the alley where Madi was killed?" When she started to protest, he stopped her and told her about the prints on the door handle. "This is what I think happened. You knew about Madi's money and his knife. When you heard that Moroka had knocked him out, you saw your chance, slipped through the back door, took his knife, stabbed him, and stole his money. You were content to let Moroka rot in jail for the killing. You are a dreadful woman! But you will spend a very long time in jail for your awful crime!"

Bongi shrank into her chair. She started gabbling, denying everything, contradicting herself, confused about the money and the knife. After a few minutes Kubu relented, calmed her down, and told her to tell her story from the beginning.

"Madi came into the bar and was all over me. I'm supposed to be working! Mma Toteng gets cross! But he bought us champagne and promised to pay her for my time. She seemed okay with that and left us alone. But a few minutes later she came back and said that Moroka was on his way, and he was drunk and angry, and Madi should run away. Madi was very cross. Said he would fight Moroka for me and win. He had medicine from the best witchdoctor in Gaborone which made him impossible to beat! Mma Toteng looked very unhappy and pulled me aside. She was afraid Madi had a knife, and that one of them would be killed. I was to take the knife from his pocket and give it to her. Afterwards she would say she found it on the floor. She also told me to suggest that he leave his money with her for safekeeping during the fight. And he did that. So when Moroka came he was ready. That's when I took the knife from him and gave it to Mma Toteng.

"Ten minutes later Moroka came back, boasting and kissing me. But then Mma Toteng called me to the back room. She was very worried. Was Madi all right? She still had all the money—ten thousand pula, she had counted it—but someone had taken the knife. It had been on the table in the storeroom, and now it was gone! She told me to go to look for Madi, and she unlocked the back door. I was worried and started to go, but just as I was walking out she pulled me back. What if Moroka came looking for me? Better I stay in the room and she would go. So I stayed, and she went out."

"Did you open the outside door?"

"I think so. But then she pulled me back."

"Was the door still open?"

"I suppose so."

"All right. Go on."

"Mma Toteng was back after only a few minutes. She said someone had stabbed Madi! He was dead! We were very frightened. We decided to let someone else find Madi's body."

"Why were you scared?"

"We were the only ones who knew about the knife! Maybe the murderer would want to stop us talking. It was best to stick together and say nothing."

"And the money?"

"Oh yes. The money." She hesitated.

"What happened to the money?"

"We split it. It wasn't like stealing! Madi didn't need it anymore. He isn't married or anything." She looked at the floor. "Anyway, he said he was going to give it to me," she improvised.

"Where is your share now?"

"I have it with me."

"You must give it to the police. Right now."

To Kubu's embarrassment, she unbuttoned the top of her dress, fished in each side of her bra, and dumped warm pula notes on the desk. When she buttoned up her dress, there was a noticeable decrease in her bust size.

◆◆◆

Detective Tau might have enjoyed the handing over of the loot, but he was at The Happy Drinker Liquor Company which supplied drink of the non-homemade variety to Mma Toteng. He easily found the man who did the deliveries. The man also took the orders, loaded the van and seemed to handle most other aspects of the business. He needed a good memory, and Tau was pleased to find that he had one.

"Yes, I did a delivery for Mma Toteng on Wednesday. She needed beer and some spirits. A case each of brandy, whiskey, vodka and gin. We were a bit short of brandy on Wednesday, so I took over a case on the Friday. Left it on the bar with Bongi because I found the delivery entrance locked, and Mma Toteng wasn't around to open it."

Detective Tau wrote it all down carefully. He was very proud to be working with the Assistant Superintendent and didn't want to miss anything.

Meanwhile Kubu was pondering Bongi's story. It neatly explained some issues, and overall it seemed so unlikely that it could hardly be invented. But was Bongi really dumb enough to fall for a story about some mysterious murderer stealing the knife from in front of their noses? The obvious deduction —surely even to Bongi—was that Toteng herself was the murderer. And where was the rest of the money? Hidden elsewhere on Bongi's body? It all seemed very far-fetched.

Mma Toteng was next. She was a tougher nut than Bongi, but when she heard that Bongi had changed her story, she cracked too.

"I knew nothing about Madi having a knife. I didn't take it from Bongi or Madi. The first time I saw it, it was sticking out of Madi's chest!" She offered a theatrical shudder. "Madi did give me his money for safekeeping. I would've given it back to him too, if he'd asked, every thebe of the ten thousand pula. But he wasn't going to need it anymore, was he? So I split it with Bongi. After all, we were his friends." Kubu indicated that Mma Toteng would need to return the money as soon as possible, half fearing another striptease. But she just nodded, saying that her share—five thousand pula—was safely locked away at the shebeen.

"When did you split the money?"

"After Bongi came back and told me Madi had been stabbed."

"She went out to look for him?"

Toteng nodded. "I sent her to see how he was. I unlocked the back door and she went out that way so that Moroka wouldn't see her. I waited in the storeroom in case he came looking for her. A few minutes later she was back saying that Madi had been stabbed. That Moroka must have had a knife. We were scared of Moroka, so we let someone else find Madi's body. Then I called the police."

Kubu got up with a grunt and left the room. Obviously one of the women was lying; perhaps the other was telling the truth. Toteng's story was more believable. The implication was that Bongi did take the knife and, knowing about the money, hoped that Moroka would finish Madi off. When he didn't, she did the job herself, with Toteng covering for her. Bongi would need to be very stupid to fall for Toteng's wiles if her story were true. Toteng's story made sense; Bongi's did not. It seemed he had no option but to charge Bongi with the murder of Joshua Madi. And yet…

Back in his office he reviewed the file, going over his notes, rereading the reports from forensics and Ian MacGregor, looking at the photographs. There was one of Bongi taken the night of the murder. She was wearing too much make-up and too little skirt. Dressed to attract men and tips. Kubu dumped it on the table and picked up one of Toteng. Her perennial frown made her look managerial, despite her traditional dress, scarf, and necklace. Kubu placed her next to Bongi. He moved the pictures around, looking for something overlooked or a clue missed. Suddenly he grabbed one of the pictures and stared at it. Just then the phone rang interrupting his train of thought, and he answered with a trace of irritation. It was Detective Tau, and soon Kubu was keenly interested in what he had to say.

♦♦♦

MABAKU WAS impressed. "Well, Kubu, I must congratulate you. How did you catch Toteng when all the evidence pointed to Bongi?"

"It was all a set-up. Toteng used Bongi's natural stupidity to get her to fall into trap after trap, while she kept all Madi's money except for five thousand pula needed to pad a bra." Mabaku raised his eyebrows but didn't interrupt. "Take the door handle. She opened the security gate, wiped the handles clean, and then persuaded Bongi to open the door only to call her back. And the evidence that Bongi was the one who went into the alley where Madi was lying unconscious gets carefully preserved behind the locked security door."

"Except…?" Mabaku had played this game with Kubu before.

"Except that Toteng claimed she cleaned the door after the big delivery on the Wednesday before the murder. But I traced the delivery man. He was there on Wednesday afternoon all right, but he was back on Friday afternoon, the day Madi was murdered. He had to deliver one case of brandy. He tried the side door, but it was locked. So he brought it through the bar."

"I see! So what happened to his fingerprints on the outside door? They were cleaned off when Toteng prepared her fingerprint trap for Bongi. Makes sense, but that'll never convict her!"

"No, but Ian's fibers will. The fibers in Madi's hand are from terminalia pods. Toteng was wearing a necklace with them that night. When she stabbed Madi, he must have come round and grabbed it. But at that moment she found the right angle between the ribs and forced the knife into his heart. Madi would have died at once, and then she could pry his fingers loose. And I'm sure we'll find much more money than five thousand pula when we search her place."

"Will she stick to her story?"

Kubu shook his head with a broad smile. "I persuaded her that we had her cold. The funny part is that she blamed it all on Moroka! Said that she was sure he'd kill Madi after the stories she made up about him and Bongi. Moroka always got aggressive when he had too much to drink, and he always had too much beer on a Friday night. But he blew it. You can't trust a man to do anything properly, is what she said."

Mabaku started to laugh. "Well done, Kubu. Excellent. Now I want to review that other case…"

But Kubu was already heading to the door. "It's our wedding anniversary, Director. We're having a small celebration at home. Joy's cooking my favorite meal. And we're having a bottle of champagne, not…"

"Yes, I know," Mabaku interrupted, "the real stuff, not sparkling wine. On your way, then. But be in my office at eight tomorrow morning. Sober!"

Kubu waved, but nothing would shift the grin from his face. The best part of the day lay ahead.

◆◆◆

BONGI FELT SHE had got off lightly, a slap on the wrist. A stern lecture from the big policeman everyone called 'Hippo,' and two nights in a holding cell. She understood it had been wrong to take the money, and she should have realized that Toteng was the murderer. Perhaps Toteng had placed a spell on her? That was probably it. She was relieved that her dubious behavior could be explained by black magic.

She hailed a minibus taxi, and squashed into the crowded vehicle. It was old and rusted, and she could see the road moving beneath her through a hole in the floor. Such things were normal to her, and she was soon chatting to the other passengers. She was on her way to see Moroka. Madi and his money were gone forever, but Moroka would be lonely and happy to see her.

But Moroka didn't look happy. He let her in and gave her a drink, but then ignored her. He sat brooding, drinking beer. Apparently not his first. Not boastful, not amorous.

Bongi was frightened. This was not like him.

"You and that bitch Toteng set me up, didn't you?" he said at last. "To get Madi's cash. I was in that stinking jail while you enjoyed his money!"

"No, Moroka, it wasn't like that! Toteng told me he was dead. That someone had murdered him. I'm sorry, darling. Love me. Make it all right."

"Where's the money?"

"The police took it. We each had five thousand pula. That

superintendent made us give it to him."

"There was a lot of money! Much more than ten thousand." The veins stood out on Moroka's head and his neck. "At least thirty thousand, maybe forty thousand! Where's the rest? I want my share! I earned it beating Madi! And rotting in jail while you and Toteng had fun." Suddenly he was quiet, still.

Bongi felt chill fingers of terror. She looked for escape, but Moroka was between her and the door. "Moroka, there was no more money! I swear!"

Moroka finished his beer in one gulp. The veins threatened to burst, and his muscular arms ended now in fists.

"I want my share!" he shouted, as he moved towards her.

Glossary:
Mma – Respectful term in Setswana used when addressing a woman
Mielie – Local name for corn
Rra – Respectful term in Setswana used when addressing a man
Shebeen – Neighborhood bar
Terminalia prunioides – Tree with striking purple pods

Dumber Than Dirt

Libby Fischer Hellmann

Derek's father used to call him dumber than dirt. His mother said he wasn't the sharpest knife in the dishwasher. Both of them said he had more luck than brains. Like the time he accidentally shoved the gearshift in reverse and backed his father's '78 Dodge Challenger into a wall. No one got hurt, but eight-year-old Derek felt his sore bottom for days. He felt something else, too. He'd only gripped the wheel for a few seconds, but the thrust of the engine was so powerful, his sense of control so profound, that Derek was hooked on cars.

As he grew up, his passion deepened. He didn't care much about the engineering, or the technology. But the cold sleek lines of a classic design, the supple leather of a bucket seat, the hum of a perfectly tuned engine triggered an urgent need in him—a need that could only be met by flooring it every chance he got. He spent his high-school years happily scouting, admiring, and borrowing the objects of his desire, sometimes without the owner's permission. But Derek never thought too much about the consequences of his actions, and when his friends went off to college, Derek went off to East Moline for two to five. He swore afterwards he'd never be seduced by a V-8's siren song again.

That summer he got a job at Lindsey's, a pub on Chicago's north side. Lindsey's sported lots of polished oak, soft lights, and a dartboard in back. They served tiny steaks with blue cheese on top, and the place was always crowded. Chuck Lindsey was a Sixties liberal who thought everyone deserved a second chance. He hired Derek to wash dishes and sweep floors. Derek found a room a few blocks away and walked to work. In Lakeview, most folks did, and the dearth of cars helped

Derek avoid temptation. He cheerfully joined the throngs of pedestrians hoofing it down the street, another skinny young man with long hair and a slightly sleepy expression.

He was on the early shift one morning, rinsing out pots, when he heard a knock at the door. He walked out to the front and squinted through the window. It was Brady, a regular who sat with Lindsey almost every night, sharing jokes and stories and drinks. The bus boys said Brady threw money around like water. Once in a while Brady's wife, a hot blond number, came in too. Today, though, Brady wasn't smiling. As Derek opened the door, he felt waves of tension eddying out from Brady.

"Lindsey in back?" *No "hello, how are you, pal."* Brady never looked at you when he spoke, as if people were annoying, things you swatted away like flies.

"He's not here."

"He must be." Brady sounded irritated, as if it was Derek's fault, and brushed past him. Derek started sweeping. Last night, he was loading the dishwasher when he heard loud voices coming from Lindsey's cramped office next to the kitchen. Then there'd been silence. A few minutes later Derek saw Brady slink down the hall, his face half-hidden by a baseball cap pulled low across his forehead.

Now Brady pushed past him again. "You hear from him this morning?"

Derek shrugged. "Nope."

Brady opened the door. "When he comes in, have him call me." Not a request. An order.

"Sure thing, Mr. Brady." The door slammed.

A few minutes later, Derek caught a gleam of silver wedged between a barstool and the foot rail. Thinking it was a gum wrapper, he leaned over to pick it up. It was a set of car keys. A small tag asked the finder to return them to Ian Brady at a post office number. Derek turned them over in his hand. One key was silver, but the other was that new kind of key that wasn't a key at all, just a finger of black plastic. Mercedes made them. Derek laid the keys on the bar. Brady would be charging back in as soon as he realized he'd dropped them.

He finished sweeping the floor. Then he unloaded the dishwasher. Half an hour passed. Brady wasn't back. Derek started to itch all over. He stayed in the kitchen and tried not to think about the keys. Twenty minutes later the itch was still there, and his face felt hot. He checked the clock. Lindsey would be in any minute, along with the lunchtime crew.

He walked back to the bar. The keys glinted in a shaft of sunlight. He ran his thumb and forefinger around his jaw-line, stroking an imaginary beard, a habit he'd picked up that made him feel smart. He stared at the keys. Then he scooped them up and let himself out the door.

The Benz couldn't be too far away. Derek walked up one block and down another. No car. Puzzled, he doubled back through the alley behind the restaurant. There it was, parked in the spot Lindsey usually kept vacant for suppliers. A navy blue coupe that looked like it just came off the showroom floor. Cream interior. Deep pile carpeting. Fat seventeen inch tires. It had to be over five hundred horsepower. That thing would fly.

He skulked in the narrow shadow from an overhanging eave, his eyes scanning the buildings across the alley. This was the hottest summer since the year all those people died, and today was already a scorcher. Everyone must be holed up next to their air conditioners with the blinds down. Derek sauntered up to the car and pressed the dot of raised plastic on the key. The locks snapped up. He swung himself into the car. The leather seat yielded to the contours of his back, as though it was custom tailored for him. He gripped the wheel and turned over the engine. It caught right away. He nudged the car out of the alley.

He headed east to the Drive, handling the Benz as gently as one of Lindsey's crystal glasses, the ones he saved for special occasions. The slightest touch of his hand prompted an eager response, as if the car was anxious for his next command. The ride was well balanced and stable, and it cornered on a matchstick. He cruised down the Drive, getting the feel of the car, then turned south on Fifty-Five.

The road opened up a few miles later, and Derek floored it.

The car hesitated for a fraction of a second, then lunged forward. Derek hunched forward and let the car eat up the highway. There was always a moment when he could tell whether a set of wheels was worth it or whether it had some defect, some flaw that made it a clunker. But this baby was perfect. Derek blew out his breath. It felt like he hadn't really breathed in years. His fingers drifted over the walnut-trimmed instrument panel, the velvety smoothness of the seats. He wasn't sure where the car ended and his flesh began.

WHEN DEREK SMELLED it, he thought it might be fertilizer from a nearby field until he spotted the warehouses flanking the highway. Then he popped open the glove compartment, thinking Brady left a burger or hot dog inside. He found lipstick, tissues, and a garage door opener, but no food.

The odor grew more rancid, and he opened the windows. That helped for a while, but when he closed them to crank up the A/C, it came back. An uneasy feeling twisted his stomach. He veered off the highway at the next exit and stopped. The smell was strongest near the trunk. He got out and opened it up.

He jumped back as if he'd singed his fingers on the trunk, then took a cautious step forward. The body of a man was curled up inside. There were brown stains all over his khaki pants and polo shirt. On his feet were black Converses, the kind Lindsey wore. The hair on the back of Derek's neck stiffened. It *was* Lindsey.

The sudden roar of a passing car reminded Derek the trunk was wide open. He pushed it down. His pulse raced. This had to be a bad dream. If he opened the trunk again, it would be empty. He did. It wasn't.

Then he glimpsed a patch of red plastic peeking out from under Lindsey's body. He pulled it out. It was a shopping bag from one of those fancy Lakeview stores. Inside was a crumpled white shirt with the same brown stains, and a large butcher's knife, it too stained with blood. Derek froze. The knife was from the restaurant's kitchen.

He stiffened. He had a big problem, and grand theft auto was just the beginning. A minute passed. He walked up to the passenger side and pulled the tissues out of the glove compartment. He edged around to the back and slid the knife out of the bag, using the tissues to keep his prints off. Clutching the knife, he jogged to a wooded area set back from the road, found a patch of dead leaves and twigs, and buried the knife underneath.

Seconds later, he was back behind the wheel heading south on Fifty-Five. Calmer now, he turned on the radio and twisted the dial to a country station. Tim McGraw was singing *I like It, I Love It*. Derek thumped the wheel to the beat. Then he noticed the cell phone built into Brady's car. His hand flew to his chin and stroked it for a moment. He punched in a number.

"Louie? It's Derek." Louie was from East Moline. They'd worked in the laundry together, listening to country all day long. It was Louie who told him he was married to Faith Hill.

"Derek, my man. Still keeping your ass clean?" Louie guffawed. He knew Derek was a dishwasher.

"Louie, I got a problem."

"Hold on, lemme get to another phone."

Derek heard a shrill voice in the background. "You already had one lousy break today. This better not take long."

"Don't mess with me, woman," Louie's voice snapped. Then he was back. "What's happening, man?"

Derek told him. There was a long silence.

"Where are you now?"

"In the car."

"Man, are you crazy? You calling me from some dude's car? What's the matter with you? Get to a pay phone and call me back." There was a click and the line went dead.

Derek drove to the nearest gas station, but a few people were filling up their tanks, and he couldn't risk someone getting a whiff of Lindsey. He sailed past it then redialed Louie's number.

"You at a pay phone?"

"Er, yeah, Louie."

"It don't sound like it."

Derek took a breath. "Louie, I don't know what to do."

"Only one thing to do. Get your ass out of that car. Fast. Dump it."

"Can you help me?"

"No way, man. Ditching cars is one thing. Dead bodies is somethin' altogether different. Screw it man. You shouldna' called me."

"Louie, don't hang up. Please."

More silence.

"Louie?"

"Yeah?"

"Where do I dump it?"

"Anywhere man. Just do it." Louie sounded impatient. "Shit. You got no clue, do you?"

Derek shook his head, not realizing Louie couldn't see him.

"All right. Listen to me good now, Derek. You remember that movie we saw in the joint?"

"What movie?" Derek loved movies. When he could follow the plot.

"Think. The one about Bernie. You remember?"

Derek thought hard, his lips pursed together with the effort. It was something about two guys trying to figure out what to do with a dead body. *Weekend At Bernie's.* "Yeah." He was proud of himself. "I remember."

"Well, where's the one place we thought they shoulda' ditched him, but they didn't?"

Derek thought he recalled some of the guys acting like they knew all about dumping stiffs, but he couldn't remember what they said. "I - I dunno."

"Man, do I have to spell it out for you?"

Derek hung his head.

"Listen. I'm not gonna say it straight out -- you never know who's listening. But you get yerself out to the airport, you hear?"

The muscles on his face relaxed. "I got it. Thanks, Louie."

"And we never talked, you got it?"

"Sure."

"Derek?"

"Yeah, Louie?"

"Long term parking."

"Right."

Derek cut northeast towards O'Hare. He might catch on slow, but he knew what to do now. He'd ditch the Mercedes then race into the airport like he was boarding a plane. Then he'd make a one-eighty and take the subway home. His problems would be over. He turned up the radio and whistled along with Garth Brooks.

But when he got to long term parking, he realized they'd just finished renovating the lots. There was now a booth next to the automatic gate, and inside sat a black man, or Double-A as Louie called them. Derek pulled up and waited for his ticket.

The man stared at Derek with narrowed eyes, and Derek felt a jolt of recognition. The guy was an ex-con. Louie said you could always tell. There was something in the eyes, something that marked you as a former inmate, and it never went away, no matter how long you were out. Derek realized he should have waited until dark. The booth might have been empty, or even if someone *was* there, they'd probably be jammin' to the music from their headphones, taking no notice of a guy in a Benz. He circled the lot and pretended to change his mind. As he looped back to the highway, he felt the guy staring after him.

Derek cruised through neighborhoods where the same house reproduced itself in different hues of paint. After an hour or so he came to an industrial area dotted with warehouses and factories. He sat up straighter. The road dead-ended just ahead. Beyond it was a field, waist high with prairie grass. Nothing else. He stopped and got out of the car. There was no traffic. Or people. He was about to toss the keys into the field and run like hell when he heard a voice behind him.

"Nice wheels, man."

Derek whipped around. A kid on a bike. The kid braked to a stop.

"A CL600 with a V-12 engine, right?"

Derek didn't know what model it was, but he dipped his head anyway.

"I know a guy has one of those new CLK350s, but this baby is wicked sweet."

Derek grunted. The kid went on about independent suspension, torque, and power transmissions, clearly trying to impress Derek with his knowledge. But Derek didn't want to shoot the breeze. He had to split before the kid smelled Lindsey.

"What are you doing around here, anyway?" The kid wrinkled his nose.

Derek's stomach flipped. He shrugged, struggling to act nonchalant. What should he say? Luckily, the kid gave him an out.

"You work around here?"

"Yeah," Derek said, almost grateful. "Yeah. I do."

"Oh. You must have just started, right? 'Cause I never seen your car before."

Derek nodded. Then a thought came to him. "You know what time it is?"

The kid shook his head.

"I gotta go. They dock you an hour's pay if you take too long on break."

He got back in the car and tried not to lay down any rubber as he pulled away.

By late afternoon, the stench from the trunk was turning his skin clammy. Blasting the A/C didn't help, and the hot angry air whipping through the window scalded his arm. He sped up Ninety-Four to Milwaukee, then backtracked south. He'd missed his shift; he hoped Lindsey wouldn't fire him. Then he giggled. Lindsey wouldn't be firing anyone anymore. By nightfall, though, he was drained. He was a prisoner in the Benz, just as surely as he'd been in the joint. He was hungry and tired, and he didn't know what to do.

It wasn't until three in the morning, occasional headlights winking past him on the Skyway, that he had an epiphany. This wasn't his problem. It was Brady's. Brady killed Lindsey. He,

Derek, was guilty of only one thing: taking the car for a joy ride. If he could somehow undo that, he'd be in the clear. He played with the idea, turning it over in his mind, like a new car you want to baby until you know its limits.

The sun was just breaking over Lincoln Park, streaking the sky with pink when Derek drove east on Fullerton. He found Brady's home easily—his address was in the glove compartment. It was a neat brick townhouse, surrounded by a wrought iron fence in front and a small garage on the side. A discreet sign mounted on the gate asked visitors to announce themselves. He parked the car, got out, and left the keys in the ignition. He pressed the buzzer and then sprinted to the corner where he crouched behind a shuttered newsstand and peeked out.

Brady's door opened; Brady and his wife emerged. Brady's wife was in a bathrobe, her blond hair in tangles, but Brady was wearing the same clothes he'd worn yesterday. Both of them looked shocked to see the Benz. His wife waved her arms in the air, then pointed a finger at Brady. Brady's arms flew up as if he thought she might hit him. Then he gestured to the house and hurried inside.

His wife waited until the front door closed. Then she strolled up to the driver's side, looked in both directions, and took the keys out of the ignition. Back at the trunk, she inserted the key and raised the hood. Ten seconds passed. Then Derek heard her scream, loud enough to carry a full block away. She slammed down the trunk and ran up the driveway, clutching her stomach with her hands. Derek thought she was going to throw up. He waited until he heard the sirens approaching before he left. He thought he might have forgotten something, but he didn't know what it was.

DEREK COULDN'T DECIDE whether to show up for work. If he didn't, someone would wonder where he was, but if he did, they'd ask where he'd been yesterday. He decided to go in and say he'd been sick. He needed the money.

The sign said Lindsey's was closed, but the place was crawling with cops. A couple of uniforms shielded the door. When he told them his name, they said to duck under the yellow tape stretched across the front. A man in a fancy suit and silk tie stood at the bar, talking into a cell phone. His skin was the shade of cocoa, his nappy black hair grizzled at the sides. His eyes were fearless.

"I know, but it's the closest thing we got to a crime scene." His eyes locked on Derek trying to slip through the door. "This is the last place anyone saw him alive." The man pointed to a table. Derek sat down. A guy taking pictures was just finishing up, while another guy started to smear black powder all over everything. "Call me back when you have something." The man who'd been talking snapped the phone closed and dumped it in his jacket pocket.

"Luke Woolston. Area Three Detectives." The man nodded to Derek. "Who are you?"

Derek stammered. "D-Derek Schroeder."

"They told me you missed work yesterday."

"Yeah." Derek refused to meet the detective's eyes.

Woolston took a swissle stick off the bar, stuck it in his mouth. "How come?"

Derek gazed past the detective. The guy with the briefcase was dusting the top of the bar with white powder. "I got no A/C. I couldn't breathe."

Woolston twirled the swizzle stick in his mouth. "You go to the ER? See a doctor?"

Derek shook his head.

"But you made a miraculous recovery." The detective curled his lip.

"I took lots of showers."

Woolston sat down across from Derek. "When was your last shift?"

"Yesterday morning."

"Where did you go afterwards?"

"Home."

The detective's cell phone rang. Woolston pulled it out of his pocket. "Good. Keep on it." He laid the phone on the table, his eyes never leaving Derek's face. "We've got a problem."

Derek looked at the cell phone.

"Yesterday we got a report of a stolen Mercedes. Brand new car. Then, less than twenty-four hours later, the car shows up. With Mr. Lindsey in the trunk." He took the swivel stick out of his mouth and pointed to the phone. "Now I hear you did two to five for stealing cars."

Derek blinked.

"You see the problem?" Woolston twirled the swizzle stick. "Let me try out a theory on you, son." He stood up, walked around to Derek, laid a hand on the back of Derek's chair. Derek had to twist around to see him. "I'm prepared to believe that whoever killed Lindsey didn't intend to kill him. I think the offender..."—Woolston took his time with each syllable—"was just out for a joy ride. And you know, I can understand that."

Derek cocked his head.

"I was into cars myself," Woolston smiled. "I was runnin' a 327 in a 'Fifty-Four Bel Air. Nothing like the feel of a Hurst shift in your hands, you know? 'Course that was a while back."

Derek felt his lips curve up in a smile.

"So," Woolston went on, "Lindsey might have seen this person in the act of, shall we say, 'liberating' Brady's car. And the person panicked. He knew he'd be sent back inside. So he did the only thing he could think of. He stabbed Lindsey with a knife." Woolston wandered back to his own chair. His eyes gave away nothing. "What do you think of that theory, Derek?"

Derek's foot started tapping the floor under the table. He tried to stop; he knew it didn't look good. He couldn't.

"You come down to the station with me, son. You can tell me all about it."

"Brady and Lindsey had a fight," Derek blurted out.

Woolston raised an eyebrow.

"Two nights ago. I was loading the dishwasher. Lindsey's office is right next to the kitchen. I see Brady comin' out of the office. All sneaky like. Then, when I'm on the early shift yesterday morning, he shows up looking for Lindsey."

Woolston sat down and nodded, as if he'd heard it all before. "What about the car, Derek? You take it for a ride?"

Derek shrugged.

The detective's cell phone rang again. He listened, disconnected, then inclined his head toward Derek. "You sure there's nothing else you want to tell me?"

Derek shook his head. His foot was still tapping.

"Like how did your prints end up on the steering wheel and the trunk of the Mercedes?"

Derek flinched. That's what he'd forgotten to do at Brady's house. It was all over.

Woolston ignored him. "Where's the knife, son?"

"I didn't kill him."

"Did you have help?"

"I didn't do it. I was set up."

"It's your word against Brady's." He dropped his chin, but kept his eyes on Derek.

"I found the keys in the bar."

"So you *did* steal the car?"

Derek said nothing. It was quiet except for his shoe tapping.

"Son, if you confess, it'll go easier on you. I'll tell the States Attorney you cooperated."

"I didn't kill anyone. You can't prove it."

Woolston stood up. "You may be right. But I can put you away for theft of a motor vehicle. And with a dead body in the trunk, I can also charge you with concealing a homicide. That's a Class Three felony. With your priors, son, you're looking at some serious time."

THE CEILING OF the cell was dimpled with tiny white pebbles that seemed to be glued onto the tiles. Derek tried counting them as he lay on his bunk but then gave up. Some of them were so tiny he wasn't sure whether they were part of the design or just mistakes. They'd transferred him downtown after the arraignment and assigned him a public defender, but his lawyer, a woman who looked too young to know what she was doing, wanted him to cop a plea. She told him it was only a matter of time until they charged him with homicide. The only reason they hadn't was the absence of a weapon. When he told her he didn't do Lindsey, she shook her head and said it didn't much matter.

He wondered whether to tell her about the knife. It wouldn't have his prints on it, but the fact that he knew where it was might work against him. He should try to be smart about this. But he wasn't feeling very smart. Or hopeful. He should never have taken the job at Lindsey's. He'd always wanted to be a lifeguard. He should have tried for that. His parents were right. He was stupid.

He was still lying on his bed thinking how you couldn't tell day from night inside when they came to get him. Woolston was waiting for him in the interview room.

"We're letting you go," the detective said wearily.

Derek whipped his head up. "Did Brady confess?"

"No."

"Someone else did it?"

Woolston shook his head.

Derek was confused. "What happened, then?"

Woolston stared at Derek, then shrugged his shoulders. "I shouldn't be telling you this—but Brady's wife found a bloody shirt of Brady's stuffed in a bag in his closet."

Derek's chin jutted forward. "A bloody shirt?"

"Yeah. It seems that Brady and Lindsey were lovers. The wife's known about it for a while. When Lindsey showed up dead, she claims she wrestled with her conscience, hoping they could put their marriage back on track. You know, forget about the past. But when she found the shirt, she realized she couldn't."

Derek thought about it for a minute. "What does Brady say?"

"He admits that he and Lindsey were lovers. And that they had a fight the other night. But he says they made up a few minutes later. In Lindsey's office." Woolston cleared his throat.

So, that was the silence Derek heard the night he saw Brady coming out of Lindsey's office. Embarrassed, he made circles on the floor with his foot.

"Of course, Brady denies killing Lindsey, but we've got this shirt..." Woolston's voice trailed off. "And now his wife doesn't want to press charges about the car." Derek got the feeling Woolston didn't believe a thing he'd just said but didn't care enough to go on with the case. "So we're letting you go. You got lucky."

Derek smiled.

"Do me a favor, though. Get out of Chicago. It's not your kind of town."

DEREK TOOK Woolston's advice and packed his things. He'd catch a bus south. Or west. But he had one thing to do before he left. He wanted to thank Mrs. Brady for not pressing charges. Apologize for the trouble he'd caused. Tell her he hoped there were no hard feelings.

She answered the door in a halter-top and skimpy shorts. Her blond hair was swept up on top of her head.

"I've been wondering when you'd show up."

She stood close enough that he could smell her perfume. Then she turned to a small table and picked up an envelope. "I'll bet you're interested in this." She smiled mysteriously and dangled it in front of him.

"What's that?"

"You know."

"No, ma'am, I don't." He was bewildered

"Don't play dumb with me. Where is it?"

"Where's what, ma'am?" He'd been hoping to impress her with his good manners, but she didn't seem to be noticing.

"Look Derek, or whatever your name is, you almost screwed this up for me. Big time. But I managed to make it work anyway."

He shifted his feet.

"Why do you think I dropped the theft charges?"

At last, she was saying something he understood. He replied eagerly. "That's why I'm here, Mrs. Brady. I wanted to – "

She cut him off. "You're damn right that's why you're here."

Derek felt like he was in one of those movies where he couldn't follow the plot. "I did you a favor. Now it's your turn. Where's the knife?"

The knife?" Derek involuntarily took a step backwards. How could she know about the missing knife? Unless—he concentrated hard—unless she knew who put it there. Which would mean she knew who killed Lindsey. Or maybe—He met her eyes and saw the answer to his question. "You killed Lindsey."

"A real genius aren't you?" She sneered, checking her nails as if she'd just had a manicure.

"Why?"

"You think I'm just gonna sit by while my husband makes a fool of me? With another man?"

Derek thought fast now. "The keys. Brady didn't lose them. You planted them. To frame him."

She flashed him a cold smile. "After he went to sleep the other night, I took the car to the restaurant and killed Lindsey."

Derek frowned.

"Oh, I had some help." She twisted around. Derek could just make out the shape of a shirtless man sprawled on a couch in the living room. "Then we planted the keys, sopped up the shirt with Lindsey's blood and threw it in the bag with the knife. I knew Brady'd be back at Lindsey's the next morning. He was so crazy about that man he called him first thing every morning. God forbid Lindsey wasn't there, he'd run over like a damn puppy dog to find him."

"But then—"

"But then you stole the car. You really had me going for a while." She tossed her head. "I had to improvise."

Derek stuck his hands in his pockets.

"Thank God it all turned out. Now there's only one loose end left."

She opened the envelope and peeled off a few bills. "Consider this a down payment." She handed them to Derek. "You bring back the knife, the rest of it is yours, too."

He took the cash. Ten grand. And ten more later. He held

the bills in the palm of his hand. She waited, an expectant smile on her face, while he thought it through. He stared at the floor, tiled in black and white. Then he lifted his eyes. She folded her arms across her chest. "Well?"

He chose his words with care. "You know something, Mrs. Brady? I'm right sorry, but the truth is, I just don't remember where it is. It could be anywhere." He smiled innocently.

Her smile faded.

"And if anything happens to me, the police might find a note telling them where the knife is and who used it... "His voice trailed off. He flipped up his hands.

She eyed him with suspicion, her hands on her hips. Derek bit his tongue. Finally, she sighed and handed over the rest of the cash. "You leave me no choice." Derek slid the bills into his pocket. "How do I know you'll be back?" she asked uncertainly.

"Oh, I wouldn't worry about that, ma'am," he said slyly. "I reckon you'll be seeing a lot more of me from now on."

She slammed the door in his face, but Derek didn't mind. He whistled as he skipped down the street. He patted the twenty grand in his pocket. So what if he was dumber than dirt? Who cared if he wasn't the sharpest knife in the dishwasher? His parents were right. He had more luck than brains.

The Snow Birds

Gary Phillips

Now one time it comes on Thanksgiving or rather two days before, and we were standing on the sidelines in the midst of our permutating as the Silver Slicers of Bowler Street went at the Rude Cru of Avenue J. Sidelines is a relative term when it comes to street polo as it was of necessity that we and the other onlookers had to at times quickly move about to avoid say a smashed toe or bruised shin. The lads and lasses zoomed back and forth, to and fro, on their steeds of battered alloy whacking the bejeezus out of a croquet ball with their homemade plastic mallets while adroitly slaloming their bikes, most of the time barely sluicing past one another, on the field of play.

We stood upon a one-time overgrown lot that had been the graveyard for discarded refrigerators, accessories from chopped Benzs and Mustangs, hype needles and used condoms. Now it was a cleared, leveled and green cityscape upon which the various organized and loosely affiliated street polo teams competed and honed their skills.

"Watch out, fool," a youngster who went by Droop, intoned as he rambled past on his bike.

Droop was not so heady into the contest that he would address us in that manner. Oh, no, we had more stature than that. He was keenly aware that such temerity would earn him a stern rap across the knuckles, or some other part of his body, from my companion.

I of course am not referring to Li'l Vet, whose feline-like indifference to most matters physical and psychological is renown, but to the other member of our trio, one Laticome Malloy Burris affectionately known in our environs as the Sour Apple Kid. The sobriquet having arisen from when he was no more

than a mere crumb snatcher ambling about the numbers empo-
rium his dear old widowed mom maintained—hidden behind a
false basement wall no less—to the delight of its neighborhood
patrons. Even as a little shaver, as he helped her keep track of
who was betting what, graduating from writing this pertinent
information on flash paper to retaining the various bets in his
voracious memory, he sucked on sour apple candy. And to this
day he has continued that avocation.

Droop bore toward the goal then suddenly back-ped-
dled furiously, as these bikes they rode are termed fixed gear,
no brakes. Simultaneously he swung that mallet with a Tiger
Woods-like élan and drove the ball through the truck tire that
had been cut in half and stuck part way into the ground to form
an arch.

"Ye-ahh. What's my motherlovin' name, chump?" Droop
trash-talked his opponent again, named Mando, belittling his
inadequate defense.

Mando did not take this jest in the spirit of sportsman in
which it had been delivered. He lashed out with a foot, scuffing
one of his new kicks, a classic Chuck, against Droop's chest. At
this juncture I'd be remiss if I didn't mention that there was an
ongoing riff between the two as, one might suspect, it involved
a dame. In this case it was a lovely young woman named Annakosta, who'd come this close to gracing the pages of a King
magazine thong special.

Subsequently she dropped Mando for Droop. To her
Mando had not demonstrated proper commiseration when
she, sniffling and teary-eyed, recounted to him how she lost
the opportunity to expose her wondrous backside to the paid
and pass around circulation, of said publication. King was not
called the illest men's magazine ever, for nothing. And so there
it was.

The two were aloft on their bikes maintaining their balance
as they squared off against each other while their respective
team mates urged them to take their beef elsewhere. There was,
after all, a game afoot.

The Sour Apple Kid looked from the potential dust up to

me. "We'll vamp on the shipment tonight. There'll be four re-frigerated bobtail Kenworths." He took a toke then passed the blunt to me, the pungent contents packed into in cherry-vanilla flavored wrap. Despite partaking, The Kid was alert, seemingly no worse for wear after his redeye flight arriving from Miami this morning.

"That's a quality truck, Li'l Vet ventured.

"Indeed," I concurred, inhaling and passing the joy stick to him.

Out on the field the polo match had resumed. Mando had rode away to be replaced by a chap we all called Ferengi because he was ugly and small like those aliens introduced on Star Trek: Deep Space Nine that I enjoyed as a youngster. Droop took no pleasure in the other's departure as he knew Mando kept grudges like 'tween girls kept love letters—forever.

There would be disproportionate payback or at least the attempt at such. Droop would have to be mindful, which did tend to crimp one's style when you were out on the town with your girl. It did help though that Annakosta, the former lady friend of the affronted Mando, knew how to handle the gat she kept in the knockoff Gucci bag she sported. Such was life here in the Tri-Quarter section of the city.

"I realize this goes without saying," I began, "but there are four trucks with two men in each and only three of us," I men-tioned this knowing the Kid had certainly calculated this rudi-mentary math, yet I was curious as to his answer. We knew that these aforementioned rigs rolled with a driver and a guard, that both were armed with the latest in firepower, and were more than happy to demonstrate their knowledge of these weapons. For these wastrels were in the employ of Sid "Dragon Eye" Ludlow, the Kid's rival in certain sundry endeavors.

Li'l Vet offered the Kid the blunt but he eschewed any more chronic. Instead he popped a sour apple hard candy in his mouth. He wrapped his tongue around it and illuminated, "Due to the holiday season getting underway and what with the number of drunk driving incidents from last year, there will be at least one if not two check points along the highway to town."

I was beginning to get the picture but Li'l Vet was not quite on the page. "What the fug does that have to do with our caper?" he inquired testily. Understand Li'l Vet was not special in special class way. But he was a meat and potatoes sort of guy and always strove to be one hundred percent clear on a job before undertaking his appointed tasks. That certainly made for less mistakes as he had never been sent to the hoosegow and did not intend to break precedent.

The Sour Apple Kid dislodged the candy from inside his cheek to address Li'l Vet's concern. "Dragon Eye Ludlow will have his drivers take the old Windhaven Road to avoid the checkpoints." The road he spoke off was in places no more than a narrow lane that allowed for only one truck's progress at a time. Indeed some of that road wound through scenic country like a bucolic scene fronting a Get Well card you'd send you're baby's mama if she had a cold or threw out her back doing a hoochie dance for a rap video.

Li'l Vet nodded his head in light of this clarification.

"When those bobtails get through Linsburgh that's where we'll hit 'em," the Kid said. Linsburgh was one of those recent suburban developments that looked like it was designed by that huckster who cranked out those syrupy sweet paintings of Smurf-like houses and landscapes. I still could not fathom why so many seemingly rational people were gaga for his stuff. To each his own for sure.

"Yes," I said, duplicating the head motion that Li'l Vet had displayed. The Kid's idea was sound. There was a piney woods section between Linsburgh and here, and it made sense to hit the trucks there. "That also means they'll be on edge, ready for an attack," I observed. I too liked to cover all the angles before these after-hours undertakings.

"I know," the Kid said but did not continue. Soon enough the Silver Slicers won two out of three games and, the Kid was in a jubilant mood. For not only had he utilized his pull among the local pols to get the lot cleared for street polo, but was also a financial backer of the Slicers. That and the Rude Cru was backed by Dragon Eye so we interpreted our victory as an omen of things to come. Said gent was not in attendance, but a few of his lieutenants were, and they shouldered the loss morosely and silently.

These neighborhood intramural contests were a proving ground for a soon to be established semi-pro league of street polo players the Kid was lining up some of the downtown swells to back as an athletic program for at-need youth or whatever the current in-vogue term was to describe the ragamuffins from our area. The Sour Apple Kid examined all the angles, and played quite a few of them in the process.

As the team enjoyed their pizzas and red soda water at Good Time Mary's eatery, we huddled in a rear booth reserved for the Kid wherein he outlined the rest of the plan to us. Our doubts were assuaged.

And so that night, actually around two the following morning, we were in place as a light snow flurry dusted the landscape. The wintry effect had been unexpected until the bubbly weatherwoman on the local eleven o'clock news proclaimed, "Gosh, folks, it looks like our Doppler Radar readings are showing the front has about-faced and it's bringing parka time with it." She smiled big shiny horse teeth into the camera while dispensing this update.

I'd smiled back at her as I broke out the proper gear. Myself, I like big-toothed women.

Dressed warmly, we were now hunkered down along either side of a bank of fresh snow. In the near distance, we heard the trucks get closer to this quiet, isolated part of the woods.

"Ready?" The Kid asked over the two-way.

"Fo' sure," Li'l Vet affirmed for he and I. As one, we adjusted our night vision goggles.

The first Kenworth rumbled past, then the second behind it. They kept a little less than a two-car length between each vehicle. As the third went past, the Sour Apple Kid rose on his side of the roadway and me on ours, and we primed and threw our homemade phosphorescent grenades. The three of us closed our eyes tight as they flared.

It goes without saying that in addition to dressing correctly, we'd also brought along the right equipment for this mission. As an example these grenades gave off little sound but did burn with a brilliant, blinding light courtesy of ignited aluminum and magnesium particles. The attack caused the driver in the fourth truck to swerve radically and smash into a conveniently stout tree, sending the passenger slash guard's head into the cracked windshield. Seat belts. Always wear your seat belts I say.

Eyes wide open, Li'l Vet, being a rather fleet-footed individual, popped up with his weapon and swiftly gained his position. He fired the tear gas launcher he aimed with practiced ease. At this juncture I should mention Li'l Vet was called this not because he'd served in the military but due to his love of his pit bulls. He raised these dogs for the purposes of gaming—of the sort a certain ex-NFL quarterback was sent to prison for doing as well.

But where the QB treated his animals cruelly, Li'l Vet, for veterinarian, was the soul of compassion when it came to the ones under his wing. But a debate on the merits or lack thereof of this underground so-called sport is best reserved for a latter time. The important thing here is that Li'l Vet's projectiles hit their marks.

He bombarded trucks three and cracked-up four. The stuff wafted back on a gentle night breeze, seeping into the truck cabs. It was not tear gas he'd unleashed, but knock out stuff. Actually that was a misnomer as the chemical we used was an opiate in vapor form, and was designed to disorient our targets. Obtained, I mention on the QT, via a prominent anesthesiologist who owed the Kid a favor for once getting his wayward daughter out of a jam.

It was my assignment to then use one of the street polo mallets to incapacitate the ruffians stumbling out of their trucks. One chap emerging from number three had his nine lose, but found he couldn't pull the trigger due to the effects of the gas. I sent him to dreamland with a deft whap and tap.

The hooligans from the second truck were proving worrisome. They'd diverted their vehicle into an opening in a copse of trees and were now out of said carriage and shooting at us.

Just beforehand, Li'l Vet and the Kid, utilizing the Glock his dear mom had bought him one birthday, had taken care of the driver and guard in the first truck. They lay nicked but alive and bound on the side of the road where we also took cover.

"Your jammer on?" The Kid inquired, squeezing off a shot for effect.

"Yes," I replied, removing the instrument from my pocket and showing him its green light. We'd purchased these cell phone signal jammers from a foreign country via the internet. We each had one on our person as well as several scattered between us and our vehicle deeper in the woods.

I said, "So they can't get reinforcements but how do we curtail their bullet melody?"

"Yeah," Li'l Vet piped in, "even out here we can't keep this racket up without the highway patrol or some nosy cop making an appearance."

"That is so," the Kid said, reviewing options silently. "Getting into a firefight with these mugs is bound to garner unwanted attention, let alone the chance one of us gets plugged."

I gulped at the suggestion.

"But they're between us and our whip" Li'l Vet pointed out. "So we got to get through them to get out of here."

The Sour Apple Kid then loaded a grenade in the RPG-7 he'd also brought to the party. The grenade launcher was of the variety originating in the former Eastern Bloc. The Kid won the weapon a few years ago at the conclusion of a successful poker game with some Russian mafia gentlemen of his acquaintance. He'd been holding onto it for just the right occasion.

"I propose," he announced, "we do something to get the cops here on the double." Without waiting for our vote, he crouched and fired the explosive charge not into the wooded area from where Dragon Eye's boys were bristling, but at abandoned truck number three. Words fail me on how best to convey the paroxysm of sound, light and fury that erupted as that diesel-powered conveyance blew up. Suffice it to say the three of us were knocked down by the concussive wind even as our mouths hung open.

"My, my" the Kid uttered, gaining his feet and helping me to do so as well. A singed turkey fell next to my foot. Several more turkeys and their parts rained about the landscape and we put our arms up for protection. Fortunate too as we turned just in time to a groan as one of Dragon Eye's men, apparently having somehow slipped his bonds, was zeroing in on us with his heater. But then a descending turkey struck him squarely in the head and made the little tweeties circle his brain.

"Hey, look," Li'l Vet said, pointing, and running over to the turkey carcass that had saved at least one of our lives. He bent and then straightened up. In his hand was a packet wrapped in translucent material of a familiar size and shape.

"Well I'll be," The Kid said as we neared our compatriot.

"Dragon Eye Ludlow's smuggling blow in the turkeys," I announced.

The Kid inclined his head in the direction of wailing sirens. "Time to make our departure."

"Indeed," Li'l Vet agreed. We three ran to our van, the rival gunman already in the wind ahead of us, and departed. The Kid's retired mother lived out this way in a house he bought for her some years ago. He'd also some time ago reconnoitered this area in case the gendarmes should happen to be chasing him and he needed an escape route. Thus we were able to avoid the fuzz and get back to town intact.

That morning the local news was filled with speculation as to what had transpired in those woods outside of Linsburgh. It was known the trucks had been stocked with turkeys. There was a rumor these birds were intended to be centerpieces in a turkey dinner giveaway for the indigent and unfortunates in the Tri-Quarters section. Some of them plucked fowls, it was breathlessly added in the accounts, were stuffed not with pre-packaged giblets but Bolivian Marching Powder. The loaded turkeys were marked with a slash on the left leg.

It was further alleged the gobblers and the weasel dust belonged to Sid "Dragon Eye" Ludlow. But he was unavailable for conformation or other comments to the newshounds camped out in front of his swank townhouse. He was doubtless elsewhere. The men captured at the scene remained mum.

THANKSGIVING IN Tri-Quarters was a splendid affair. The down and outers, the addicts, the boozers, the recovering, the enablers, the street walkers, the under-employed and the non-employed, the folks who helped these folks, and the Kid and his crew including dear old mom, enjoyed a fine meal of turkey—fried, soaked in brine or traditionally prepared—and all the fixings. Tables and chairs had been set upon the cordoned off street polo field. This was the third such shindig the Kid had put on.

When he'd received the tip that Dragon Eye was looking to steal some of his thunder by putting on his own Thanksgiving feed, the Kid had been beside himself.

"He can do Christmas or Easter or Chanukah, but not Thanksgiving," the Kid had bellowed. This day, you see, was the date his brother, a social worker too enthralled to the bottle and too burdened by the plight of his charges, had passed out drunk in the streets and perished from exposure. He'd broken out of classy rehab facility The Kid had placed him in, and not for the first time. The Thanksgiving feast was his way to honor him and give back to our neighborhood.

All along the Kid and us had wondered why was Dragon Eye going so far out of town to get his turkeys? Sure, his scheme was to have his dinners prepared on the down low as all the soup kitchens and homeless pantries in Tri-Quarters were lined up to cook the meals the Kid was bankrolling. But until that tom broke open, we didn't have the answer as to why Dragon Eye had procured his fowl from afar—killing two birds with one stone as it were.

"Here you go, mom," the Kid said as he handed the gravy bowl to his mother.

"Thank you, son," she said, beaming with pride.

Li'l Vet tapped the Kid's shoulder as a black Lincoln glided to a stop along the avenue. He started to reach for the roscoe under his coat but the Kid stalled that with a look.

The smoked back window of Henry Ford's finest went

down part way and out glared one large bulging orb nestled in burnt, scaly skin set next to a squinting one. Dragon Eye Ludlow took a few moments to take in the festivities, and then the window went back up and the car started off.

I breathed again and took a sip of my brandy. The Kid had flown to Miami as part of the plan. On the sly he obtained a monogrammed cufflink belonging to a brigand who'd threatened to muscle in on the Kid's and Dragon Eye's action in the past. I shall not go into detail as to how this item was obtained, but it involved a lady who is the spouse of said kingpin, but who, it's asserted among some, has an affection for the Kid.

Early on Li'l Vet and I tried to tell the Kid if we did intercept the turkeys, even though we wore masks and gloves, Dragon Eye would be awfully suspicious that cufflink or no, it was he and not the Miami bent nose behind this. But the Kid was insistent on doing this and so the presence of the snow added verisimilitude to the frame we'd constructed.

The Lincoln was heading in the direction of the airport.

Pinked Off

Maureen Fischer

Fedora Dierberger was the antithesis of what an interior designer should be.

Not skinny or stylish but squat and German, a Mack truck commandeering our house, thumping down swatch books and catalogs on our kitchen table. Fedora fueled my mother's disenchantment with the Betty Crocker life. After her visits, Mother disliked our Hotpoint appliances and orange Formica, wanted rid of our brown davenport in the den and stopped baking devils food cakes.

This was the Sixties when the economy boomed beyond today's imagining, a time when my mother employed a cleaning lady, a summer girl and a decorator.

"Monica wants a pink room?" Fedora asked her one afternoon though I'd just told her that. I stared at the woman through harlequin glasses that enlarged my eyes the size of fifty cent pieces. My mother brushed hair out of my face and motioned for me to sit up straighter.

"Yes, bright pink. And see this?" I opened a Penney's catalog and pushed it next to Fedora's pack of Viceroys. "See this white furniture with the gold handles? I want that too. And please, pretty please, a really shocking pink room."

"She'll have it," Fedora said, winking at my mother, slapping shut the catalog and depositing it out of sight. I remember laughing with delight even though her cigarette breath was gagging me. Her scarlet nails (chipped) tapped ashes into a tray and missed. Her Cadillac always needed a wash.

Unlike Fedora, my mother Shirley was meticulous, never a crumb on the floor or a spot on the furniture. But she was jittery and prone to migraines. She'd already had a nervous breakdown—or so it was whispered—and came out of it thanks to the birth of a caboose child, my little sister Celeste, nine years younger than me. My mother viewed most of life as pressure: having friends over for dinner, golfing in the nine-hole group, bridge club, church guild. But the birth of Celeste calmed her down for years, and so did Fedora.

I remember one day they discussed the kitchen.

"I love blue and green, Fed," Mother said, feeding formula to Celeste and stroking her bald head while I did dishes.

"We'll stay in the blue-green family, hon, but I think you want turquoise and chartreuse here in the kitchen. I know you, Shirl. You don't want what every other lemming in this suburb wants. You're artistic." Fedora patted her grey bouffant and stubbed out her cigarette. "I'll bring wall paper samples on Friday."

She had my mother's complete trust from the beginning. When she tackled my bedroom as a warm-up to redoing the entire main floor, I was excited. I slept on a mattress in my parents' bedroom for three days waiting for my room to be done.

I moved out my record player and 45s, my jewelry box and Princess phone so nothing would be damaged. My bedroom door was locked when I got home from school to ensure the surprise.

◆◆◆

Even now forty years later, I can still remember the day I first saw my new room. My fifth grade teacher had slapped me that day for stretching out my legs on the embankment where her favorite, Theresa Kettler, wanted to sit. We were watching the eighth grade boys' baseball tournament. The slap came from behind like a board against my cheek.

"Move your feet. NOW!"

I retracted them; others had been slapped but never me. Theresa sat down with a smile for Sister. That morning I'd turned in my report on world religions using information from *The World Book* on Buddha, the Koran, even Voodoo. My report came back slashed with a D+; my enthusiasm for

Haitian Voodoo had struck Sister Steven Marie as sacrilegious. Only the prospect of the workmen finishing my new room helped me make it through.

"I can't wait. Mother, thank you!" I'd hugged my mother hard that morning on my way out, but she'd been bouncing Celeste on her lap and couldn't hug me back.

I felt so special. Neither of my brothers or the baby were having their rooms redone. No more olive rug with threadbare patches, no more apricot bedspread with holes near the hem, no more dolls on the floor because I had no shelves. Now since Mother had met Fedora at a country club cheese tasting event, my dream was coming true. And it was all going to be a surprise; I hadn't even set eyes on a fabric or carpet sample. All that was left to Fedora, goddess of taste.

◆◆◆

It was November and almost dark as I ran home through the leaves in the Mullikins' yard, squeezed through the hole in their buckthorn hedge and burst in our back door. I threw my book bag on the floor and ran upstairs, took the hallway like a running back and inhaled the fragrance of wallpaper glue.

The first look stunned me. I pressed my temples, shut my eyes, then reopened them. The sight of it hurt like one of my mother's migraines. I remember collapsing on the edge of that grayish pink, nubby silk bedspread and wanting to rip it and stain it with tears. There was no shocking pink, just shades of tepid ugliness; no ruffles or flounces, just panel curtains in off-white taffeta; no pink carpet but a rug the hue of the squid in my science book. Fury shook me. But it wasn't the rage of a brat, it was despair. I had trusted my mother and a stubby woman named after a hat.

My doll collection had been heaped in my closet to make room for the fake flowers on the Ethan Allen dresser. I mourned for the Penney's wall unit with gold handles. I took out my dolls and they cried with me. Even the global dolls from foreign countries ordered off the back of Chef Boy-R-Dee boxes hated my room.

When my mother arrived home from her hair appointment at Ben-ri Coiffures and met me at the top of the stairs, I was curled in a ball sobbing.

"Oh my God. You ungrateful little whelp."

I snuffled and gasped, trying to stop. She had a temper and my father was out of town on business.

"What's wrong with her?" my brother asked, jumping over me and heading downstairs.

"She's being a brat. Go get the groceries out of the trunk, Robert. And Monica, you stop it this minute. Damn it! How many girls would kill for a room like yours?"

Not one, I thought.

The room became a moot point; I would live in it until I left home. Meanwhile, Fedora and my mother hired workers to antique our kitchen cabinets a dirty white with turquoise interiors. Blue and chartreuse wallpaper turned our kitchen into a Peter Max painting. Fedora and Mother finished off with plastic bricks glued like wainscoting along the breakfast room walls.

My mother never spoke about my room and neither did Fedora, the object of my hatred. With her short arms and legs and tan even in winter, I began to think of her as a breed of alien from Rod Serling's "The Twilight Zone."

Periodically she returned to lay siege to our five-bedroom saltbox. In tenth grade, she and Mother gutted the one room Dad held sacrosanct, our den, where he read *Life Magazine* and watched "The Ed Sullivan Show." One week when he was out of town, they had Goodwill cart away his brown couch and replaced it with a scratchy orange divan and gold and turquoise wing back chairs firm as pincushions. They hired Manpower to pry up the red and white linoleum in the amusement room—great for cartwheels and dancing—and laid carpet squares. Only Dad's bar and bar stools were left intact.

My brothers, Bobby and Denny, didn't care about the redecorating because they were always out with friends. Neither did five-year-old Celeste who was into ballet and Barbies. But my Dad and I suffered. When I left for the University of

Wisconsin, I told Mother to give my room to my little sister, by then a cheerleader and boy magnet. Like Mother, Celeste had blue-black hair, bewitching eyes and skin like a peach.

♦♦♦

Three months later, I was home for Thanksgiving, roomless and sleeping on the studio bed in my brother's old room. When I glanced down the hall to my bedroom, pink light spilled into the hall like a Day-Glo waterfall.

Under the ownership of Celeste, the room had been papered in electric pink. A white wall unit with gold handles, shelves with knick knacks and a built-in desk like in the Penney's catalog replaced my maple set. Pink carpeting popped with color. Fuchsia sheets clashed deliciously with rosy tie back curtains puffing in the breeze. I stood paralyzed. Celeste came in and flopped on the bed and the sheets lent a neon glimmer to her face.

"Mom and Fedora did it," she said. "Do you like it?"

I nodded, unable to speak.

"I didn't pick any of it. But it's my dream room." She admired her polished nails, then looked up. "How could you stand it the way it was?"

My throat constricted. Tears welled but I didn't blink. I realized then that Celeste was Mother's favorite and always would be. The idea that parents love us all equally is a charade. The certainty of that ricocheted in my brain like the steel ball banging in my little brother's pinball machine down the hall.

♦♦♦

At twenty-five, my walnut eyes pretty behind contacts, my posture erect, my hair auburn and gleaming like in the Prell commercials I'd written for a Chicago ad agency, I had totally forgotten the room. Celeste was a Tri Delt at Arizona State, Bobby a dentist in Milwaukee and Dennis, a golf pro in Santa Barbara. I hadn't been home in more than a year. My Dad wanted me to visit so there I was, chewing a mouthful of steak at the country club's chuck wagon buffet with my parents when

I learned Fedora was in a coma.

An old guy in a hounds tooth jacket hobbled by midway through dinner holding a shaky plate. "Ned," my Mother said. He turned a stiff neck.

"Shirley. Jim. Hello. Is this your lovely daughter?"

"This is Monica. Monica, this is Ned Dierberger, Fedora's husband. You remember Fedora," my Mother said.

"Hello, Ned."

He smiled, then set his plate down and took my mother's hand. "She's still comatose. It's tragic." His voice caught and his face looked like a bloodhound's.

"I'm so sorry to hear that." My mother squeezed his hand in both hers. Dad's thigh nudged mine under the table. He'd made out a lot of checks to Fedora. He'd felt terrible about my bedroom and I'd been upset over his den.

"It's been more than a year now. I'm afraid we'll have to . . . pull the plug soon. Shirley, she always said you were her favorite client." Ned's chin trembled.

"She was so talented."

"She always made her clients very happy." He patted my mother's hand, then drifted off.

Dad and I looked at each other. He didn't smile but his russet eyes did, the crow's feet on either side crinkling. Mother told me Fedora had been ill off and on for years: stubborn bronchial problems in her forties, then digestive troubles to the point of needing to have part of her stomach removed in her fifties, and then, finally when she'd regained energy and clients, she keeled over into her steak tartare at Chez Bonnet at sixty-two with a stroke.

"You never told me she was ill," I said.

"I knew you wouldn't care."

I beckoned to the waiter for another scotch and water.

"I'll have one too," Dad said.

"It's such a shame," Mother said, then launched into a description of Celeste's sorority sisters, courses and boyfriends.

◆◆◆

Back at our house, which was for sale but not selling, I left my parents watching Johnny Carson and went upstairs to my old room. I groped around in the back corner of the closet amidst the hems of Celeste's prom dresses and found the compartment I'd gouged in the drywall behind the molding in fifth grade. No one had redone the closet. I pulled out the German doll with its stolid face and gray hair from my global collection. It was scrunched and flattened but intact. Three of my mother's straight pins punctured its stomach and throat and temple. The temple pin jutted out the other side.

I sat there staring at it, my heart racing, my hands clammy. I marveled at how much the German doll with its stunted arms and legs, loud dress, and Sixties hairdo resembled Fedora. Then I thought of finding a doll that looked like my mother and piercing its heart.

Santa's Little Helper

Anne Frasier

'TWAS THE NIGHT before Christmas and Santa lay sprawled on his back in the middle of Savannah's Chatham Square, a pool of blood under his head. It didn't take a coroner to pronounce this one.

"Dead." Detective David Gould straightened away from the body.

Most criminals had a line they wouldn't cross. For some, animals were off limits. For others it was children, old people, or crazy people. Santa? What kind of sick bastard killed Santa? In front of a buncha kids, no less?

Elise Sandburg was bent over the body, visually examining the bullet-mangled face. David found her lack of revulsion oddly attractive. They hadn't been partners all that long, but they shared a dramatic history. She'd saved his life in more ways that one. Would he ever tell her that? Probably not.

At the moment they were the only ones near the body. Just their own cozy little Christmas Eve get together. Coroner, medical examiner, and crime-scene team hadn't yet arrived. A few cops were working the crowd looking for witnesses while others fanned out to search the immediate area.

Elise shook her head, echoing David's disgust over the Santa slaughter.

"Come on," he teased. "This can't possibly be the sickest thing you've ever seen."

"Why do you say that?" She didn't look up, but he could hear the annoyance and suspicion in her voice.

"I was talking about Savannah, not your heritage. You're too sensitive about that root doctor stuff." But people said she could work spells. Mojos. He sometimes wondered if she'd worked one on him.

She got to her feet. "You seem in an awfully good mood for being called out on Christmas Eve." Her eyes narrowed. "Have you been drinking?"

When you were an addict, everybody waited for you to relapse. "Please, I'm trying to find a new stereotype."

"Prescription drugs?"

Their conversation was low and deadpan. The casual observer would think they were discussing Santa.

"Can't I just be high on life?"

"If you're delusional."

"Maybe I'm happy to be spending Christmas Eve with you."

"I invited you to dinner tomorrow."

"I'm coming. I was making cranberry bread when you called."

Her brows lifted. "Right."

"Hey, I can be very domestic. You'd be surprised."

From somewhere in the distance a Bing Crosby song was playing. Delicate white lights had been strung in tree branches and wrapped around narrow trunks. Some kind of flowers were blooming, and the scent was sweet and heavy.

Ah, Savannah.

The coroner van pulled to a stop in the middle of the street, and Elise returned to her visual exam of the body.

"Interesting angle to the trajectory." She pointed. "Entry here, under the chin. Exit here." She pointed to the blown eye socket.

"Perpetrator could have been holding the gun low, about hip level." David demonstrated with his hand. "To keep the weapon hidden."

She nodded, but didn't look convinced.

Sirens sounded, radios squelched, and lights strobed in the darkness as more police arrived.

A door slammed and an officer approached. "Dead?" he asked too loudly.

Elise glanced at the crowd and nodded.

"Santa's *dead*?" a little kid wailed from the other side of the yellow crime-scene tape. "*Dead*?"

Another kid started bawling. That cry was taken up by the next and the next.

David ducked under the tape. "He's not the real Santa," he told them.

"Mommy said the Santa in the square is the only real Santa. That all the other ones are helpers." The kid turned to the mob. "He *was* the real Santa."

"So we don't have to be good no more?" The question came from a boy who was too old for Santa, but probably wasn't ready to admit it at the risk of no gifts.

"You still have to be good," David said. Then over his shoulder: "Can somebody cover him up?" The medical examiner and coroner were finally tending to the victim. "It's Christmas Eve. There are kids here."

"I sat on Santa's lap."

David looked down at the little girl tugging on the hem of his coat.

"I sat on Santa's lap and showed him what I found." She pulled out a Colt Defender.

Adult gawkers gasped and stepped back in a wave.

David calmly crouched in front of her. "Let me have that, sweetheart."

She didn't want to let go, but David managed to pry the gun from her tiny fingers. It was sticky from blood spatter and candy.

"You shot Santa," one of the boys said.

"U-uh." Her lip trembled.

"Right in the eye," the same boy elaborated. "Killed him dead."

The little girl began to wail.

A young female elf appeared and held out a lollipop. "Quit your cryin'. He ain't the real Santa."

The child stopped sobbing and reached for the sweet.

The 17ᵗʰ Rule of
Highly Effective Bank Robbers

Troy Cook

Are you nuts? We can't have a nine-year-old kid on this robbery!"

Tara bristled, crinkling her eyebrows. "Can, too!"

Wyatt patted her on the head. "It's okay, honey. If I decide to do this job, you'll definitely be a part of it. You and me are a team."

Tara beamed, then stuck her tongue out at the greasy-haired stranger in their living room. He blinked a few times, shaking his head.

"I just don't see how this is gonna happen, Wyatt," the stranger said. "I know we got mutual friends and that you're highly recommended, but this is a kid we're talking about."

"Then maybe this won't work out, Guy. I'm telling you that she can handle herself. You either trust me or you don't."

The stranger, Guy, leaned back in his chair. "Come on, Wyatt…"

"No. You listen, here. She's a really bright kid. And I've been training her, making her a nice set of rules she can use to prepare for jobs. She even has experience."

"That's right. Three banks!" Tara said. "And I'm almost ten anyway."

She stared at Guy and tried to act tough, but the man ignored her.

"Fine, whatever. You're her daddy. If you want her in a dangerous situation, who am I to tell you what's what?"

"Damn straight," Wyatt said. "So what's the job?"

Tara grinned and plopped down in the corner. Grabbing

her Barbie and Ken dolls, she pretended to play but kept her attention on the conversation between Guy and her daddy.

"This is a good one, Wyatt. Half a million to split."

"Bullshit. Banks don't keep that much cash on hand."

Guy grinned. "Course not. That's why we don't hit the bank. We hit the armored car company instead."

Wyatt knocked back a shot of Jack Daniels. "No."

"Now I know you're partial to banks. But this is where they keep the money for *twenty* banks. We're just cutting out the middle man."

"Twenty?" Tara said. "I bet they'd have a lot more money than we got at the last bank."

Wyatt shot her a glare. "Keep quiet, Missy. Or go to your room."

Tara pouted, but kept silent.

"You've got my attention," Wyatt said. "Convince me."

Guy pulled out some schematics and spread them across the dinette table. "You're gonna love it. This plan is foolproof."

Wyatt snorted. "I'm sure it is."

"Just listen for a minute, okay? Here's the big picture—I've got a man on the inside who will short out the alarm at a key access point. This small-town place doesn't have much security. If we do it at the right moment, all we have to do is bust through two locks and take out three guards. It don't get much simpler than this."

"What about your inside man? What makes you think they won't figure out he's part of it?"

"Because we take him out, too."

Tara gasped and brushed her long brown hair out of her eyes so she could get a better look at Guy. "Daddy? Does that mean what I think it means?"

Wyatt's eyes narrowed and his hand moved toward the gun in his waistband. "A man that would take out his partner…"

"Whoa, hang on. That's not what I meant. We're going to take them out with tranquilizer pistols. Here, I brought one with me."

Guy reached under his jacket and slowly withdrew an

aluminum-barreled tranq gun. "These are single shots so we'll carry one in each hand, plus one in the waistband, just in case. But don't miss."

"How long does it take to kick in, bring someone down?"

"It slows 'em down immediately and keeps 'em from using any fine motor skills, like firing a weapon But, a big guy like you might take a minute or two to be completely out."

Tara frowned, uneasy with the way that was phrased. Guy was a little creepy.

"All right," Wyatt said. "I'm in, provided the details back up what you've been saying. But one question. Why tranquilizers?"

"This way we can shoot my man without killing him. Also, if something does go wrong, you get a lighter sentence if you don't use lethal weapons."

Tara stomped her foot and pointed her Barbie doll at Guy. "If something goes wrong? But you said it was foolproof."

Guy winced. "All right, you caught me. *Practically* foolproof." He turned to Wyatt. "She's a real firecracker, ain't she?"

Wyatt nodded. "You got that right. She's makes me real proud."

Tara glowed, basking in the praise. *He's proud of me!*

◆◆◆

THREE DAYS LATER, Tara bumped along in the back of a cargo van with a tranquilizer gun in her hand and a nervous smile on her face. *Oh boy, here we go again.*

A large jolt almost knocked her over and she found herself wishing she had a seat like Guy and her daddy had up front. The bumps were making it awfully hard for her to get her hair hidden beneath her cowboy hat.

The van made a hard right and Tara squealed as she banged into the side of the van.

Guy growled, "Girl, we're almost there. You're supposed to be ready now!"

Tara wedged herself into the back corner of the van and rubbed her forehead. "If you had seatbelts, I'd be ready already."

Wyatt made his way from the passenger seat and knelt beside Tara. He grabbed her hair and shoved it under her hat. "I know you hate being dressed like a boy but it's the perfect disguise for you."

"I know. You've only explained it a hundred times. But I still don't like it."

"I know, Sugar, but it's important." Wyatt placed the mask over her eyes and secured it. "You been going over the rules?"

"Yeah."

"Good girl. What's Rule #1?"

"Mmmm, don't close my eyes when I shoot?"

"That's right," Wyatt said. "Hopefully, you won't have to shoot. But don't forget that your gun is your friend. Treat him right and he'll take care of you."

Tara looked down at her feet. "If I tell you something, promise you won't get mad at me?"

Wyatt grabbed her chin and looked her in the eye. "What is it, Sugar?"

Tara hesitated, then blurted out, "I'm sorry, Daddy, but this job is making me real scared."

"It's okay, Honey. You've been nervous before. You'll do fine."

"No, it's not that. Well, actually I am nervous about that. But…" Tara leaned in close and whispered, "I'm really scared of Guy. I think he's going to do something bad to us."

Wyatt nodded. "You're one smart cookie, you know that? Those are your instincts kicking in, and they're right on the money. I don't trust this guy either."

"So what do we do?"

Wyatt tapped his finger on her tranquilizer gun. "Just pretend you're watching the guards but keep one eye on Guy, okay? I'll do the same."

Guy brought the van to a stop and killed the ignition. "All right, it's go time. You ready, Girl?"

Tara nodded.

Guy pulled a Barbie doll, still in its box, from a bag sitting next to him. "If you do a good job today this baby will be yours."

Tara clapped her hands as Guy dropped the doll on the seat, then jerked a ski mask over his head and jumped out of the van. Wyatt tugged pantyhose over his face, slid open the side door, and hopped out. Tara ran after them, running as fast as she could to keep up.

Tara was breathing heavy when they finally stopped at the back entrance. Guy crouched down and got to work on the lock.

"You sure your partner shorted out the alarm on this door?" Wyatt asked. "I hate trusting someone else to get the job done."

"Yeah, damn it. He's already called it in and it'll be fixed by this afternoon. It's now or never."

"Then quit talking to me and get 'er done already."

Guy grimaced and got back to work. Twenty seconds later, and with a triumphant grin, he popped open the door. They rushed inside and paused at the next corner. Tara could hear the buzz of a video camera around the corner and her heart felt like it was going to explode.

Guy checked his watch and whispered, "All right, my partner is going to leave his station in about one minute. We'll only have thirty seconds, the time it takes him to grab a cup of coffee, for all of us to move quietly down this hall and blow the door to the guard room. I've got the charge ready to go but I won't have any time for questions this time. I need to concentrate on the task at hand."

Wyatt chuckled. "No problem."

"And remember, the big, bald guard is our inside guy. Shoot him last and don't hurt him. Shoot the little guards first."

Wyatt nodded. Tara took a couple of deep breaths, trying to calm her herself.

Guy looked at his watch. "Five, four, three, two, one. Go!"

The three of them snuck down a long, concrete hallway. Tara watched the camera that was pointed right at them and prayed that no one was watching.

Guy knelt by the last door on the right and pulled the bomb from his pack. He placed the putty around the door lock, wired it up, and scooted back about ten feet. Guy and Wyatt placed their tranq guns at their feet and her daddy motioned for Tara to do the same.

"Cover your ears, Honey, and close your eyes."

Tara cupped her ears as Guy held his hand up and counted down with his fingers.

Three...two...one...*BOOM!*

Even with her ears covered, the sound was louder than she expected. Tara grabbed her gun off the floor and followed her daddy into the large, smoke filled, money room.

Tara waved her gun around and tried to ignore the burning sensation in her eyes. The room was a madhouse—guards yelling and reaching for their guns as Wyatt and Guy took aim and shot at them. The guns made little *pffftht* sounds that might have made Tara laugh if things hadn't been so scary and chaotic.

Wyatt ran toward one of the guards and launched himself into a little guy who was reaching for an alarm switch.

A few seconds later, it was over. Tara looked around the room and had to laugh at the guard bent over a chair with a feathered dart sticking out of his butt.

Wyatt smacked the limp guard he'd tackled, a dart stuck in his chest. "Wow, that was fun! What a rush."

Wyatt grabbed a key from the guard, unlocked the money cage, and went inside. Guy pulled a guard off one of the flatbed carts and rolled it over to the cage, just in time to be knocked over by Wyatt on his way out.

"What the hell is this? There's nowhere close to half a million in here."

Alarmed, Guy raced into the cage and cried out, "What the hell? These are mostly singles, and bags of change!"

Wyatt rolled over the big, bald guard and smacked him a couple of times across the face. "Where's the money, Baldy? There can't be more than a hundred thousand in there."

Baldy, drugged out with his eyes rolling back in his head, started to giggle. "Hey, man...I don't know what happened... it's some kind of big payroll day or something...the banks took it all this morning…weird, huh?"

"Are you kidding me?" Wyatt started kicking Baldy, repeatedly, with as much force as he could muster.

Tara flinched and sat next to one of the downed guards. She turned away from the beating. There was another *pffftht* sound and a groan from her daddy. She whirled around and found a puffy, feathered dart sprouting from her daddy's neck.

Wyatt slumped onto a flatbed cart.

Tara cried out and aimed her tranquilizer gun at Guy, who had a big grin on his face and an empty tranq gun in his hand. She squinted her eyes and squeezed the trigger, only to watch the dart hit a clock on the wall behind him.

Oh, no. I only had one shot!

Guy reached into the cage and grabbed the canvas bags filled with bills, ignoring the heavy change bags. "I'm gonna pretend you didn't shoot at me, Tara. You didn't have to be here. That's something your sicko father made you do. In fact, maybe you should thank me for rescuing you."

Tara threw the empty tranquilizer gun at him, nailing Guy in the left shoulder.

"Hey, stop that. I'm giving you the chance to walk right out of here, Tara. And I suggest you take it, unless you want to be carted off to a juvenile detention center."

Tara shuddered, watching her daddy's eyes roll back in his head. She tried to think of what she could possibly do to stop Guy and save her dad. *I need another gun.*

The guards!

Tara checked, and sure enough the guard she was sitting next to still had his gun in his holster.

"Come on, Tara. Just 'cause I'm screwing your old man over doesn't mean you and I can't be friends. I'm trying to help you."

Thinking fast, Tara screwed up her face and started to bawl. Pretending to cry wasn't as hard as she thought because she was so close to tears anyway. She threw her body onto the guard as if she was throwing a Class A temper tantrum, kicking and wailing.

"Look, I don't have time for this crap, Tara. If you want to get out of here, you've got about one minute to do it. Because that's how long it'll take the cops to get here once I push this alarm."

Not the alarm! She grabbed for the gun and whirled around to face a surprised Guy.

A sharp crack from the revolver and Guy dropped to the ground, blood gushing from his thigh.

Ohmigod.! I can't believe I shot him.

"I'm so sorry, Guy. I had to. I couldn't let you push the alarm."

Guy moaned and pulled his shirt off, tying it around his leg to staunch the blood flow.

Tara paled, looking at the pool of blood. "Now I'm going to give you a chance, Guy. If you leave right now, I won't shoot you again. You can even take the money."

Wheezing, Guy gave her a sickly grin. "You got it, Girl."

He grabbed the bags of money and hobbled out the door while Tara rushed to her daddy's side.

"What should I do, Daddy? I don't want the police to catch you."

Wyatt focused his eyes for a second and mumbled, "Use this cart I'm laying on and just roll me on out of here, Honey. Roll me as far down the road as you can and then hide me in the best place you find and wait for me to wake up. If you can do that, we just might make it."

"I can't do it."

Wyatt's eyes defocused and his head lolled to the side.

Tara stared at the flatbed cart and climbed to her feet, shaking her head. "I'll do the best I can, Daddy."

She dropped the gun on the cart and tucked his legs underneath him so they didn't drag on the ground. It took her a great deal of effort to push the cart around the corner in the hall, but once she got past that obstacle she didn't think it looked like too hard of a job. In fact, there was a slight downhill slant to the road that made it easy to lead him away.

♦♦♦

TARA SLUMPED ON the couch with her dinner—a bowl of Cheerios she'd prepared herself—and wondered if her daddy was okay. She clicked on the television and flipped through the channels, looking for some cartoons, but all the channels had either commercials or news reports of the robbery of an armored car company.

"Booooring."

She was about to turn off the TV when her daddy slipped through the door. His face was covered with scratches and a gash in his shoulder bled down his arm.

"Are you okay, Daddy?"

"I am now, Honey."

Wyatt ripped open a couple of garbage bags and dropped the canvas bags of money onto the orange shag carpet. He pulled an unopened Barbie doll from one of the bags.

"Guy said he wanted you to have this."

Tara jumped up and down, clapping her hands. "And did he say he was sorry?"

Wyatt smiled. "Why yes he did. Over and over."

On the television, a news reporter said, "We take you live to the scene of the second shootout in Pitkin County. The deceased has been identified as Guy Richards, suspect in today's earlier shootout."

Rule #17: Don't trust nobody. Truth is as hard to come by as thirty-year-old virgin. The day you believe some lying sack of horseshit is the day you get put in the ground, permanently.

Puck

Pat Dennis

"She's here!"

Edith Mae flattened herself against the entryway wall. Her bulbous arms spread out against the white and gold embossed wallpaper like a vulture stuffed by a bad taxidermist. She turned her head sideways in fear her profile could be seen through the door's tiny peephole.

Meanwhile, Ralph scurried across the floor from the living room, racing toward the stairs to the basement. "Just answer it! She knows we're in here."

Her jaw clinched tight. "Of course she does, you old fool. You left the living room curtains wide open."

Ralph halted. "How many times do I have to tell you, I like to look outside?"

"How many times have I told *you*, if you can see out, *they* can see in?"

"They," he repeated right before he bolted down the steps, "are our neighbors, not some friggin' foreign invader."

"Humph," she hissed as the sounds of the Westminster chimes jolted her and a few seconds later, jolted her again. Ralph was right. The woman outside would keep pushing the doorbell till doomsday. There was no escape.

"Mrs. Iverson, I know you're in there." The chipper sing-song voice pierced the thick oak. "You can't hide!"

The giggle that followed disgusted her. It was the kind of laughter a person shares with a treasured friend, not used as a ploy to open a door.

Puck!

She relented, carefully opening the door, allowing only half of her to be seen. She smiled sweetly considering she'd like to kill the impish woman who stood in front of her, clipboard in hand, eyes wide and earnest. "What is it Mrs. Zarimba?"

"Call me Puck. You've known me for five years so I know you know my nickname. And in fact, it's very fitting today because I'm here to ask you to…"

"I can't donate to any of your environmental causes or buy any of your trinkets or order any of those nasty cookies from your kids. I told you before, I'm on a fixed income."

She didn't fail to notice that Puck took a quick glance at the two new BMWs sitting in her driveway.

Hockey Moms! They expected you to drive a beater so their kids could waste their days skating around inside a stupid arena instead of on a lake as God intended.

"I'm here for a good cause. The Little Beavers Hockey Team is going to Brainerd for the state tournament. We're selling these adorable frames to raise money for expenses."

Puck held up a flimsy plastic picture frame. The sides were hockey stick replicas. The top and bottom were a line of miniature hockey pucks.

"For only $30.00 you can buy four of these and support the team at the same time. Aren't they just the sweetest things ever?"

She didn't respond. How could she tell Puck that she'd never seen such a piece of crap in her entire life or that the price was totally outrageous? Nor did she ask what was the value in teaching kids to manipulate people into buying junk.

"Of course, if you'd rather just donate money, you certainly can. I already have over $1500 in cash donations that…"

This time she didn't hesitate to respond. "I'll buy four of them. Do you want the money now?"

Puck smiled widely, "Yes, please."

"I'll get my purse."

Fortunately, a twenty and a ten were always hidden in the bottom of her purse. It was an emergency stash in case she needed to bribe a cop who stopped her for speeding, or a grocery store worker who noticed lamb chops peeking out from inside her cleavage.

At 66 years of age, she knew what kept the world spinning. She always had. Good old money, plain and simple.

It was why hers was held onto so tightly.

A thousand dollars was hidden in a coffee can on her kitchen shelf. Thousands more were buried in the backyard. Even underground, the money was as easy to find as the dough stashed in the Folgers can. On top of each financial grave, she'd placed laminated cardboard tombstones with words like Forever Fluffy or Mittens the Kitten. She never owned a cat, alive or dead. In fact, she prided herself on not liking pets or people.

No one or nothing could be trusted, including the banks, her husband or her kids. Her dad taught her early on that everyone in the world was looking out for themselves. If for a moment she drifted from her inherited inclination of distrust, her grifter of a father would remind her with the backside of his hand what people were really like.

She grew to understand that most folks would steal from their own grandmothers. Or from their neighbors, which is exactly what she planned to do as she stood at the front room window, watching Puck trek across the cul-de-sac and back home.

"What if she catches you?" Ralph said, shuffling to his Lazy Boy with a six-pack of Miller Lite. "I don't want to shell out for a lawyer to get you off the hook."

"I won't need a lawyer. I've done this before," she reminded him.

"Swiping $1500 is a lot different than stealing a cup of Cocoa Puffs…"

Or sugar or a can of tuna or whatever Edith Mae needed in a pinch. Over the years she'd found it easier to sneak into a neighbor's kitchen than drive the four miles to the grocery store. Besides, she knew that if she were a friend to the people on her block, they'd gladly have given her what she needed.

She was just sidestepping the friend part.

"How's she going to catch me? She's never home, she's always out driving around in that friggin' vehicle of hers."

Nearly thirty years earlier, the surprising arrival of the first minivan in her neighborhood convinced her that life, as she knew it, was over.

Gone were the good old days when Scotch was the drink of choice, not Merlot. Ended were the days when mothers naturally took more interest in themselves then their children.

Good manners dissolved as well. No one could smoke a cigarette or two without being considered offensive. And daily, kids were being turned into sissies by being belted down in cars or forced to wear stupid helmets as they rode their tricycles a half-a-mile an hour.

The worst, as far as she was concerned, was the invention of the puffed-up, pregnant-looking station wagons, with their super high seats and DVD players.

DVD players!!! It was as if the hyperactive latte injected hockey moms would commit suicide if their kids weren't entertained 24/7.

Hockey moms. They were as bad as minivans.

"I don't think you should do this," Ralph stated as he flipped the channel to a rerun of *Friends*. "Someday, you're going to get caught and then where will we be?"

She didn't answer his question. "Haven't you seen that stupid episode at least a hundred times already? Here's a clue, moron. In real life, they're not friends."

"Neither are we," Ralph mumbled in a hoarse whisper.

She spun around. "What did you say to me?"

"Nothing important," he answered, pulling up the tabs on each of beers. He arranged them in a single row on the coffee table in front of him. "Nothing you don't already know."

♦♦♦

LATER THAT EVENING, Edith Mae waited patiently, stationed behind her bedroom curtains. She peered through a small opening, her binoculars barely visible to the outside world.

She'd used them before, on all of the neighbors. It was fascinating how quickly people would forget there were other people in the world while prancing around in their undies, showing their secrets to the world.

If she stood on a chair and stretched, she could see straight inside the Hartman's bedroom window. Of course, nothing happened in that room. She wasn't surprised.

The Olson's master bedroom was a different matter. The husband and wife fought constantly. She assumed the battles were about her. She was right.

Mrs. Olson made it known to everyone on the block that she wanted to move out of the neighborhood, or even the state if possible. She was tired of being sued in small claims court by her hostile neighbor.

Yet, Edith Mae continued her litigations, telling the judge her health was being destroyed by the presence of a portable basketball hoop at the end of the Olson's driveway. She insisted her daily two-hour naps were constantly being interrupted by high-pitched yells and irritating laughter. As far as she was concerned, the once quiet cul-de-sac had been turned into a ghetto playground.

When she shifted the binoculars she saw Puck run out of her house and jump into the minivan. All three of her children followed, as well as her husband, Lance, and their yappy dog Dixie.

She noticed Puck leaned over to turn on the radio. More than likely, she had chosen the obnoxious Radio Disney. The entire family and dog were popping up and down like prairie dogs in the Dakotas as they took off down the street.

She decided to wait a good half-hour before going over.

"You're gonna fall off that chair," Ralph's voice loomed behind her.

She almost did.

"You almost made me fall! You're such a negative person. Can't a woman peek through the curtains without you making a big deal about it?"

Ralph pointed toward the tote bag on the bed. "You're taking tools to break in?"

"I don't need tools. You know no one on this street locks their door." Edith Mae carefully stepped down. "It's like those Generation X'ers think a locked door is politically incorrect or something. Sometimes, I think they want us to meet in center of the sac every night at ten to sing *Kumbaya* to each other."

"We don't lock our doors," Ralph reminded her.

"No one would dare to break into this house."

"That's probably true," he conceded, with a shrug.

Edith Mae waddled to the bed and sat next to the bag. She pulled out a flashlight and clicked it on and off a few times. She slipped it back inside the tote. While seated, she checked herself out in the full-length mirror, pleased with her choice of black slacks and top. It was already dark outside. She definitely wouldn't be seen.

"You're going too far this time," Ralph insisted. "Groceries and trinkets are one thing but that's a lot of cash you're planning on stealing."

The cold stare from her ice blue eyes nearly sliced Ralph in half.

"It's not cash, it's a donation for the betterment of a neighborhood. Mine."

THIRTY-TWO MINUTES later, Edith Mae was at Puck's side door. She opened it easily and slipped inside.

The layout was familiar. She'd broken into the home at least a dozen times before, sometimes for ingredients or sometimes just out of boredom. *Out of boredom,* she'd remind herself on those occasions, not because of some inner need to connect like some wacky shrink once suggested to her.

There was no way she could connect to someone like Puck anyway. They were too different to ever be friends. Puck lived in some sort of optimistic fantasy world where good things happened to good people. Edith Mae knew better.

Besides, she needed no one. All she really needed was to get in and out of the house as quickly as possible without being detected.

Normally on one of her excursions, she'd take the time to find a piece of chocolate or two. She knew Puck loved Godiva. But, tonight she was in a hurry. The house was large and the loot could be anywhere.

Still, a little treat would be nice; maybe a cream-filled truffle or two.

No, she'd resist. Fifteen hundred bucks would buy a lot of chocolate.

She'd noticed that Ralph was even cheaper since he retired, fretting over every dime. He claimed they only had enough retirement for one to live on in-style, much less two. If she wanted pin money to blow on some shopping spree, she'd have to find it herself.

Quickly scanning the kitchen counter, she lifted the lid on each canister. The only things inside were what should have been. She opened every kitchen drawer as well. Although she was in a hurry, she'd stop to read personal notes, to do lists or check out the pictures of the kids plastered across the refrigerator.

She decided Puck kept the money in her home office, a small room off the master bedroom upstairs. The room and its activities were fully visible from across the street. Puck's husband would sit at the computer, staring at it for hours. Sometimes, Puck would stand nearby as he held up bills in the air, waving them back and forth.

Too bad she and Puck weren't friends, she would think at those times. If they were, she'd tell her all men are like that and it's best just to ignore them.

In fact, the last time she was in the house, she clicked on the computer herself. She discovered Puck and Lance were $13,053.00 in credit card debt, far less than most of their neighbors.

She thought Puck would be happy to know her little family was better off than most. But, she never told her.

The hockey manifest was kept in the office as well as the list of names of her kids' soccer team, or the names of the latest environmental nut cases Puck had befriended. If the money was anywhere, it was probably sitting right on top of the desk.

It wasn't.

It was inside the desk drawer.

Her heart jumped for joy as she grabbed up the stack of

bills and shoved them into her tote. She grabbed a few still-packaged hockey picture frames as well. Eventually, she'd sell them on eBay.

She made it to the office doorway when an envelope caught her eye, a festive blue one with her name on it.

The words *Edith Mae Iverson* were written in red crayon.

Her hand reached out and lingered over the pastel envelope. She carefully picked it up and slowly pulled out the enclosed card.

Emblazoned across the front were the words *Thank You* surrounded by glittery flowers. Inside, were the signatures of all the children from the Little Beavers Hockey Team, as well as Puck's. At the bottom someone had handwritten *Thank you for being so generous, Mrs. Iverson.*

She was speechless. It was the first thank-you note anyone ever wrote to her. It contradicted what she always knew, that she was only meant to give and to expect nothing in return.

She studied it for a while, the tiny signatures, the stupid little smiley faces, and Puck's name, written in all caps. Slipping the card back into its envelope, Edith Mae placed it back on the desk. Out of her tote she grabbed the stack of money and picture frames. She peeled off a twenty from the pile and slipped the rest back into the drawer. Twenty was enough for a small box of chocolates. The good kind, the kind she'd share with Puck, her new best friend.

A smile crossed her face until she heard Ralph's voice booming out to her from downstairs.

"Get out, now!"

She didn't stop to think. If she had, she never would have bolted out of the room. She would have wondered instead why she didn't hear the minivan drive up or why she didn't see the vehicle lights reflected through the upstairs' window. She would have questioned how Ralph had gotten into Puck's house in the first place. She had locked the door behind her.

The shock of hearing her husband's voice overcame her logic. And she was more than surprised to see him standing at the bottom of the stairs, hockey stick in hand. She was just as shocked when she slipped on one of the many hockey pucks that weren't there before.

She felt herself tumble over and over. As her body slammed into the wooden floor she realized Ralph had been right all along. She had gone too far.

She decided, crumpled on the floor and barely breathing, so had her husband. Ralph stood only a few feet away from her, holding the stick in the air. She heard him mumble sorry as he slammed a puck into her temple.

Yet, it wasn't Edith Mae's life that passed in front of her eyes before she died, but Ralph's future. At the inquest, he would claim his wife mistook Puck's house for their own. After all, she had done it before.

She envisioned him providing a verbal confirmation to the well-known rumor that her memory had been failing as fast as her devotion to alcohol rose. She saw him smile ever so slightly when the judge declared her death an accident.

She knew that as soon as she died, Ralph's life would change for the better. Her life insurance policies insured that. And, the stash of cash that only she and Ralph knew about, hidden around the property, would be icing on his cake.

With her last breath, Edith Mae saw Ralph would become a generous man, as well as a good neighbor. He'd keep his curtains open as well. And he'd buy every single trinket being sold at his front door. He'd order boxes and boxes of those Girl Scout cookies—the ones he always loved, the minty kind, the kind that she always hated.

Why I Write Mysteries, by Gordon Matthews

Pete Hautman

Every Sunday afternoon, riding in the back seat of the Oldsmobile with the twins, Mom and Dad up front, we would visit the houses of the dead. Dad would stop the car across the street from the house, or the apartment building, or some other place if they had not died at home. Sometimes it was an office building or a park or a liquor bar or a bridge over the Mississippi River. Usually, though, it was a house or an apartment. I came to understand that violent death occurs often in small homes. A lot of them needed paint.

"Here," Dad would say, double-checking the newspaper clipping, "is where Teresa Groth was killed last Thursday night. She was shot in the stomach and was lying in a pool of blood when the police arrived. They think her boyfriend did it."

The five of us would stare out through the smudged windows of the Oldsmobile, looking at the yellow police tape on the door.

"A Hail Mary for Trudy Groth," Dad would say, taking the rosary down from the rear view mirror. We would put our hands together and pray.

I was maybe six years old when Dad started taking us to the houses of the dead. During the week he would read the daily newspapers—there were two of them back then—and clip articles. Sunday afternoons, after dinner, he would herd us all into the car and take us to the sites he had selected from his collection of clippings. It was something we did together, as normal and as regular as going to church. I remember how surprised I was when I learned from my classmates in the second grade that other families did not do the same.

I was twelve the first time I refused to go. There was something else I wanted to do that day, I don't know what. Maybe it was a touch football game over at Scott Park, or a matinee at the Boulevard. To my surprise and immense relief, Dad did not seem to mind when I told him I did not want to go with the rest of the family to pray for the dead. He was surprised, though—I could tell because he touched the tip of his nose with his forefinger and held it there, looking down at me for a long time before nodding, slowly. But he seemed to accept it.

After that I went to pray for the dead less and less often, and at some point during my high school years I stopped going altogether. When I left home to attend college in Arizona I put the prayers for the dead behind me, thinking of it only rarely.

After two years at the U of A I dropped out, took a sales job in Phoenix, got married, got divorced, and started writing murder mysteries. Never exactly made a living at it, but I keep cranking them out.

Christmas would draw me back to Minneapolis for a few days, but the rest of the year I stayed in the West, flexing my shallow roots in the warm and arid soil. One Christmas I asked Max, the Thoughtful Twin, whether Mom and Dad still went out to pray for the dead. Max was in his late twenties then, and had his own place a few miles north on Highway 10. We were sitting in Mom and Dad's rec room watching the Vikings lose to the Bears. Max was drinking a Budweiser. He looked fat. Mike, the Mechanical Twin, was in the basement with Dad trying to fix the washing machine. Mom was out forcing her fruitcakes on the neighbors.

"I don't think he does it anymore," Max said. "He still goes through the newspapers and cuts out the articles, but I don't think he goes out. I think Mom finally put her foot down."

I nodded.

"They're getting older, Gordy," Max said. "Dad's sixty-nine now, you know. Their friends have started to die. Every month another funeral. I guess that makes a difference. Your friends start to die, you don't want so much to pray for strangers anymore."

"Do you ever wonder what he was thinking about, taking us out to where all those people got killed?"

Max shrugged. "I don't think he was thinking much of anything. I think it was something just happened to him."

"What do you mean?"

"You know. Like one day you start scratching your ear because it itches, and the next thing you know you're doing it all the time and pretty soon you got a sore on your ear and you can't keep from picking at it. Or you sprinkle a little salt on your beer one day because you see the guy sitting next to you at the bar doing it, and pretty soon beer doesn't taste right without it. You sit around trying to figure stuff like that out, I don't know, a guy could go nuts."

Max was the Thoughtful Twin. If I had asked Mike, the Mechanical Twin, the same question he would have said, "I dunno. What you driving these days, Gord?"

Everything was sticking to me, the said and the unsaid.

As soon as I got back to Phoenix I immersed myself first in work, then in another woman, washing away the smells of my parents' airless, hot, humid little Minnesota house, clearing my pores to let in the dry desert air. It took a week to start feeling clean again, and another week for my past to find its cell and close the door.

Other people have had worse childhoods. A woman I was dating once showed me scars on her back that she said came from being beaten by her mother with a television antenna. They looked like the kind of marks you would get from sleeping on a wrinkled sheet, but they would never fade. This was after I had told her about my family's weekly prayers for the murdered souls. She had asked me why I had left Minnesota and somehow I had come out with the murdered souls bit. I was complaining about a weekly tour of the city in the back seat of my father's Oldsmobile and she tells me about having her ten-year-old back split open by a crazed and drunken mother. I finally learned to keep my childhood locked away, it had neither the joy nor the horror to justify public airing.

In late February I received this email from Max.

Gordo,

How are you? It's snowing like a S.O.B. here, and my snowblower is broke. Good thing I got 4WD on the Bronco. Mike keeps promising to fix my blower, but you know Mike. So anyway, I got time to write now which I been meaning to do.

You remember you asked me about Dad taking us to all those places where people got killed? Well, I asked him about it while we were watching the Rose Bowl. Did you see that? Man! So anyways I asked him if he still went out to pray and he said not since Mike and I moved out.

I asked him why and he said the only reason he did it was for us. He said it was part of our education, if you can believe that. What the hell do you suppose he thought he was teaching us? Wonder if he'll ever say.

Gotta go, bro!

Max

Well, the first time I took the family on a field trip it was kind of an accident, y'know? We were coming home from church, I remember Gordy was about ready to start the first grade and the twins were just born, and I got to thinking about, you know, being a good father to these kids. I had this idea that the best thing would be to educate them, so I started thinking about what kind of things we could learn, you know, together. So I said, halfway to home from St. Mark's, I said, what the hey, let's go on over to Minnehaha Falls.

Well now, Mary, she didn't know what to make of it.

"You mean now?" she said.

"Sure," I said. "Why not? Go get some history, the three of us."

"But what about Kathy?" Kathy Aronson was the girl we had baby-sitting the twins.

"Call her up," I said. "Tell her we'll be a little late."

So we went to the historical Minnehaha Falls that Sunday

and looked at the statues and I read what the carvings said out loud to Gordy. He seemed to like that, and I learned a lot too.

That was our first Sunday field trip, and it was a big success except Mary refused to walk down the steps to the base of the falls in her Sunday shoes.

So I started taking the family out regular after church. One Sunday we would visit historical Fort Snelling, and the next day we would drive by the Governor's mansion, and the next Sunday we would go stand on the very spot where Captain Zebulon Pike met the wild Indians. I was learning a lot, but I noticed that Mary and Gordy got a little bored sometimes no matter how exciting the history was. I use to try to jazz it up a bit, you know. Tell them Zebulon Pike was strong as Paul Bunyan, tell them he rowed himself up the Mississippi in a hundred foot canoe. That kind of stuff seemed to light up little Gordy, but Mary didn't care for it. But I was doing the best I knew how, trying to give my kids the advantage.

After a while I started running out of famous historical places to take them, so we started going to see things that I found in the newspaper. One day we went to see a cheese factory that had burned to the ground. The building, what was left of it, was surrounded by black mounds of burnt cheese that had flowed out like hot lava. Everything smelled like Cheez-It crackers. Gordy liked that one a lot, and when we got home we ate Cheez-Its.

Another time I was reading the paper and saw an article about a St. Paul lawyer named Berglund who had been charged with hiring a man to kill his wife. The police said that he had paid a man $1500 to kill his wife so that he could collect a million dollar life insurance policy. So the next Sunday, after church, I took Mary and Gordy and the twins to the house in St. Paul where the murder had happened and told them the story.

Course, I had to jazz it up a bit.

"...the killer came into her bedroom, quiet as a cat, and raised up his ax, and Mrs. Bergland woke up at that very moment and saw the gigantic blade coming down, the last thing she would ever see, while the wicked lawyer sat drinking fancy cocktails at his country club..."

I tell you, you never saw such a wide-eyed face as the one on Gordy. Even Mary got caught up in it. Max and Mike, the twins, were only about one and a half then, but they seemed interested even if they didn't know what I was talking about. We sat there staring across the street at that house for, I don't know, a long time. Gordy kept asking me about the blood.

"Was there a lot of blood?"

"Blood was everywhere. On the mattress, on the walls. They had to throw the bed away."

"Did the blood squirt all the way up to the ceiling?"

I was thinking, about then, that maybe Gordy's education needed something to balance off the blood and guts, and that was when I got the idea to say a prayer for Mrs. Berglund. So we said an Our Father, and that seemed to calm us all down.

I don't know how it happened, but pretty soon nearly all of our field trips were to places where people had died. We had found something we could do together as a family, something we all enjoyed. I know that some people, people like my brother George, and all of Mary's relatives, thought we were pretty strange, but I didn't let it bother me any. Some parents just send their kids to school, but I say the important lessons of life are learned in the home. Some families, they just don't do anything together.

Eddie's Dungeon

A Jerry Scott story

Chris Everheart

Icry at funerals. I cry at weddings. I cry at bar mitzvahs and kindergarten plays. I'm not divorced. My kids talk to me. I've never been in prison or even wrongly accused of a crime. Unlike the great "private eyes" of fiction, my name isn't Sam or Max or Dick. I can handle myself in a fight, but I'm not what you would call a tough-guy. I still get the job done, though.

I'm a working private detective named Jerry Scott. I do divorces, criminal background checks on rich kids' nannies, insurance frauds and the occasional bail-jumper. I deal with rotten characters sometimes, but I try to look for the best in people—if only because it helps me get through the day.

Bail cases can be complicated. I don't want to get into all the details, but basically the way bail works is someone pays the court a bond to get out of jail. The bond is a guarantee that offender will return to court when scheduled. A bondsman puts up money for bails that people can't afford on their own and takes the ten percent deposit for his trouble. The risk is that if the defendant doesn't show up to court, the bondsman doesn't get his money back, so he has to track down the bail-jumper himself and bring him in or he's out the thousands of dollars he put up. There's a profit in this kind of business, but the clientele is not the prettiest.

Take Eddie Prentiss, for example. Nice enough guy when he's not on meth, crack, pills or booze... Ah, who am I kidding? He's always loaded, he's always a jerk and he's always in trouble. He steals cars, beats up his girlfriends, runs drugs into small towns in Northern Minnesota and has a half-dozen kids all over the five-state region. With no permanent address, he can be almost impossible to find—especially when he's due in court.

That's where I come in. I have a nose for wrong-doers. Maybe it's because I think positive and the negative always stands out. I know Eddie because I've tracked him down before. In his own way, Eddie likes me because when I catch him I don't beat him up or lecture him or embarrass him. I take him in, turn him over to the desk sergeant and collect my fee from the bondsman.

This time Eddie did something bad enough that his bail was sky high and once out of jail he didn't ever want to be found. He was up on federal drug charges when he got out and immediately disappeared. The problem is that a girl who was planning to testify against him—Lisa Miller—also disappeared the same day. He must have really pissed this girl off to make her risk her life and become a snitch. But she's missing—presumed dead—and Eddie didn't show up for his hearing. The authorities didn't think any of it was a coincidence and issued a warrant. So now he's got two problems—the US Marshals Service and *me*.

Ordinarily I would let the Marshals handle one this ugly—it's what they do best. But Bobby Bright, Eddie's bail bondsman, is dangling fifteen thousand dollars in front of my face to bring him in first so he can collect the bond now. He would prefer to wait for the Marshals too, but he's going through a nasty divorce and needs to drum up some cash without selling any of his chick-magnet toys. See? *Always treat her right the first time around,* I tell these young guys.

That's how I find myself crawling into the tiny basement window of an abandoned house in a seedy North Minneapolis neighborhood. My wife is going to kill me when she sees this new shirt. She made me put a bag of grubbies in the trunk of my car for just such an occasion, but I don't have time to change clothes. Earlier this afternoon I got a tip from a friend who works for the city as a meter reader. He saw a guy who looked like Eddie's newspaper mug shot hanging around this house with a young lady. That's as good an ID on Eddie and Nora Larson—his latest wife-never-to-be—as I'm going to get. I need to nab him before he and Nora move again. I'm counting on the fifteen grand from this quick collar to build an in-ground swimming pool at my house.

I know it seems like it would be easier to knock on the front door, but the element of surprise is crucial, especially when working alone. If I suddenly appear, gun in hand, in the living room or bedroom, screaming my head off and threatening to shoot, the suspect is much more likely to give up than if he has time to peek out the window and figure out that someone has come to take him in.

The basement windows on these old houses are tiny and the opening is tight. To squeeze through, I have to take off my windbreaker and pull my 9mm, holster and cuffs off my belt. I lay them in a neat pile next to the window, stick my feet in and slide through on my belly, scraping every square inch of exposed skin and, OUCH!, I think I just gouged my arm on a nail!

That hurts! But I'm through and it's too dark to see the bleeding so I'm not going to worry about it right now. I collect myself and stand on my tiptoes, reaching back through the window to grab my jacket and gun, but it isn't there. But *something* is. A leg!

I flinch away from the appendage but it's too late. I hear a gunshot and my arm convulses with the impact. I snap my arm back into the basement as three more loud cracks fill the dank cellar. I pull away from the opening and pin myself against the cold concrete wall for protection. I'm pretty sure I'm not hit again, but someone's got my gun, they know where I am and they're OK with killing me.

Eddie Prentiss—who else would be that stupid and desperate right now? I can't feel the pain in my arm and that means it's bad. I've got to do something.

I edge toward the window and take a quick look outside. I don't see any feet or legs. That's good, but I rule out the possibility of crawling back through the opening. It's too small, my arm already feels weak and I'd be a stuck pig—half in and half out, an easy target for Eddie and my gun. There might be another window down here, but hell, I couldn't get out any of them. I could yell for help but it would give away my position to Eddie and, in this neighborhood, there's no guarantee anyone would respond even if they did hear me.

Well, as someone once said, "The only way *out* is *through*." So, in the low light, I start searching for the staircase—there has to be one, even in this dump. I shuffle a few feet away from the window, catch my toe on something and fall to my knees. I turn myself around, scraping the shins of my new slacks, and feel at the bulky obstruction on the floor. It's large and has a familiar, sort-of *spongy*, quality. I run my hands along it in the inky dark and discover a familiar feature.

Yes, it's an arm, I tell myself logically, *a human arm.* I run my hand down to the fingers and discover they are small and covered with jewelry, little rings as cold as the basement concrete. I casually reach for the other end of the mass and feel the long, curly hair. I suddenly flinch, jolted with the realization that this is a *person*, motionless and cold.

This is Eddie's handiwork. It has to be Lisa Miller, the missing witness. I recoil and flap my good hand in the air as if to shake the death off it. I've discovered dead bodies before but never like this. It's like being in Dracula's dungeon.

My brain is popping with sick possibilities. I try to think clearly. The wound in my arm is starting to burn. This basement is as silent as a vault. I can hear blood rushing in my ears and my own heavy breathing. I have to get out of here and, to do that safely, I need to know where Eddie is.

I feel my way to Lisa's feet, mumble an apology and pull off a sneaker. I throw it at the dimming window. It bounces clumsily in the sill and another roaring gunshot breaks the silence. He's still outside, waiting for me to come through.

On a hunch, I scramble in the direction of Lisa's feet and, thank God, find the stairs. I start clawing my way upward, dust spitting at me and splinters digging into my hands and knees. I see a crack of daylight and hope carves a small niche out of the terror now filling my brain.

Eddie's girlfriend, Nora, may be in the house—may even be involved in Lisa Miller's death—but I hope she won't give me any trouble. I should never have come here without backup. It was *stupid*. But an image of me sitting next to a sparkling new swimming pool flashes across my mind. I watch the kids playing in the water with their inflatable toys. And there stands my wife—looking pretty hot in her bikini, I might add and...

I gotta get out of here!

I throw myself against the door, not bothering with the knob, and the thing explodes open. I crumple to the filthy hardwood of the first floor. The late-afternoon light blinds me and I'm momentarily disoriented. I try to figure out an escape route. I pick myself up from the floor and feel the deeper, jarring pain in my arm. I look down at the wound and instantly regret it. There's a hole in my left forearm the size of a nickel and the whole thing between the elbow and the wrist is misshapen and swelling up fast—shattered inside, probably. I turn my arm over, shuddering with the pulses of pain, and see the jagged exit wound. There's surely some bone missing. The blood is streaming down my wrist and pooling in my hand. I have to get out of here before I bleed to death!

That's when I hear footsteps creaking on the front porch. Eddie's coming! But at least now I know where the front of the house is. I start heading in the other direction, looking for the back door and hoping I don't run into an armed Nora.

The rooms in this old dump are nondescript, long ago stripped of furniture and fixtures. I can't find the kitchen, where there has to be a door. I start to panic. I shuffle from room to room and try to calm myself. I see the swimming pool again—my new favorite happy-place. My heart skips a beat as red stains appear in the blue water and I realize that I'm standing in the kitchen and there's *no door*—just one solid wall of plywood. Oh, my God!

The hinges on the front door hiss and howl as Eddie opens it. I can imagine the look on his face on the other side of the decaying walls—*satisfaction*. One more obstacle to freedom is about to be cut down and tossed on the pile in the basement. I search the barren room as the front door slams shut with a ragged BANG!

Eddies footsteps march on my accidental redoubt. I glance around frantically, looking for a two-by-four, a two-by-two—I'll even take a *one*-by-two right now if I can get it—anything to swing. Then I spot it—a rusty iron pipe poking stiffly out of the floor where the sink must have been.

I lurch for it and my bad arm stings deeply. I grab the pipe with my good hand and grip it like a lifeline. I pull. It barely moves.

Footsteps.

I pull again, thinking of Bruce Banner, and it gives a little. FOOTSTEPS!

One last mighty wrenching and it's free! I have my weapon, if you can call it that. I try to move for the near wall to make a surprise attack at the doorway, but too late! I stumble backward and coil myself in the far corner as the footsteps stop and there in the doorway stands Lisa Miller, *the witness*—not the least bit dead—with my gun in her hand.

I freeze, arm and iron club cocked above my head. Lisa sees the look of utter shock on my face and freezes too. Then her eyes narrow and she steps forward, pointing the gun at my chest and squeezing the trigger.

I slam my eyes shut and see wife, kids, mom, dad and dog by the pool and I wave goodbye as—BANG!—footsteps—BANG! BANG!—and the sickening sound of a body hitting the floor.

I open my eyes and let out a shocked breath. It's not me on the floor, but *Lisa Miller*. She lay there limply, pumping shallow, agonized breaths. It doesn't make sense until I look up through the doorway. Standing in the backlight of the other room with a smoking pistol in his hand is Eddie Prentiss.

"Damn it," Eddie sighs. He crouches down and gently brushes Lisa's cheek with his calloused hand. "Why'd you do this, babe? Why'd you shoot Jerry?"

"She's here, Eddie," Lisa says weakly. "She's here and you

lied to me. You said you weren't gonna see her no more. You lied, Eddie."

Eddie looks up at me with a big question on his face.

"In the basement, Eddie," I say, sliding down the wall as my legs turn to noodles. "Nora's down there, dead."

Eddie turns his hurt eyes back to meet Lisa's.

"I had to, Eddie. You lied," she whispers, "you said you wouldn't…" She shudders and her final breath wheezes out.

Eddie stands up, blocking the backlight again. "I saw your car out back, Jerry. You shouldn't-a come here. I was almost out of town. I was almost… SHIT!"

I flinch involuntarily at his howl. I can feel my body and my logical brain shutting down. I'm going into shock. I can't move to defend myself—I don't know enough to be scared anyway. Eddie walks over to put the final bullet in me. But instead he grabs me by my good arm and hauls me up across his shoulders. I see Lisa's dead eyes staring up to the sky as I fly over her. Then everything goes dark.

◆◆◆

EDDIE WAS SPOTTED at a gas station near Eau Claire in my stolen car, using my stolen credit cards on his way to Chicago. Next stop he made was at a rest area outside Madison. When he came out of the men's room, there were a half dozen Wisconsin State Troopers waiting. He went for his gun and that was the last of Eddie Prentiss.

I got the news from Bobby Bright, who called me at my room to let me know. Before he skipped bail for the last time, Eddie drove me to the hospital in my own car, dropped me off at the ER door, gave the orderly my driver's license and insurance card then took off with the rest.

I'm in pain, pretty messed up, but I'm alive—thanks, in an odd sort of way, to Eddie. You see? It never hurts to treat everyone well, because even the bad guys can return the favor once in a while.

Contender

William Kent Krueger

I'm alone in the gym. Working the heavy bag with my left. Waiting for Marzetti.

There are mirrors on the wall so the fighters I train can shadow box. When I look at my reflection I see what I always see. A face like a Halloween mask. Mostly it's the result of letting too many gloves get to me in the ring. An unfortunate tendency to drop my right and leave my kisser open. But the honest truth is I got an early start toward ugly compliments of my old man. Far back as I can remember, he was laying into me with his bare knuckles. Me and my ma. Beat us like dirty rugs. If you wanted to paint the legacy he left me, two colors would do it. Black and blue.

I rest my left glove against the heavy bag and stare at the gym door. Still waiting for Marzetti. I'm sweating but it ain't from working the bag.

I should have taken care of my old man but I was scared. My ma finally resolved the matter. Killed the son of a bitch. Waited for him to come home drunk which he did more nights than not and when he passed out on the sofa she plopped a butcher knife through his heart. They sent her to the women's prison in Shakopee. Me they sent to a string of foster homes. I was fourteen. Got into a lot of trouble. Boosting cars mostly. Spent time in the reformatory outside Red Wing, which wasn't too bad. That's when I learned to box. Had a chaplain there who was a Golden Gloves champ. A good guy name of Father Di Salvo. Di Salvo trained any kid who had an interest and after the beatings my old man gave me, I definitely had an interest. I ended up trusting the priest and one day I confessed to him that I felt guilty it was my ma who'd killed my old man.

"Should've been me," I told him. "I should be the one doing hard time."

Father Di Salvo thought about that. Then he said, "The Lord has something else in mind for you, Corrigan. I'm guessing there'll come a day when you know what that is. In the meantime try to remember not to drop your right."

After Red Wing, I took what Di Salvo taught me and got myself professional trainers and a manager and turned myself into a real boxer. Fought under the moniker Kid Corrigan. Middleweight. Eleven years. '46 to '57. Last match was the day Sputnik went into orbit. I stepped away with a record of 37 wins and 25 losses. Every trainer I had said I could've gone farther except for dropping my damn right.

I bought this gym in Frogtown. Not the best part of town. I've been broken into a couple of times so I keep a little snubnose .38 locked in the bottom drawer of the desk in my office. Like Father Di Salvo, I began training fighters. Kids mostly which I found I liked. Even if they didn't show promise, they showed heart. One especially.

His name was Frankie Marzetti. Slender. Black hair. Dark eyes. Fifteen when he first walked into the gym. Stands there beside the ring watching a couple of my boys spar. At first I'm concentrating on my fighters and giving pointers. Then I spot the bruise splashed across the new kid's cheek and I watch him instead. Every punch gets thrown in the ring, his own fists move. The kid's got fight in him. And that bruise has me interested.

I walk over. "Name's Corrigan," and I shove my hand in his direction.

He holds back. Trust ain't an easy thing especially if you're used to some man's hand coming at you in a hard ball of knuckles. I leave my paw out there open. He finally takes it. Nice firm grip.

"Marzetti," he says.

"You fight?"

"No."

"Want to?"

"Sure. But…."

"What?"

"I don't have money."

"Can you push a broom?"

"Yeah."

"Then you can work off the cost of training."

"When do I start?"

"What are you doing now?"

Frankie Marzetti had more heart than talent. I've had kids with better footwork and harder punches but I never had a fighter showed more guts than Frankie. He was intense. Focused. Sometimes I'd play jokes on him just to get him to lighten up. When he laughed, which wasn't often it was a good sound. But as fast as good humor came to him it left. The kid didn't trust happiness.

One afternoon Frankie's sparring. He's dripping sweat. It's clear he's working off something angry inside. He's taking hits he could duck and he's swinging wild not smart. I keep yelling at him to protect his face. Keep that right up. Suddenly there's this woman standing next to me. In a gym a woman's about as common as a tattoo on a nun. She's watching Frankie. She's got black hair like him only long over her shoulders. She's got a profile like the kid but more delicate. She turns to me and she's sporting the same kind of bruise I saw on Frankie's face the first day he walked into my gym. Her eyes are dark like Frankie's but they don't have his fierceness.

"You must be Corrigan," she says. She's got a voice reminds me of how talcum powder feels.

"Guilty," I say.

"He's not doing his homework. He spends all his time here."

I nod to let her know I think it's an important thing to consider then I say, "What he learns here is a good education in its way. But I'll tell him not to neglect his studies. What's with the shiner?"

"I walked into a door."

"Same one Frankie walked into a while back?"

"I'm going to take my son home now," she says.

She calls to him and Frankie looks at me. I give him a nod. He don't like it but he doesn't gripe. Takes off his gloves. Steps out of the ring.

"You got a good kid there," I tell her as she starts to leave.

She stops and turns back. Gives me this long deep look.

With women, I've always kept my right up. You got a kisser like mine you understand that no woman's going to think soft thoughts about you. You ain't never going to be a contender for her affections. But I look at Frankie's ma with her face half-shadowed by bruise and I let my guard down.

"Thank you, Mr. Corrigan," she says. That's all. That's it. Thank you Mr. Corrigan. But I hear those words and I feel a blow to my heart worse than any punch I ever took in the ring.

After they leave I call to Doyle, an old fighter who helps me out sometimes in the gym. "Take care of things. I'll be back in a while."

I catch up with them at the end of the block. "Mind if I walk you home?"

"We don't need an escort, Mr. Corrigan," she says.

"I happen to be going the same way."

"Suit yourself."

Frankie walks on one side of his ma with his hands stuffed in his pockets. I walk on the other. We cross University and head up the hill toward Summit Avenue. The ritzy part of town. It's fall and we're kicking through leaves and our feet make little crunching sounds like we're stepping on tiny bones.

"Is my Frankie a good fighter, Mr. Corrigan?"

"He's got heart. That's important."

"Heart." She looks at Frankie and thinks about this. "I'll just bet he does."

Their place is huge, like about one room shy of Madison Square Garden. All brick with flower beds out front. Yard like the felt on a pool table.

"Thank you, Mr. Corrigan," Mrs. Marzetti says. She takes my hand. Her own is small and delicate. Reminds me of a soft cat's paw.

"That bruise. Don't put raw steak on it okay? Nothing to

that old saw. Ice it maybe twenty minutes every hour."

"I'll remember that," she says.

"See you tomorrow, Frankie."

But Frankie ain't listening. He's looking at a car pulling into the drive. A black Chrysler big as an aircraft carrier. "Shit," he says real quiet.

Two men get out. First guy's huge. Chest wide as the grill on the Chrysler and arms like buffalo thighs. He opens the door in back and the second guy gets out. Slender. Good looking. Thick black hair. A lot of Frankie in his face. He's wearing an expensive three-piece. Diamond stud in his tie tack.

"Cozy," he says coming up the walk. "Am I intruding?"

"Corrigan's the name." I offer my hand.

He doesn't touch my mitt. Just lets it hang out there empty. "Whatever you're selling, Corrigan, we're not buying."

"I'm Frankie's boxing coach."

"Boxing coach?" He looks at Frankie who looks at the ground. "I don't know anything about a boxing coach."

"I got a gym other side of University," I tell him.

The guy with the Chrysler-grill chest says, ""Corrigan's. I've seen it."

Diamond stud says to me, "Is Frankie a good boxer?"

"He has potential."

"And how much will it cost for him to realize this potential?"

"Frankie works a little for me around the place. I train him in return."

"Quid pro quo," the guy says. Whatever the hell that means.

"I should be getting back." I turn to Mrs. Marzetti. "A pleasure meeting you."

"I'm sure it was," Mr. Marzetti says looking at his wife. I've seen fighters at the end of a vicious match with kinder looks in their eyes.

"See you tomorrow, Frankie," I say.

When the kid doesn't respond his old man prods him, "Answer the man, Frank. Will you be there tomorrow?"

I can see Frankie's hands balled into fists in his pockets. "Maybe," he says.

I leave them standing there. I can't help feeling like I've abandoned Frankie and his ma.

All night long I toss and turn. Thinking about Mrs. Marzetti. About the soft voice, the soft hand, the soft skin on her face and that bruise that showed the dark leak of blood beneath. And I think about Frankie and those balled up little fists jammed where his old man couldn't see them.

Frankie doesn't come around the next day or the next. In the afternoon I take a walk to the Marzetti house and knock on the door. Frankie answers. I don't see any new bruises and I'm relieved.

"Missed you at the gym," I say.

"I'm not coming anymore."

"You still got a lot to learn."

"Who is it, Frankie?" Mrs. Marzetti steps up behind her son. Her right wrist is bandaged and her arm is cradled in a sling of white cloth. Her look tells me I shouldn't be there.

"Wasn't a door did that, Mrs. Marzetti."

"Please go," she says.

"Leave him," I say.

"And go where, Mr. Corrigan? I have no money and we have no other place."

"You stay with him and one day he'll go too far. If he doesn't kill you it'll be Frankie he kills."

"We tried to run before," Frankie says. He looks at me desperate. Like some kid on a refugee poster.

"I can help," I tell them.

She shakes her head. All that beautiful black hair rippling. "Go away, Mr. Corrigan. You'll only make it worse." She gives me a look I've seen on plenty of fighters in the ring just before their managers throw in the towel. She closes the door against me.

I spend the afternoon making calls to guys who know guys. What I learn about Marzetti makes my skin crawl. The bastard's officially into real estate but what everybody understands is that he's connected. People in high places protect him. He's untouchable.

So there I am sitting in my office stewing. I'm thinking about the woman who got herself into a corner she can't get out of and about Frankie who's got nobody in his corner. I'm thinking about how much I hate a guy like Marzetti. I'm thinking about his bodyguard and those arms like buffalo thighs. And I'm thinking there's no way I can turn my back and forget.

Marzetti's real estate office is in the phone book. I call and tell the woman who answers that my name is Nelson. I'm from the city planning commission and I need to talk to Marzetti about a problem with one of his properties. The woman's got a voice like silk panties and I figure that working the phone probably ain't the only thing she does for Marzetti. I get the man and I give him a few one-twos. Call him everything in the book. A coward son of a bitch who'd beat a woman and a kid but wouldn't stand toe-to-toe with a man. Tell him he wants to do something about it he can find me at my gym. I hang up while he's in the middle of his bluster.

I tell Doyle to clear out the gym and take the rest of the day off. I put up a sign on the door says the place is closed but I don't throw the lock. I change into my sweats and haul out the biggest pair of gloves I got and get them ready. I figure a guy like Marzetti's going to show up when it's dark. Won't want witnesses to what he's going to do to me.

Long about dusk I put on the gloves I've prepared. I start working the heavy bag with my left and waiting for Marzetti and thinking about Father Di Salvo and what he told me years ago. That the Lord had something else in mind for me. I'm thinking maybe this is it.

He shows up after dark. Chrysler grill comes in first to check things out. Marzetti's behind him. Chyrsler grill locks the door. Marzetti walks my way. Chrysler grill follows him like a huge shadow.

I leave off jabbing the bag. "A real man would've come alone, Marzetti."

"No, a stupid man would have come alone." He gives me

a slimy grin. "I don't know what your interest in my family is, Corrigan, but I bet you'd love to do my wife. Let me clue you. You've got a face with so much ugly it could derail a train. No woman let alone my wife is going to come within kissing distance of that kisser." He laughs and his big shadow laughs with him. "Corrigan. Goddamn Mick name. I hate Micks. Know what I'm going to do, Corrigan? First I'm going to have Lou here beat you bloody. Then I'm going to have him put a bullet through that stupid Mick brain of yours."

Corrigan's bodyguard reaches under his jacket and brings out a piece. A big revolver.

"On your way to hell, Corrigan, here's a little something to chew on," Marzetti says. "When I'm finished with you I'm going home and I'm going to give my wife a fat lip and maybe my boy too and the only reason I'm doing it is because you've pissed me off."

"You like the feel of hitting a woman, Marzetti? Hitting a kid? Try hitting me. I guarantee it ain't going to be the same."

"I'll enjoy watching what Lou here does to you. He was a fighter himself you know? Heavyweight. Only you'll notice he's not wearing gloves this round." He gives me that grin again.

They're both standing a good six feet from me. Way beyond my reach. "Let me give you a pointer first," I say to the man called Lou. "Something every guy I ever fought knew about me from the get go. Kept me from ever hoping for a title fight. See when I get ready to jab with my right I drop my glove and leave myself open to a left hook. Like this."

I face Marzetti's shadow and bring my gloves up near my face. Lower my right and in slow motion show him what I mean. When my arm is fully extended my hand's still three feet from the big guy's heart. Then the end of my glove explodes in a puff of leather and stuffing and Marzetti's shadow looks stunned and looks down at the hole in his jacket the bullet from my little .38 has made and drops in a heap like a fighter I've just KO'ed. When he's down, I put one more in him for good measure.

"See I brought a friend too, Marzetti," I say.

Marzetti looks down at his bodyguard. Then he looks at the exploded end of my glove. Then he looks at me. For a guy used to doing all the talking he's suddenly pretty mum.

I step to the dead man and kick his gun across the gym floor. I remove my gloves, careful to keep the snub-nose on Marzetti, and then I surprise him. I toss the gloves and drop the gun on the floor beside the heavy bag.

"I'm going to give you a shot at the title," I tell him. "You knock me down, the gun is yours."

In Marzetti's thinking he's a big man. People jump when he snaps his fingers. Women and boys bruise or break when he hits them. And I can see in his eyes that he thinks he has a chance, that his size will save him. He lunges and swings.

It feels like heaven the way the bones of my raw knuckles shatter the bone of his long jaw. He staggers and turns and comes again and this time I flattened his nose and as he reels he sprays bright red blood. I work his body, cracking ribs, and when he bends to protect his torso I give him an uppercut that would dent a steel beam. His head snaps back and his body follows and he's on the floor, staring up, dazed. I walk to the sparring ring and grab a bucket of water from the nearest corner and splash him so that his eyes focus. Then I turn and pick the snub-nose off the floor and stand above him.

"That was for your wife and Frankie," I tell him. "Maybe you'll do better against the palookas in hell."

And I put a bullet between the bastard's eyes.

I fish in the bodyguard's jacket and find the keys. The big Chrysler's parked in the alley. I load the bodies in the trunk then take care of cleaning up the gym floor. I drive the car to a side street off University a couple of miles west and leave it. I walk a few blocks and drop the damaged right glove in a dumpster and catch a bus back to the gym. It's almost a week before they discover Marzetti and his shadow. Never able trace anything to me. Hell they never even look my way.

I follow the case in the papers and wonder about Frankie and his ma. I think about them both pretty often. Considering the odds, I figure I fought a good fight and it's okay I'm alone after. Was always that way.

Then one day a few months later I'm working the heavy bag to keep myself in shape and I glance in the mirror and see Frankie and his ma walk in the door. They're both looking happy. Both looking relieved.

"I'm wondering, Mr. Corrigan, if you'd be willing to resume training Frank. I have money to pay you now." She looks like a dark-haired angel and my throat's all choked up and I can't even speak.

Frankie smiles at me and I think if I ever had a son, I'd want him to look at me just that way. He says, "I still have a lot to learn."

"You already got what's important," I tell him. "You got someone in your corner and you always will."

"You'll train him then?" his ma asks.

"Sure."

"And I wonder if you'd like to come to dinner some evening soon. Even though I'm not Italian, I make a pretty good lasagna."

I lower my guard completely and tell her God's truth. "It would be my greatest pleasure."

And we all grin like idiots.

Den of Iniquity

Lori L. Lake

After she recognized Gordon Chasney, Ava Tanner spent weeks trying to figure out a way to kill him and get away with it. Shooting? Stabbing? Poisoning? Mow him down with her car? Her favorite method involved crushing him. She imagined him in a giant vise, screaming as bones cracked and blood spurted. The vision was so ruthless that she shuddered and felt nauseated even while she maintained a fascination for every murderous idea she teased into being.

But murder would be too quick. What she really wanted was to hurt him, make his pain last, humiliate him the way he'd shamed and abused her. Most of all, she wanted to relish the fact that he'd know who she was and be aware, before the end, that he was paying for what he'd done.

But she couldn't think of a single way to accomplish this. He was well over six feet tall, built like a lumberjack, and had physical power and agility she could only dream of. Though only five-two, she possessed an unexpected wiry strength, but she knew her 125 pounds was no match for him.

Ava had finally tabled her dreams of murder and brainstormed for another solution . . . which was why she broke into Gordon's house. If you could call it breaking in when no breaking was involved. She was amazed at how casual he was about security. Her own doors were never left unlocked, and the windows in her small apartment didn't open far enough to allow anyone over two years old to wriggle in. Not so at Gordon's.

She'd watched him off and on for weeks. One day, while he mowed the backyard, which was nicely secluded by tall hedges in which she was hidden, his mower ran out of gas. He walked off toward the gas station four blocks away, red can in hand.

Ava waltzed right through the back door into Gordon's unlocked kingdom.

The house smelled of stale beer and burnt meat. On the stove, a pair of wizened bratwurst sausages surrounded by a heap of dead sauerkraut lay in a black frying pan, burnt almost beyond recognition. From the spatter around the pan, it was clear they'd been there a few days.

Wrinkling her nose, Ava passed through the kitchen, then hastened through the living room and down a hallway where the smell wasn't so strong. The crappy-brown shag rug cushioned her every step. Somebody had probably paid big money a couple of decades earlier to lay this expanse of carpet throughout the house.

A pair of crooked shades blocked the morning sun, but she could still make out stray socks and little clumps of underwear here and there. What was it with him? Didn't he see anything below knee level? Items on his dresser top—watch, pen, pocket change, penknife, checkbook—sat in orderly fashion, and in the bathroom, he'd lined up his shaving cream, razor, aftershave, deodorant, and toothbrush holder in a row on the counter. But she had seen dust balls scattered liberally throughout the house, and she nearly kicked over more than one empty beer can sitting next to furniture.

The next room, instead of being a second bedroom, looked like a cross between a sportsman's paradise and a home office. A den of iniquity, she thought. An eight-point deer head mounted on the wall was flanked by two fish so shiny they appeared to have just leapt out of a lake and suddenly found themselves attached to ovals of decorative wood.

Gordon's desk bulged. Paper, envelopes, old phone books, and other junk overloaded every drawer. A stack of receipts and a three-ring binder, obviously from the auto parts store where he was employed, were piled on the computer desk on top of random slips of paper and a handful of music CD jewel cases. The corner of a photo peeked out from under a pile. Ava hastily donned a pair of latex gloves she used when she changed toner in her printer and lifted the papers on top. Gordon had printed out a picture of a naked woman, her breasts pendulous and her private parts splayed open for all to see. Feeling queasy, Ava covered the photo, careful not to let any of the paper pile cascade to the floor.

She forced herself to stop focusing on the stacks of junk and the wildlife rotting on the walls, and moved to the computer, which she was delighted to find was humming away. One touch brought up the screen. Still standing, she opened a browser, typed in an address, downloaded and installed a program, and closed the browser.

How long had she been inside? Ninety seconds? More? She calculated that it would take Gordon six or eight minutes round trip to the gas station. To be on the safe side, she set her watch timer for three more minutes. She swiftly examined his computer applications and files.

Within thirty seconds, she found his cache of dirty pictures. She didn't bother to open the multitude of video files, but she clicked on the first in a series of photos. With a gasp, she plopped into the desk chair, feeling light-headed. There was no doubt—Gordon Chasney was the one. Shots of naked women and frightened-looking teenage girls—beaten, bound, and sexually used—made her so sick to her stomach that her breakfast rose up in her throat.

"Not here, not now," she said aloud, then looked around, shocked that she'd spoken. Even though she still had another minute, she'd seen enough. Now if she could only find his keys. She took a deep breath to center herself, closed the photo files, and hustled from the room.

He made it easy for her. A key rack hung next to the front entryway. She hunted through all the dangling metal, searching for a backdoor key. She took his ring and several individual keys to the kitchen door and started fitting them in the lock. Voilá. Not only was there a backdoor key on his ring, but also a spare, which she tucked in her pocket.

Her watch alarm went off, and she silenced it. She returned the keys to the rack and headed for the back exit, noting an open door she'd missed before. She saw it led to the downstairs level and to the tuck-under garage.

She had barely slipped into the hedge when Gordon rounded the corner of the house. Oh, shit, she thought. That was a lot closer than I intended. As he filled the gas tank, she tried to calm down. Once he had cranked up the mower, she moved through the hedge and away from Gordon Chasney's den of iniquity.

That was the start of it.

♦♦♦

OVER THE NEXT weeks, Ava came to believe Gordon was the most obvious man she'd ever known, so why didn't anyone else see it? All you had to do was watch him closely, and it was clear there was something off about him. Had he been this obvious during her childhood when he'd stalked her, gained her trust, and then molested her? She wished she could remember the details better, but she couldn't. Whenever she thought of that day—being grabbed, held down, the relentless probing—her stomach clenched and sometimes she very nearly passed out. All she knew for sure was that he'd initially been very smooth. He'd had to be, or even at age ten she would have seen his true intent.

She watched him now as he walked briskly around the neighborhood park, his eyes glinting with interest as he surreptitiously glanced toward little girls on the swings, on the slide, twirling on the merry-go-round. Ava wanted to scream at the parents in the park. People, she wanted to say, can't you see him? He's a sexual predator!

But she had no proof, and he looked completely innocent as he kept to the sidewalk, hands in his windbreaker pockets, smiling and nodding pleasantly. Couldn't anyone else see how his eyes followed the children like a voracious grizzly seeking flesh to devour?

She couldn't waste another moment worrying about perfecting a plan. He was on the prowl again, and she needed to act. If she couldn't kill him and get away with it, there had to be another way to stop him. Luckily, her self-employment as a website designer gave her time and flexibility. Tuesday nights Gordon bowled in an eight p.m. league at the Leapfrog Lanes. No more dithering. She needed to get back in his house and take care of business.

◆◆◆

THE PROGRAM Ava had installed during her first foray into Gordon's domain yielded all sorts of good information. Every time he typed something, the spyware monitored where he surfed and what he searched for, and every keystroke he made transmitted over the Internet to her. She knew his home and work computer passwords, banking information, credit card details, and what he'd bought online. If she wanted to, she could install a program that would allow her to update his computer remotely . . . but she didn't dare use that for what she had in mind.

Tuesday night she dressed in a long-sleeved gray shirt, black slacks, tennis shoes, and a baseball cap. When it was sufficiently dark, she drove to the side street near Gordon's house and waited until she saw his truck turn the corner and pass her car. Show time. She gathered her courage, picked up a clipboard, and got out. She strode into his backyard as though she had every right to be there. Had anyone seen? She stood on his back porch stoop, hardly breathing, expecting someone to call out. A dog barked in the distance. Over the hedge she could see the second-story windows lit up in the house behind Gordon's, but no one seemed to have noticed her.

She pressed the back doorbell and heard the muffled ringing inside. The house stayed dark, and no one came to the door. After waiting one sweat-filled, oxygen-deprived moment, she put on her gloves, inserted the stolen key, and was surprised to find that Gordon hadn't locked up when he left. She giggled nervously. All that work to get his keys, and he doesn't even bother with security. What an arrogant man.

Ava slipped into the house and turned on a penlight to find her way through the kitchen. He'd left a light on by the front door, and for a moment that worried her. What if he came home unexpectedly? When he parked in the garage underneath the house, she thought she'd hear the door go up and know to get out. But what if he parked on the street and came in the front door?

In all the time she'd watched him, he'd never parked on the street, so she had to assume he'd do exactly what he always did.

The computer was on. Did he ever turn it off? Didn't he know that hijackers could put all kinds of spyware on his computer much more easily when he left it on? Since he went to porn sites, his computer would likely be stuffed full of bots and malware. She checked his cookie file. Sure enough, he had all sorts of problems festering. This pleased her.

Now it was time to do the one distasteful thing she'd been avoiding. She entered keywords that she hoped would bring up kiddie porn chat lists. She knew they'd be difficult to find, that they were well-hidden. But with some persistence, she expected to at least come across some Internet groups where she could advertise her plan.

She should have set her watch alarm. So deep was she in her searching and inquiring that when she felt a strange rumble beneath her, she didn't pay attention at first. Then far away, below, a car door slammed, and she came to her senses. She leapt from the chair, grabbed her clipboard, and tiptoed toward the kitchen.

She heard him coming up the back stairs. Quick course correction. She ran to the front door, opened it, and pushed at the screen door. A light came on behind her. She stepped out to the porch as she peeled off her gloves. Over her shoulder, she saw Gordon's foot as he came up into the kitchen.

She whipped around, between the front door and the open screen, the gloves balled up in one hand. His eyes met hers, a surprised look on his face. She froze.

"Can I help you?" he asked.

"Cable company, sir." She looked down at her clipboard. "I got the call that you're having trouble with your TV reception and Internet." She pulled down the brim of her cap and hoped it shrouded her face.

He moved to stand in the hallway only a few feet away, wearing a puzzled look. "Isn't nine-thirty kind of late for repair work?"

She glanced at her watch. "Dispatch said this was an emergency, and that no matter what, I was to get in and fix the problem. We work 'til ten, so here I am."

He rested a big, meaty hand against the edge of the door. His eyes looked glassy, his face relaxed. "I didn't call."

She smelled beer on his breath. Maybe he wasn't so with it after all. Heart beating fast, she lifted a page on her clipboard. "1289 Birch, cable and Internet out."

He made a snorting sound. "Look, lady, this is 1289 Franklin. Birch is a couple blocks thataway." He gestured behind him with a big thumb. "Better get your ass moving if you want to fix 'em up before ten."

Ava stepped back and let the screen door flutter closed. "Thanks, mister." She stumbled off the porch feeling giddy and amazed. Oh, my God. Had that really happened? She'd almost been caught. Unbelievable.

She was hunting for a parking place in front of her apartment when she realized she'd left her penlight behind.

◆◆◆

AVA SPENT THE next week alternating between feeling triumphant and trying not to melt into a puddle of stress. She made herself focus on her work with her Internet accounts, but she couldn't help thinking that her entire plan was in danger due to a damned penlight. How could she have been so stupid?

The next Tuesday night she repeated her preparations, though every time she realized what she was contemplating, she shook, and just before she left her house, she threw up. Still, she forged on. When Gordon departed for the bowling alley, she entered the house quickly. This time he had locked the back door. Maybe he was educable after all.

She didn't have the penlight to guide her, but she crept through the house to the den of iniquity. A touch of her gloved hand brought up the computer screen, and it shed enough light for her to search by. She moved piles carefully and looked under the new detritus.

The penlight wasn't on the desk.

On a hunch, she knelt and felt around the carpet, wincing at how dusty and crud-flecked the shag was. She had almost given up when she saw a glint of silver along the front of the desk pedestal and found the penlight half-hidden in the long fibers.

Ava pocketed the light and checked her watch. She had a lot to do, but in order to complete the transactions, she had to wait until Gordon would be on his way home. The timing would be maddeningly close, but she wouldn't be taken unawares again.

Over the next hour she prepared to set up a merchant account using Gordon's credit card, built a bare-bones Internet storefront and got it ready to post, then created his very own e-mail address—gordyluvsgrrls—at a popular free service.

The worst part was finding and downloading online photos of degraded women and girls and writing disgusting comments to advertise what was for sale in each of the packets she created to sell at the storefront. She felt guilty about using the pictures, even though justice would ultimately be done. If she had any way of knowing who the women were, she would apologize, but of course each was as anonymous as the abusers who raped and hurt them.

Ava had just enough time to send out an advertisement to a few pervert lists before her watch alarm sounded. She went to the front window and peeked out the edge of the closed curtains. When she saw Gordon's truck come to a halt at the stop sign down the block, she ran back to the den, sent all her creations, and waited during maddening seconds for them to be approved. The sound of the garage door cranking open set her heart into overdrive, and she mashed her lips together to stop their trembling. When the approvals flashed on the screen, she quickly closed each program, and ran to the front door before Gordon even got out of the truck. She was in her car driving away, penlight in pocket, before another minute passed.

♦♦♦

THE NEXT WEEK Ava went back to Gordon's house to field orders off his merchant account. She was disgusted to see 412 orders, from all over the world, totaling in excess of four thousand dollars.

She selected U.S. customers only and used Gordon's equipment to print out smutty photos and type up envelopes from his desk in which she enclosed photos of children, girls, and women. Before he arrived home, she had prepared thirty orders. She drove directly to a mailbox in a neighborhood far from her own and dropped in the first makeshift packets, knowing that the recipients would be furious upon receipt. They'd paid $9.95 for poor quality photos on regular laser paper. It was only a matter of time before her carefully contrived plan would blow up in Gordon's face.

THE NEXT TUESDAY night in Gordon Chasney's house, Ava managed to mock up fifty-one packets and transfer $11,074.35 to his savings account. His gordyluvsgrrls e-mail account also had eighteen messages from outraged customers. The noose was tightening.

She deleted her original key-logger program and other traces that she'd been on his computer. When she heard the garage door, she got away, headed to the mailbox, then went home and slept her best night of sleep in years.

THE FOLLOWING Monday, Ava opened the newspaper to see the headline she'd longed for: *Local Man Arrested for Running Kiddie Porn Racket.* She scanned the article. Multiple counts of mail fraud . . . illegal possession of child pornography . . . possibility of decades of imprisonment if convicted . . . more charges to come.

"A-ha! Gotcha, Gordy-O. You're toast. Woo hoo!" She danced around the house, laughing with unbridled glee. Her level of elation was so great that she skipped breakfast, put on a sweat suit, and went outside to jog.

The sun shone down upon her, and the chilly breeze wasn't cool enough to penetrate. She quickly worked up a light sweat in a two-mile loop, and by the time she came back past the neighborhood park, her muscles were pleasantly fatigued. She stopped at a bench to stretch, and that's when she saw him.

Square-shouldered and beefy, the man had a hard face and predatory eyes. He strolled along the sidewalk, glancing periodically at the children frolicking on the playground equipment. He seemed particularly interested in one tiny girl who lay on her stomach over a swing, legs dangling, arms wrapped around the swing's wood slat. Her long, golden hair nearly touched the ground as she sang a little song and periodically stuck a foot down to keep the swing moving. Ava watched the man with growing alarm.

She wondered how long it would take to find out where he lived.

You *Can* Be Too Thin

Gary R. Bush

My feet were on my desk as I watched the brunette aerobics instructor going through her paces in the studio across the street. I admit to being a bit of a voyeur. The brunette glanced my way and gave me a wave. I guess she recognized a manly guy when she saw one.

My reverie was broken by the two men who entered my office. One was a goon with shoulders so wide he barely passed through the door. The other one was tall and thin with a nasty scar on his left cheek. "You Dryden?" Scarface asked.

"Me Dryden. You Jane?" I replied.

"Funny man. They didn't tell us you were a funny man. Did they, Leroy?"

Shoulders answered without moving his lips. "No."

"I try to live a life of humor. What can I do for you gentlemen?"

"We hear you been snooping around the Wilson matter. It would be better for your health if you lay off."

Myra Mae Wilson, once the shy daughter of a wealthy family of eccentrics, became a wild child after her divorce from Mr. Wilson. Now, she was being blackmailed. Judge Gaffney, the family lawyer, had asked me to look into it.

"If I don't lay off?"

"Then Leroy and I will see that you do."

"Why don't you two run along before Daddy has to spank?"

"Thinks he's a tough guy as well as funny, huh, Leroy?" Scarface pulled a flick knife from his pocket.

"Yond Cassius has a lean and hungry look," I said, as I stood.

"Huh?" The thin and scarred one asked.

"He's quoting Shakespeare," a voice called from the doorway. I looked up to see a tall Mohawk Indian leaning against the jam.

"Hello, Raven," I said.

"The Redskin your muscle?" Scarface asked.

"Sometimes I'm his muscle."

"Enough of this shit." He came at me with the knife. I easily blocked it with my left forearm. He did, however, slice the sleeve of my Fox Creek leather bomber jacket. I hit him hard with my right and broke his nose. Blood spurted, spraying my desk. It pissed me off so I followed with a left.

Leroy wasn't as dumb as he looked. He pulled a Glock from his jacket, but going up against Raven was a fool's errand. Before Leroy could get off a shot, Raven slapped him down and pulled his own piece, a Desert Eagle .50, and shoved it between Leroy's eyes.

"Who sent you?" I dragged Scarface to his feet.

"Screw you," he wheezed.

"Him no talk, maybe me scalp-um." Raven pulled a Bowie knife from his jacket.

"No!" Scarface cried. "Some guy at Cracker's Bar paid us to rough you up. He didn't give a name, just a grand each. He was a big guy going to fat, smoked a big cigar. Don't let the Indian scalp me!"

Raven laughed. "OK, you moron. I won't put my manicured hands in your greasy hair. Now, pick up your friend and scram before I change my mind."

They ran from the room and Raven gave a war whoop.

"'Me scalp-um?' What, you been watching B-westerns?"

"Quiet, Long Knife."

"Long Knife? I prefer *He-Who-Laughs-At-Danger*."

"In Mohawk that would be *Igg-bay-Itter-shay*."

"Mohawk? Sound's suspiciously like Pig Latin to me."

"You're the detective, you figure it out."

We left my office and went to Harry's Gym to hit the heavy bag and spar a few rounds. I had fought Archie Moore back in the day and Raven learned his style in the streets. Neither of us really knew who would win in a real fight against each other and neither wanted to find out.

After we showered, I changed into an Armani Collezioni dark blue wool 3-button suit with flat front trousers, a Madeleine Finn Hooksett Nantucket shirt, blue silk Hermes tie and Moreschi Cordeno dress shoes with a matching belt.

"Very understated," Raven said as he emerged from the locker-room.

"You as well," I commented. He was wearing black dyed buckskin pants, a yellow silk shirt and a long black buckskin coat. His boots were of soft rawhide and laced up to mid-calf.

◆◆◆

SANDRA AND Raven's latest were to meet us at our favorite French restaurant.

Raven and I walked into the bar, where his date was waiting. This month, he was seeing a twenty-something blonde Estonian named Kaija. The woman was getting her Ph.D in physics. They exchanged a few words in her native tongue, followed by his tongue half-way down her throat.

When they came up for air, Raven looked at his Rolex, "Where the hell is Sandra?"

"C'mon Raven, you know it takes time for her to put her makeup on," I reminded him.

He shook his head, "Don't you ever get tired of waiting?" And he turned back to Kaija.

Did I get tired of waiting? I suppose, but Sandra was so perfect, I excused her little idiosyncrasies.

I ordered a Jenlain Ambree—a French beer, rich in caramel malt showing spicy hops—and looked around the bar. Here, the beautiful people gathered. A redhead with dangerous curves gave me the eye and I gave it right back to her. By the time I was on my second brew, she had taken the stool next to mine.

"You're kind of cute," she flirted. "Big muscles, rugged face, you've been around."

I nodded, taking a sip of my beer.

"How would you like to go around with me?" There was no subtlety in her approach.

"Sorry, honey, he's taken," Sandra said, and kissed me full on the lips. I hadn't noticed her enter the room, but everyone else had.

She was elegant as always, dressed in Cecilia Yau, model thin, high cheekbones. She walked as if she was Moses and people in the room would part before her like the Red Sea.

She looked so good; I forgave her for being late.

However, Raven made a point of looking at his watch. She smiled sweetly, and gave him a peck on the cheek. She shook hands with his Baltic beauty, sized her up, and knew that she was still the best-looking woman in the room.

We went to the dining room, where Pierre was waiting, menus in hand.

"Ah, Monsieur Dryden and the lovely Dr. Silverstein, how nice of you to dine with us again. And Monsieur Raven and your lady. *Bonsoir.* You know your reservation was for a half-hour ago."

"Well, Pierre," Sandra said. "Being late is fashionable."

"And Mademoiselle is always fashionable," Pierre answered, showing us to our booth. Did I detect a hint of sarcasm in his voice?

I ordered Skip's Island Creek oysters with aged sherry vinegar and Italian caviar for an appetizer, butter-poached Maine Lobster with caponata and fresh heart of palm with smoked cockle vinaigrette and another Jenlain Ambree.

"Dryden," Sandra admonished. "You should be drinking something light."

"He's a growing boy," Raven laughed. "And we just came from Harry's Gym."

"OK," Sandra said, but she wasn't happy, since she wants me to cut down on my caloric intake. But I'm still at my fighting weight.

Raven and Kaija had soft shell crab tempura with white anchovies, pineapple and mango salsa, followed by Hawaiian Kajiki with black-eyed peas and sweet corn and littleneck clams. He also ordered two bottles of Beaumont des Crayères grand rosé brut rosé champagne.

"Excellent choice, Monsieur," the sommelier said. "This is a most elegant wine." Sandra said, "I'll have an arugula salad with a touch of sherry vinaigrette on the side."

She had only finished half the salad and a sip of champagne by the time the rest of us had polished off our dessert of chocolate and praline semifreddo with green tea fiancière.

"Do you want a taste?" I asked.

"Don't be silly, that stuff is so fattening."

"A taste isn't going to hurt you," Raven said. "For crying out loud, Sandra, eat something. A stiff wind could blow you away."

"Dryden likes me just the way I am." Turning to me, she asked, "Don't you, darling?"

I nodded, but Raven had a point. Sandra could stand a few more pounds.

♦♦♦

WE WENT BACK to her place and made love—as always, it was perfect. Well, almost perfect. First we had to lock Ruby, our Irish setter, out of the room. Sandra didn't mind her being there, but I drew the line at her presence.

Later, as she lay on top of me, our naked bodies pressed against one another, I sensed something was wrong. "What is it?"

"Do you think I'm fat?"

"Asked Jacques of Orlando in *As You Like It*, 'What stature is she of?' And replied Orlando: 'Just as high as my heart.'"

"That doesn't answer the question, Dryden." She rolled off of me.

"No, you are not fat. You could gain a few pounds."

"That's ridiculous. I have five pounds to lose. You can't be too thin or too rich."

I groaned inwardly. Not the Babe Paley cliché again. But with a smile on my face, I said, "As long as we have each other, we're rich."

"And as long as we have each other, I shall not be fat," she answered.

I threw my arms around her and felt her ribs beneath my grasp. Thin she was, and thin she'd be. She got up to let Ruby in. The dog jumped on the bed and lay between us the rest of the night.

◆ ◆ ◆

THE NEXT MORNING, Sandra agreed to go with me to see Myra Mae Wilson. I wanted her professional opinion; after all, Sandra was a brilliant therapist.

Sandra wearing only her bra and panties, leaned into the mirror 'til her nose was pressed to the glass, and began to apply make-up. An hour later she emerged from the bathroom and held up a black Valentino suit. "What do you think?"

I thought I could see her heart beating under her bra, but I said, "Fine."

She nodded, went into her dressing room and thirty minutes later, came out wearing the suit and a white silk blouse. She slipped on a pair of Michael Kors Babar black leather pumps with three-inch heels, grabbed her purse and said, "Well, what are we waiting for?"

I almost said, "Waiting for you to get your damn act together."

◆ ◆ ◆

MYRA MAE WILSON wasn't born a beauty. She had been gawky and birdlike in her movements, but what nature couldn't provide, plastic surgeons had. She even changed her name from Myrtle to Myra, more modern she thought.

We were seated in the parlor of the old Victorian mansion she had inherited from her mother. The place smelled of old ladies and lavender. Her lawyer, retired Judge Gaffney, sat next to her. He was at least 90, and his skin had become so translucent you could make out every vein in his skull.

Myra twisted a handkerchief in her hands. "I should never have divorced Duane. But after my mother and uncle died, I took the money and had work done." She pointed to her face and breasts. "Duane was the first man I ever knew. With all the money and looks I thought I could do better, but I was wrong." She began to sob.

Judge Gaffney put his arm around her. "There, there Myrt... I mean Myra girl. Young people sometimes do foolish things."

Myra wasn't that young, she was past forty. On the other hand, she had led a sheltered life.

"Who do you think sent the pictures?" Sandra asked. I had asked the same question, but Myra always said she didn't know.

Myra twisted her hanky tighter and shook her blonde curls. "If my uncle was still here he'd know what to do. That friend of his..."

"Myra," the judge cautioned, "don't go there."

She nodded. "I think it was Lofgren," she whispered.

"Taxi Lofgren?" I asked.

She nodded again. "I know I should never have gotten mixed up with him. He's an evil man and those pictures..." The tears flowed even harder.

I knew Lofgren. He was a second-rate hood, with good looks and as charming as a cobra. I could see how Myra Mae could fall under his spell. "I'll handle him."

"Take Raven," Sandra said. "I'll stay with Myra Mae."

◆◆◆

TAXI LOFGREN HUNG around the Plymouth Rec, a pool hall downtown. His old man used to have a taxi stand out front. Lofgren was practically raised in the joint, so he bought it as a front for his nefarious activities—blackmail, taxicab "insurance," and murder for hire.

Lofgren was at the bar when Raven and I walked in. His thugs were scattered about the room, playing pool or cards, but they all tensed up when we entered. All but Lofgren.

"Well, well, if it ain't the Lone Ranger and his faithful Indian companion, Tonto." Lofgren laughed and lit a cigar.

His boys laughed too, but Raven wasn't smiling. "Me prefer Native American, paleface."

"Huh?" Lofgren said.

"You ignorant ass, when you speak to me, address me as Mr. Raven, or I'll be forced to shove that Havana down your throat, followed by my fist."

"Moe," Lofgren called over his shoulder, "show this yahoo proper manners."

Moe was a hulk of a man. I remembered him when he was a ham and egg fighter—hard punch, but no speed.

"Better call in Larry and Curly," I said, stepping back.

"I don't need no help," Moe said, taking a swing at Raven. Only he missed. Raven saw it coming and cracked Moe's jaw with a single punch and the ex-pug fell to the floor.

"Heap big right hook, Injun," I said.

"Me go on warpath soon," Raven laughed.

"OK, you two are funny as a rubber crutch. What the hell do you want?" Lofgren wasn't laughing.

"The pictures of Myra Mae and the negatives."

"Fat chance. That broad got what she wanted out of me. I had to fuck her for a month—that should be worth the two hundred grand."

"You're a gentleman of the old school, Lofgren. But hand over the pictures now. This is your last warning."

Lofgren moved his head and his boys reached for their guns, but Raven and I were quicker. My Browning was in my hand. "Hold it!" I called and they all froze but one, who went for his gun. Raven put a .50 caliber slug between his eyes.

When the smoke cleared, Lofgren was on the floor, blubbering like a baby. "Don't kill me," he pleaded.

"I want the pictures and the negatives."

"Anything you say, Dryden."

He turned over the material. "Lofgren," I said, "I don't ever want you bother Myra Mae Wilson again. If you do, I will see that you die. Am I clear?"

"Yeah, I'll never bother her again. But what about my guy, Charlie? What do I do with his body?"

"What you've always done with bodies. Take him out and bury him."

"Not before I take this," Raven said, as he pulled his knife and dug the bullet of the thug's skull.

"Why did you do that?" Lofgren asked.

"I don't need you to try and blackmail me with the slug," Raven said, pocketing the bullet.

"I'd never do that."

"Right," I said. "Oh, and those punks you sent around to see me, tell them I won't be so easy on them next time."

"Huh?"

♦♦♦

"That's that," Raven said.

"No, I don't think so. Lofgren seemed puzzled when I mentioned the goons who paid me a visit."

"So, you think someone else sent them?"

"Yeah, I think I'll pay a visit to Cracker's Bar. That's where they said they met the guy who hired them."

"I'll tag along," Raven said, as he ran a cleaning rod through his automatic.

"Good, but I want to pick up Sandra. I left her with Myra Mae."

"She'll love Cracker's," Raven hooted.

"She'll be fine," I said.

We picked up Sandra and headed downtown. "Myra Mae is delusional," Sandra said. "She sees things. I think I'll recommend rest for her. I'll call a colleague, Dr. Sanderson. He runs a private sanitarium."

"I don't think she's as nuts as you think," I said.

"What do you mean?" Sandra was indigent. "You're not questioning my diagnosis?"

"Let's take care of this first." We pulled up in front of Cracker's. It was a narrow joint, a long bar, a few tables and a couple of booths in the back.

"You bring me to the nicest places, Dryden," Sandra said, looking the place over.

"Well, the décor ain't much, but the cuisine is terrible. We won't go wrong with beers and burgers."

"What is wrong with you, Dryden?" Sandra asked. "I'm not eating one of those greasy burgers."

"How about jerky? I'll bet they have some behind the bar."

"Now you're just being ridiculous," Sandra said.

A curvy blonde waitress came over. "Hi, nice to see you again, Dryden. What'll it be folks?"

"Nice to see you again, too, Lulu. Burgers, fries for Raven and me."

She looked at Sandra.

"A salad, no dressing, water."

"Not even on the side?"

"Do I look like someone who wants dressing?" Sandra hissed.

"Sure, honey," Lulu smiled nicely. "Be back with your drinks."

"Lulu? You get around, don't you?" Sandra asked me.

"A man in my business has to get around."

"Yes, but Lulu," Sandra condescended. "Why, she must be a size twelve."

"Marilyn Monroe was a size twelve," I retorted.

"Please," Sandra replied. "I'd be jealous, if I didn't know your heart was clean and pure." Raven snickered, just as Lulu returned with the drinks and gave me a wink.

"If you were a little jealous once in while, it might make thinks more interesting" I picked up my beer.

"How can I be jealous? When you have the best already," Sandra answered seriously.

"If this conversation gets any more saccharine I'm going to lose my lunch," Raven grimaced.

A large man walked in smoking a cigar. He sat down at the bar, ordered an egg and onion sandwich, a glass of beer and a martini.

"That's who I've been waiting for." I went over to see him.

"Hello, Duane," I said, taking the seat to his right.

"Hello, Pal." He looked me over. "Do I know you?"

"You should, the name's Dryden. You sent a couple of hoods after me."

"Oh, you're that guy." His back was up. "Yeah, I sent them, I was told you were bothering Myrtle…I mean Myra Mae. She's a nice girl. I wanted to make her happy. I didn't. But leave her alone."

"She was being blackmailed. Judge Gaffney hired me to find out by whom and deal with it. I did."

"Oh, jeeze. I'm sorry. I got the story wrong. Harvey told me, but I guess I was too drunk to get it straight. I suppose you want to have me arrested."

"Nah, Mr. Wilson, it was an honest mistake. But you know Myra still cares for you. Why don't you go back and see her?"

"Yeah? What's that, Harvey?" He looked at the stool to his left, listened and then turned back to me. "Harvey agrees with you, Mr. Dryden."

"Harvey's a smart Pooka, Mr. Wilson."

"He is. After Myra's uncle Elwood died, Harvey asked to join me. I couldn't say no."

I nodded. "Now why don't you go home to Myra and smooth things over? And tell her she won't have to worry about blackmail anymore."

"What the hell was that about?" Sandra asked, sneaking a bite of my burger. "Who is Harvey?"

"Wilson sort of inherited Myra's uncle's Pooka."

She nearly choked. "Pooka!"

"Yeah, Harvey. He's a six-foot rabbit."

"My God, Dryden, you've gone off the deep end."

"You didn't see the rabbit? How about you, Raven?"

"I saw him."

"Are you both delusional?" Sandra was angry.

I laughed. "Some people see giant rabbits. Others see fat that's not there. Still others," I pointed to myself, "think they lead perfect lives. It was Christian Nevell Bovee who wrote, 'No man is happy without a delusion of some kind. Delusions are as necessary to our happiness as realities.'"

"Delusions?" Sandra snapped. "Our life is a delusion?"

Before I could answer, the door opened and a dark-haired woman burst in. "Indian, you killed my Charlie. Now you die." She pulled a small .25 automatic from her purse and began to fire in Raven's general direction. The bartender ducked behind the bar. Mr. Wilson kept eating his egg and onion sandwich as though he hadn't a care in the world. I rolled to my left, drew and fired. The bullet caught the woman in the face and she went down in a bloody mess.

"Everyone all right?" I shouted.

"Dryden," Raven said, his voice choking. "Sandra, she's dead."

Later, the medical examiner told me if Sandra had five more pounds of flesh, the low caliber .25 wouldn't have penetrated her heart and she could have been saved. As it turned out you can be too thin.

Jibber Jabber

Reed Farrel Coleman

His father was a collector of things, all sorts of things, but James McCabe collected nothing. He did not relate to things, not even the splayed fingers he sometimes fanned before his opaque blue eyes. If not for the laws of physics, he would not relate to the floor on which he knelt, intermittently rocking his days away with inexhaustible energy. He was disconnected, unattached, self-contained, an eight year old universe unto himself. The doctors, shrinks, therapists, and teachers at the developmental center could only speculate about the nature of that universe. His was a silent universe, disinterested in revelation and selfish of clues.

He had cried at birth. It was the only sound ever to have escaped from inside him. He had never cooed or grunted, coughed or called out. His next sound would be his second. His next word his first. His mother fooled herself that she could divine the mysteries of her son's moods and desires by the rhythm of his rocking, by the shadows his fingers cast on the walls, even by which room James wandered into. She might as well have rolled animal bones.

James McCabe's father had long since cut ties with his son. He treated the boy with the utter disinterest which the boy himself displayed. If only the boy could have shown minimal contempt, that would have been enough for the father. He understood contempt, but he could not stomach disinterest. Love was never an issue. To his father, James was less than the least of his possessions. Objects are created without the potential for emotion. One's own love, pride, and vanity had to be enough for both you and the thing itself.

The day the two universes collided, each forever changing,

James McCabe, temporarily inert, found himself in a dark corner of the room that held his father's most prized possessions. The glass and oak case was more shrine than display. People came from all over to stand and gawk at the things in the case. Two sets of eager footfalls thumped against the big cabin's floorboards. As was always the case, it was impossible to know if James was aware they were coming toward him.

"Here we are, Mr. Smith."

Peter McCabe made a rather too formal gesture with his arm, but he couldn't help himself. Although he had shown his collection to many strangers, he could contain neither his pride nor his avarice. To see Peter McCabe's shrine cost you. It was a c-note just to stand near the case and peer through the glass. Five times that if you wished to handle pieces from the collection.

McCabe handed Smith a fresh pair of white gloves and put on a pair himself.

Reading Smith's expression, McCabe said, "Yes, it's always hard to know where to begin. This is a personal favorite. Here." He reached for a meticulously preserved hardcover, carefully covered in acid free plastic.

"*Mein Kampf*."

Smith was unimpressed.

McCabe did not overreact. "Yes, but not just any copy. Notice that the inscription is to Neville Chamberlain and that Hitler's signature is particularly bold and powerful."

Smith was still unmoved. McCabe replaced the book in the case and began nervously reciting a laundry list of other pieces from the collection.

"There's the sutures removed from Hitler's body after the attempt on his life, one of Eichmann's prototypes for the Death's Head hats, an ampule of blue dye Dr. Mengele used to inject into the eyes of children, a pair of the doctor's spectacles, Martin Bormann's Luger, a bar of human soap, a pelvic bone ashtray, a bottle of ashes from Crematorium Number Two at…"

So distracted was McCabe by his own narcissistic recitation, that he was unconscious of Smith removing his top coat.

And though the reflection of the yellow star sewn onto the chest of Smith's suit jacket was plain to see in the spotless glass of the case, that too escaped McCabe's notice. He missed it as his visitor slid the tire iron from beneath his right sleeve and into his white-gloved hand. He barely noticed as Smith screamed "Never Again" so loudly that his wife could hear it in the shed. Even as Smith raised the crooked metal rod—his bland, hollow face transformed into something barely recognizable as human—McCabe was oblivious. With the nauseating thud of the iron against his skull, it was already too late to rue his lack of attentiveness.

Peter McCabe's face smashed directly into the case, loose shards embedding themselves in his flesh. Jagged glass wedged in place peeled away parts of his neck and right ear as gravity pulled him to the floor. So much blood appeared in an instant that the oak and glass itself seemed to bleed. But Smith was far from finished. He swung the iron again and again, smashing almost every breakable object in the shrine. He dropped the iron, pulled a flask of gasoline out of his inside jacket pocket, and doused the case. He patted his pocket, feeling for a pack of matches. He became frantic when he could not feel that familiar shape in any of his pockets.

He found the matches in the pocket of his bulky top coat he had dropped behind him. As he struck the match, something else caught his attention. He heard James before he saw him. Rather he heard the floorboards creaking as the boy began rocking in the corner. James' unseeing eyes transfixed Smith. Not recognizing an ounce of humanity in them, Smith realized what he had become. A mist of profound shame filled his lungs. He wanted to approach the boy, but could not move. His hesitation proved fatal.

"You son of a bitch!"

The spell was broken and Smith looked toward the open door. The shotgun blast nearly took off his head and the inertia nudged his lifeless body into the ruined display case. His shame and the heat of the match on his fingertips consumed Smith's last moment of consciousness. The gasoline ignited. The spread of the buckshot and the impact of Smith's body finished the work he had started. The few shrine items that had remained in tact, either exploded or crashed to the floor. The room quickly filled with smoke.

THE FIRE WAS WELL extinguished and Peter McCabe had been helicoptered to the area trauma center. Mr. Smith's burned body had long since been delivered to the medical examiner's office. Smith, really Avi Pearlmutter, was the grandson of concentration camp survivors, a full time cultist, and part-time schizophrenic. James and his mother had both been treated for smoke inhalation and released.

The miracle was patient in coming. It waited until the stillness of night had fully descended and James' mom was halfway to visit her comatose husband. It waited until James' Aunt Greta had stripped off and burned her eight-year-old nephew's smoke-corrupted clothing. It waited until she led James into the upstairs bathroom, the shower already running. Then all patience evaporated and the miracle fairly exploded. James McCabe, the eight-year old universe, came undone.

The instant his bare feet touched the cold tile floor, James spoke. Well, it wasn't speech, exactly. He wasn't saying words, not so's Greta could make them out, anyway, but they weren't just random sounds either. They were like make believe words. And, there was another change in James, maybe even more profound than the nonsense words. His whole body posture, the manner of his movements changed. The awkward, ungainly jerkiness with which he had moved his entire life was gone.

"One minute he was one of them fidgety little birds and then he was a swan," she would later tell her sister. "First he started to jibber-jabber and then. . . Lord Jesus, sis, he moved so graceful-like."

And, the movements, like the sounds that came from his mouth, were not random. Although he was naked, James removed invisible clothes. He pressed them, patted out wrinkles, hung them on unseen hooks. He balled up see-through socks, placing them in phantom shoes.

"Then he looked me straight in the eye and started that jibber-jabbering all over again. It was spooky, sis, like your boy was asking me a question. I didn't know what to do, so I just showered him. When he got out, he dried himself all up and put back on them invisible clothes and started them spooky questions again. When I told him his momma would be home tomorrow, he smiled. He *smiled* at me, sis. The boy don't never smile. He went right to bed."

There was dark-clouded joy on the outskirts of town for a month or two. Although he had been burned, hit by stray buckshot, and suffered a seriously fractured skull, Peter McCabe's prognosis for survival was improved. His prognosis for a full recovery was less rosy. The damage to the skin and musculature of his face and neck would require several reconstructive procedures. The trauma caused by the blow to the back of his head, the subsequent collision of his forehead with the case, and the blood loss had left him addled, aphasic, weak.

On the other hand, James McCabe's metamorphosis was international news. Yet for all the coverage, each story filed bore a marked similarity to the ones before and after it.

"...the eight-year-old son of a white supremacist diagnosed with a severe form of Pervasive Developmental Disorder or autism, as it's more commonly known, witnessed a brutal attack on his father by. . . In the hours immediately following the attack, James McCabe, who had never uttered a word nor made a sound after his birth. . ."

So it went, at least at first. Then the tabloids moved onto the next sensation, but before they all left, *The World Planet Star* made the McCabes one hundred and fifty thousand dollars richer. Next, came the religious fanatics, cultists, and crazies. They were harder to bear, for they came with their own predetermined agendas, agendas having nothing to do with rating points and ad revenues. One group erected a likeness of James nailed to a wooden yellow star. Another took to acting out James' newfound undressing rituals. In the wake of the crazies came the intelligentsia, the critics, and the academics. They came to piss on the whole spectacle, on the McCabes, and each other. The academics, without ever examining the boy, concluded that this was no miracle, that the original diagnosis of PDD was completely misguided. Ultimately, James McCabe was judged a freak, an oddity, a future roadside attraction like a two-headed snake.

McCabe's Miracle, as it had come to be known, had become his mother's nightmare. For as the months went on, James' speech and rituals grew exponentially. From one minute to the next; his voice, his tone, his posture would change. The syllables that poured out of him seemed endless and endlessly senseless. There was no more understanding him now that he spoke than when his mother read his finger shadows. She found herself yearning for his past silence and hating herself for it.

And, her husband's rehab had all but consumed the largess of *The World Planet Star*. His problem was quite the opposite of her son's. Although he had yet to speak again, Peter McCabe was less confused and had come part of the way back to his old self. Unfortunately, his face still looked like a train wreck.

The next change in the collision of the two universes happened in the personal hygiene aisle of the supermarket. It took the shape of a bent old man, his posture that of a twisted tree limb. Even before he approached her, James' mother noticed the crooked man. So out of place, she thought, so shabby; the band of his black hat stained with sweat, his white shirt gone yellow with age. As she pushed the cart ahead of her and he hobbled towards her, she saw the dandruff on the shoulders of his threadbare black coat and the age spots on his ashen, unshaven face. She reached for the soap.

"Soap!" the old man exclaimed. "You know they made soap from human beings, the people your husband so admires."

She knew about the soap, the lampshades, about all of it.

"Get outta my way or I'll call—"

"But if you call security, Mrs. McCabe, I wouldn't be able to help you with your son. And if I don't help him... I don't think a woman like you could take much more of him, his talking and talking. Am I right? I can see in your eyes that I am right. Here's my card. I'm staying in the Best Western. If you want my help, I'll be there until Thursday."

She hesitated.

"Take it. Take it!" he said, shoving the card in her hand.

She did just to be rid of him. He touched the brim of his hat. She saw his hand was gnarled, scarred by fire.

"I'll await your call. Good day."

She did not turn to watch his retreat. Instead she stared at the card, as frayed and ragged as the man who had given it to her.

CHAIM FEINGOLD

That's what the card said, as if saying his name alone were enough. It would have to be, for it gave no address, no phone number, no fax, no email address, no website. She made to crumple the already withered card, but she did not. She would call. She knew she would as sure as Feingold, whoever he was, knew she would. She was desperate and desperation makes for strange allies.

Feingold came to the cabin that night after dark. Once again he put his fingers to his hat in the way of greeting and deference. That was his only concession to manners. He brushed past her, moving his ancient bent frame with an unexpected grace and power.

"Show me where is the room!" he barked.

"The room?"

"Where the husband was clubbed. Where he kept his foul things and the boy was in the corner. Show me!"

She led the way. "But it's all been—"

"Mrs. McCabe, do you want my help? Yes! Then please do as I say."

When they got to the room that had once held the shrine, Feingold had Mrs. McCabe describe in detail about where everything was situated, where her husband had fallen, where her boy had been, where Pearlmutter's body had come to rest. . .

"And your husband's horrible trinkets, they were all destroyed? The soap, the ashes, all of it?"

"All of it," she said. "The room filled up quick with smoke.

I got my husband out first. He was bleeding so. Then I came and got my boy."

"So, the boy was in the room here for some time, no? A few minutes maybe, yes?"

"A minute or two at least."

Feingold rubbed his cheek, grinning a contemptuous grin. It was a grin that frightened James' mother--a woman who didn't frighten easily.

"Mr. Feingold, how did you find us?"

"On the TV. I saw him on the TV and I recognized... Well, the way he moved and spoke. You wouldn't understand. Let's just say I became a student of your son and his miracle. Where is the boy?"

She hesitated.

"The boy!" he shouted. "Where is the boy?"

"In the bathroom. He seems his most comfortable in there."

"Comfortable, ha!" His laugh was as bent as his spine.

Both of them stood at the open door of the bathroom, Feingold staring in stunned disbelief as James ran through a never ending series of undressing rituals, each different from the next, and nonsense questions asked with wildly different intonation patterns. Silent tears streamed down the old man's cheeks. It had been one thing to see the boy on TV and something else again to stand in the room before him. Feingold's whole body shook. Although she was standing behind him and to one side, Mrs. McCabe could see the old man's reaction in the bathroom mirror.

The old man collected himself, walked up to the boy and placed a gnarled hand on James's shoulder.

"*Wos iz dien nomen?*" he asked the boy.

A pause. Then he continued with his rituals.

"*Was ist Ihr Name?*"

Another pause. Back to the rituals.

"*Wat is uw naam?*"

James crooked his head slightly as if he almost understood, but continued.

"Barmilyen egyezes kiejtes nelkul?"

James stopped dead in his tracks, looked over each shoulder as if making sure no one was watching or listening. When he was secure that only Feingold could hear, he whispered a blue streak. Feingold gave the boy a long avuncular hug and, in the same foreign tongue with which the boy had whispered to him, told James to put his clothes back on, that his shower could wait. Dutifully, he did as the old man instructed, sitting himself down quietly on the cool tile floor. He told the boy not to worry, that he'd be right back, and closed the bathroom door behind him.

Mrs. McCabe was on her knees in the hallway, head upturned to the rafters, hands folded prayerfully. When she was done muttering, she turned to Feingold.

"How did you—What did you—"

"I asked his name, what it was in Yiddish, German, Dutch, and finally Hungarian."

"But he doesn't—"

"—speak Hungarian. He doesn't speak English, yes? He doesn't speak at all. He still does not, Mrs. McCabe."

"I don't understand."

"Why should you? How could such a person as you or your husband understand? The boy, *your* boy, is not speaking. At the moment, that is not your son, but a thirteen-year-old girl from Budapest named Magda Nagy whose father was teaching comparative literature at the University of Warsaw when the Nazis invaded. For her, it's nineteen forty-four. Less than an hour ago, her whole family got off the train at the gates of Auschwitz. Her father, mother, and older brother were taken away and she was sent for a delousing shower."

"That's crazy!"

"Crazy! You know what she asked, Magda? First, where her family had gone. Then, what hook number she should place her clothes on. That's what the bastards would tell the unfortunates before they herded them into the gas chambers and locked the steel doors behind them. 'Remember what hook number you placed your clothes on so you can retrieve them when you come out of the shower.' That's what they told them, these people you and your husband admire. She's not even a Jew, Magda."

Mrs. McCabe did not have the strength to argue. "But how did you know? Until you just now spoke to James—Magda, whoever, he, I mean, she didn't speak Hungarian. That was jibber-jabber coming out of my boy's mouth."

"Yes and no. It was Yiddish and German, Dutch and Hungarian, Polish and Russian, Romanian and ten other languages jumbled together, sometimes spoken backwards with no native accent. It was the languages of all the people what bodies became ashes and lampshades, soap and . . . It is the language of the smoke."

"But how did you know? How could you know?"

"That is my business alone. I am going in that bathroom now. And when I come out, maybe we will both have back something we lost: you only a few months ago, me a lifetime ago."

When Chaim Feingold stepped back into the bathroom and closed the door behind him, he stood up on the bathtub's edge. In the Yiddish of his youth, Feingold shouted as if above the din of a crowded room crammed with people, though only James McCabe was there to hear him.

"Is my sister, Shandel Feingold here? Shandel!" he called, hoping that the girl he had recognized on TV in the guise of James McCabe could be reached. "Shandela! Shandela!"

"Chaim! Chaim! Here, over here I am," she answered across time and space.

And for hours, the crooked old man held his dead sister in his arms.

◆◆◆

IT WAS THREE more months before Peter McCabe was deemed well enough to come home. And when he arrived, he found a very different cabin and a very different family than the ones he had left. James had returned to his silence, but the opacity of his blue eyes was gone. You cannot have the dead speak through you and be unchanged. He was no longer a universe unto himself and had learned to indicate through gestures his likes and dislikes. Peter swore the boy almost smiled at him.

Mrs. McCabe had found the God she had run away from twenty years before. She went to church every day, asking forgiveness for herself and her husband. She had taken what was left of the money and donated it to the Holocaust Museum in Washington in the name of Magda Nagy. She sold most of their property to pay for her husband's rehab.

Still aphasic, McCabe asked his wife, "My 'hings, 'hat 'appened 'o my 'hings?"

"They're gone and we're never to speak of them again."

He grew very agitated, his arms flexing and shaking. Then she told him about Feingold and how he said James' jibber-jabber was the language of the smoke.

Peter McCabe began laughing wildly, crazily. His eyes got wide, his face red. Then he started choking, coughing. His wife was frantic not knowing what to do. Eventually, he settled back down, tears in the corners of his eyes.

"Lang'age a smoke." He shook his head. He didn't have the heart to tell his wife that he had made the soap himself and that the bottle of ashes had come from their own fireplace.

The Surrogate

Anthony Neil Smith

I hired a private eye to tail the woman who would be the mother of my wife's unborn child. You know, to make sure the baby would have a good home. The private eye had to drive over from Minneapolis because I lived in a small prairie town tucked away in Minnesota's southwestern corner, and everyone here knew pretty much everyone else. People might see her around, and maybe they would ask questions, but they wouldn't know the full story.

I asked her to meet me at the Eagle's Club downtown that night. It was closed for a private party, the local clinic's employees doing a late New Year's thing, but the bartender was an old friend of my dad's and let me in. The folks there had a taco bar and a DJ. They invited us to eat because they'd catered for more than enough people. So we did, then sat at a booth out of their way. A woman on her way to being drunk carried her plate back to her table, stopping at each one along the way to say, "God bless your meal. God bless your meal, all right?"

After she'd passed us, the private eye said, "Don't you have a lawyer who handles stuff like this? Isn't there a contract?"

"No lawyers. It's just a contract we did on our own. People lie, though. There's a lot of putting best feet forward."

"You think she's lying?"

"I don't know." Shrug. "More like...its peace of mind."

She raised her eyebrows. "What do you care, though? This was all invitro, so it's really hers anyway. Why would you doubt someone who's willing to pay you how much?"

"I'd rather not—"

"Fine, fine." She slashed her hand, then picked up a taco.

The soft shell dropped on the backend and sopping wet taco meat plopped onto her plate. "The best in town?"

"Sure, for catering."

She set it down and wiped her hands with a napkin. "So I just watch?"

"And follow."

"What should I expect to find?"

I took a long pull of beer, then looked at her a few moments. She was probably in her forties, I'm guessing divorced by a man who ran off with a younger lover. She had that short, manageable haircut that lower middle-class women all seemed to get up here. Added ten years, but at least it was easy to fix. Would she understand? If I told her what I really expected, would she bite too hard or just run away?

So, I told her, "If I knew that, I wouldn't need you, would I?"

She sighed, tried lifting the taco again. The DJ must have taken a break, because the bartender put Alan Jackson's "Gone Country" on the CD player and it had been on for ten minutes—near the end it kept skipping back to the second verse. No one seemed to notice. I wondered if I was being ridiculous, tailing Janine like this. But I had to be sure.

After what had to be a less than satisfactory bite, the private eye swallowed and said, "Jesus, Mike, if I didn't have a mortgage past due, I'd turn you down flat. Find something better to do. Take up woodwork."

I let it go. *She's gone country, look a'them boots.* Over and over through a torn speaker, and it still wasn't as hellish as what was going on in my head.

♦♦♦

AT HOME, Kath was listening to some CD she'd picked up at the Goodwill—something about *Smarter Babies, Happy Babies.* They sang songs about grammar and phonics. Shit. I could hear it even out in the entryway by the garage where I shook snow off my cap and kicked my boots off.

She was on the floor in the living room, reclined against the couch, her neck on the edge of the cushion. Her giant belly almost a full moon, only a sliver of silk pajama top on the upper crescent.

"Have a good time?" Hands rubbing her belly, talking slow and breathy like some sort of hippie Earth Momma.

I shrugged, sat in my Laz-E-Boy, picked up the mail from the coffee table. Hard to ignore her when she was like this--naked below the waist. This pregnancy had opened up her sexuality. She loved her body when she was pregnant. If my love for her hadn't already shut down several years before, I would've loved it, too. That plus the fact that even the routine sex had been shut off this go round because "we're protecting an investment."

We'd had two kids already—the oldest a boy who was now off in grad school. Could hardly believe it. Wanted to be a poet, and I have no idea what side of the family that came from. The youngest a girl just starting college. She refused to stay in town at the local state university and save us some money. No, she had to go just over the state line into South Dakota, out of state tuition for barely an hour's drive. She was getting C's in basic courses and couldn't choose a major. That was enough for us. For me, anyway. I don't think I ever took to being a dad, really. I loved those kids and did my best, but if you were to ask them if I was the most involved or affectionate father, I'm sure they'd have to think about it awhile.

Here I was, forty-seven and finally comfortable as a man, but uncomfortable in this house, this marriage, this fatherhood. Maybe it was the promotion five years ago, the business trips to Chicago and St. Louis and Tempe. The one night stands with other sales reps and middle managers, just to keep from being so goddamn bored, keep my mind off the trip home.

It never occurred to me to leave my family and start over. No, that wasn't it at all. More like a superhero costume—put it on, have a more exciting life for a little while, then take it off when that got too stressful. But to Kath, it must've seemed like I was a boring old fart who lost his sex drive. If she only knew, right?

"Your team didn't win?"

"Huh?" I had to remember I'd told her I was down at the

Nickel watching hockey. "See, I started talking to Bill, you know Bill, and just flat out forgot about the game. It wasn't that good anyway."

"Forgot, like drank too much? Like you shouldn't have been driving?"

I closed my eyes. "It's half a mile."

"I'm just saying. All of us right now, we can't afford to blow this."

Opened them again, turned to her. Hands still on her belly like a bobcat was threatening to pounce. "Blow what?"

"I mean, you hit someone or get pulled over, that's going to cost us. What would that do to me?"

"Or the baby."

"Yeah, see?" Nodding. If you didn't know her, you'd think she was high. And horny. I think she just felt important again, and that helped. No longer a *mom*, a high schooler's mom waiting to empty the nest. Once that happened, well, there we were.

Kath was only five years younger, but somewhere in her thirties she saw what her life had done to her body—nothing major, just the effects of gravity—and she didn't like it. We talked about plastic surgery, lipo, stuff like that, but in the end she surprised me—and everyone, I think—by tackling it naturally, changing how she ate, exercising more. It took a couple of years, but she kept at it, single-minded, and I was grateful she didn't push me along the way. She kept cooking my meat and potatoes even if she wouldn't touch a fork to it.

As if to say I was fine just the way I was. Which meant she hated me.

Oh, she would never say it. Back then, there was even the tidal wave of rekindled affection because of her new lingerie and new energy. But I soon saw through it, just the way she'd keep her sentences short, or not launch an insult or quip about my lazy ass when in the past they were landing like smart bombs left and right. Her new method of improving me—leaving me the hell alone, crossing her fingers I'd want to better myself to catch up.

Fuck that noise.

I sighed. I'd been doing that a lot. I reached for the remote.

She said, "I'm not finished."

Jesus. "Okay." I got up and started for the basement, where we had set up our old TV and broken-in couch on some carpet remnants, just in case. Only got past the threshold to the kitchen.

"Mike, wait."

I turned around. Waited. Crossed my arms. She rocked left and right, gripping the couch behind her with one hand, pushing off the floor with the other. Not having a good go of it. She blinked, looked at me, blinked again, eyes back down, on and off until I finally stepped over, took her hand and helped her up. Then I let go and retreated to my spot in the kitchen, trying to drown out the carousel-like music encouraging me to do my multiplication tables.

"Please, baby."

"What? I'm here. What do you need?"

She shook her head. "It was very important that we do this. That was a lot of money. We're going to be so much better off—"

"You already said. We've already said that. I know."

"Then what...why do you seem miserable?"

All the things I could say: *I can't stand the way you look at me. You think you're better than me. You flaunt your body but won't let me have it. Not that I'd want it. If I wanted a younger woman, I would've run off with coeds already. That's why I fuck women my own age when I'm traveling, so they won't remind me of how fucking old and unimportant I am.*

On the tip of my tongue. Right there. Come on, just start...say *I*.

"I..."

Okay now. Keep going.

I sighed again. "I don't know what to say. I'm fine. I'm tired. I tired of talking about *this* over and over."

"But this is real. It's happening. I need you to help me."

"I do. I have. Why is it never enough? Never?"

She looked away. "It is, honey, it is. But...what's wrong with more? Enough is great, but why not more?"

I took a step back. "It already feels like more to me. Hey, I want to watch that show I like. It's almost on."

I prepared myself for the *What's more important to you* line that was sure to follow, but instead, she stood there breathing through her nose and staring at me like a teacher stares down a bad child. I looked at my watch.

Kath finally said, "I'll turn this off. You watch TV in here. I'll go up and take a bath."

Great. Fuck. Great. "Honey, you finish. I'll be fine downstairs."

Three times three is nine, you see. Three times four is twelve—it's swell!

"No, you bought the big screen for the HD. You should enjoy it. I'll be fine."

She walked over to the stereo, bent over and turned off the music. I'm sure the ass was for me. Another pleasure denied. For the first few months of her being pregnant, I always looked. Lately, I turned away.

I didn't question her or thank her or any such. Just took my place in my Laz-E-Boy, turned on the TV while she was still in front of it replacing the CD in its case. Right before she set it down, for a weird moment, the light for the TV radiated around her like she was an angel. Maybe she felt it too, because she looked up at me with soft eyes, hand back to her stomach.

I changed it over to the Speed Channel to watch drag racing.

Tire screech didn't do much for the angel thing. Kath pinched her lips tight and moved away towards the stairs. I turned up the volume.

Just a little while to myself, you know? A little while without talking about what's good for the baby we're not even keeping. The one I had no say in. I don't want to talk about how young my wife feels, and how this new life could renew our relationship if I'd just be open to letting out the angry teenager inside me. Yes, she said it like that. Kath wants to see my angry teenager again. Shit, she never saw him in the first place. We met after college.

No, let me sit and watch hockey highlights and think about another woman. The one I've been fucking right under Kath's giant belly.

Janine. The one who's going to take the baby when it's all said and done.

Yep, been seeing her since the second month. And I had a good damn reason to put a private eye on her, too.

Let me stew on that while watching another hockey brawl.

It wasn't three minutes when Kath called down, sing-songy, "Hun-neeey?"

Closed my eyes. "Yep?"

"Scoop out the cat box, remember?"

♦♦♦

THIS DAMN CAT. "Astrokitty" was eight years old. Her urine smelled like ammonia mixed with stale beer. She was blind in one eye, sounded like a parrot with throat cancer, and shed enough fur to make a new floor rug every day. I had no idea how she could lose that much and not be bald already. But all I knew is that when I was on my knees in front of the box, scooping away and trying not to inhale, the cat just kept pacing up against my leg, leaving an inch deep layer of fur on my pants.

It was Kath's cat, and she used to do the scooping, but not now that she was pregnant. Apparently, there's some germ in the cat pee that can make the baby retarded. It didn't hurt her when we had Shoebox (we bought him from a guy who let him sleep in a shoebox) the first time she was pregnant.

But fine. It was Janine's baby anyway, and they were going to pay a pretty big sum of money, and I didn't want either of these women pissed at me, no matter how much willpower it took to keep from punching both.

Scoop. Stirring it up made it worse.

I looked down at Astrokitty. "I mean, it's just water and

kibble, right? How can you screw up water and kibble this bad?"

She rubbed her face against my sock.

Another whiff. Holy God.

Look, I'd never actually hit a woman. Hell, I hadn't hit a man since some guy in a bar grabbed Kath wrong a dozen years back. But...in my mind, that's the thing. I see myself doing it and it worries me. So I shut off even more around Kath than usual, and I just got wound-up as hell around Janine on the afternoons we were able to sneak away together, usually out in her giant SUV on the edge of tall corn fields before the harvest. This past month, we'd been sneaking off just over the border to South Dakota and checking into cheap hotels.

I couldn't put my finger on it, but something had changed the past two weeks. Sex had become less lusty, I think. She wasn't trying any more. She asked more questions about Kath's exercise routine and eating habits than she did about what would make me happy in bed. Plus, she cancelled on me earlier in the week. A bunch of stuff she had to do, buying baby furniture or some shit. Her voice gave it away, though. We were having a rough patch.

Fuck, I didn't have an affair to get into another passive-aggressive tug of war.

The cat had rubbed me so much that she built up static electricity. Shocked us both. She leapt about a foot in the air. She also let a little more stinky pee out, dribbling on the floor.

I nearly stopped what I was doing. Fuck the scooping. Fuck the litter. This cat was done. It was past done. All it needed was coaxing—an open door, a toilet seat left up. Or one swift kick.

Took in deep breaths to calm down. That smell overwhelming me, sticking in the back of my throat. I fought it. Coughed. Fought some more. Then finally tied up the plastic bag of clumped shit and piss. Astrokitty didn't hesitate. Hopped right in and let off a lethal stream.

I stood, walked into the kitchen, and then dropped the bag into the trash can and went for napkins so I could wipe up the cat's little accidents.

♦♦♦

THE PI CALLED my cell a few days later saying she had nothing to report. "You still want to pay me to keep looking for whatever I'm supposed to be looking for?"

"You're complaining?"

"It just seems a waste. But I won't turn down a job, not these days."

I let out a breath and stared out the sliding back door into my backyard. I'd forgotten to move my grill into the garage before the last big snow, so it was covered damn near up the grease-drip can, shin deep.

"Just…" Cough. Felt like something caught in my throat. But it was probably just acid. "Tell me what you actually saw."

"It was nothing. She came home at night. She ate lunch at work. She went to the store. She went to dinner."

"Dinner?"

"Yes, at the Bistro. Her husband took her to dinner around seven, they had a nice time, and were home by nine."

More acid. Another cough. "When was that?"

"Two days ago. Who cares?"

"Did you see what they had to eat?"

"Uh, no. I wasn't watching them through the window."

"Okay, but after. How about after?"

"They. Drove. Home."

"Shit, woman, *details*." Cat rubbing up against me again. I pushed her aside with my leg.

"They had a good time, then stopped by the video store, then went home."

"How do you know they had a good time? You just said—"

"They were laughing, all right? Smiling. Listen, Mike, I'm not so comfortable with this."

"Tell me about when they got home." Astrokitty couldn't take a hint. I had to kick this time.

She took the phone from her face, let out what sounded like nervous laughter. Then said, "They got out of the car, the husband hugged her, kissed her cheek before they went inside."

"After that?"

"Hey!"

I didn't say anything.

She didn't either.

Until she finally said, "Why are you doing this? They're not bad people. They're a great couple who would provide a good home for the baby. That's what you want to know, right?"

Maybe she was getting it. Maybe not. In any case, it had been enough. "Okay, yeah. I'll mail you a check."

"How about I come pick it up tomorrow?"

Should've been fine with that. I should've. But I had to say, "How about one more night? But I need to see what's going on inside. When the lights go out."

The PI breathed loudly into the phone for awhile, then said, "Just mail me the check. I need to get back to the Cities, forgot about some business. Take care."

She hung up.

I stood, walked out to the entryway to put on my boots. Then I got in my truck and drove over to see Janine.

◆◆◆

JANINE WORKED AT the local college in Admissions, and I found her on the phone. She was good at multitasking, as I'd seen her have a normal, dull, conversation with her husband on her cell while I was giving it to her in their bed, my lips inches away from the phone, and he never knew a thing. This time, Janine's eyes widened and her lips curled into a witchy sneer, but she didn't miss a beat. "Yes, I see what you mean. We can mail a certified letter, I suppose. No, I can't hound her. No, I…well, I appreciate the concern, but sometimes, failing them is the only message they understand."

I sat in a chair and pretended to look at the diploma and photos on the wall. I'd seen them all before. Yeah, here too. On the desk when she was supposed to be at lunch.

She finished the call and turned to me. "Close the door."

"Maybe I don't plan on staying that long."

She shook her head and stood, walked over and closed it

herself. Beige slacks, white blouse, looked like she had chosen the outfit from the costume department of an Eighties TV show.

Instead of coming back around the desk, she stayed on my side of it, sat on the edge and crossed her arms. "What are you doing here?"

Whatever bluster I'd had on the way in evaporated in that chair as she stood over me, a little too much make-up and her hair dyed a dark auburn. A powerful woman. Not conflicted, not pining for her youth. The only thing was that she had an emergency hysterectomy in her early thirties, and since then a couple of adoption attempts—Russia, Guatemala—fell through at the last second. All of that had been tough on her marriage. She had told me that a number of times after the four of us initially met and made the deal. I became a steam valve for her. An outlet to get rid of all the bad that had been clouding her.

I said, "I've just missed you."

"Shut up. *Shut up.*" Hissed at me. Turned her head away and closed her eyes.

I shut up.

What else was I supposed to do? Tip my hand? Tell her I know she's rekindled the spark with Donald? They were always good friends, so even with a sexless year there was no question of them staying together. It was never that. I simply hoped the sexlessness would continue and I would be the one she turned to time after time, something neither of our spouses could fault us for, not really. We filled needs for each other we weren't getting at home. So it appeared she was getting it again. Getting it good. She was glowing. I couldn't compete with that. What we'd done together was *animal.* We didn't laugh before, during, or after.

Janine said, "You can't take a hint? How obvious do I have to...Mike, listen, like we'd always said, right? It wasn't forever. Jesus."

I nodded. "Mm hm."

"I was a mess, you were a mess. God bless Katherine, right? It's an amazing thing she's doing for us. If she were to find out—"

"You want some food?"

"What?"

"I thought we could go for Chinese. The buffet."

A hint of a grin. "I had lunch, thanks."

"They've got dessert. It would be nice."

"I'm not hungry." No more grin. "What are you up to? I'm telling you we should back off. That's all. Our family, we have to prepare for the baby. It's a wonderful thing, and everything's different now."

"You said you didn't need the baby."

"Mike." Janine dropped her chin. "What I said was I learned the difference between *need* and *want*. I'd always thought I *needed* a baby, but now I know I just *want* one, and that want will make me love the child even more than if it were just something off a checklist of stuff to do before I die."

Sounded like she got that from a movie. I stood, shifted my hat further back from my forehead. "So that's it?"

Even though we were nearly touching, she didn't move away. She looked up into my eyes and said, "That's the way it is. That's the contract."

I mean, her tits were brushing against my jacket. Her breath was on my cheek. All either of us had to do was...

But I understood. I didn't have a snappy line to end it on. Not even a good-bye. I stepped around her, opened the office door, and let it slam as I stomped off. I knew what I had to do.

◆ ◆ ◆

I WENT TO the public library. We didn't have the best library in town, but I didn't want to get caught hanging around the better one on campus with Janine already wearing the Queen Bitch crown of the day. Maybe she would change her mind. Maybe the baby wouldn't be the magic spell she expected, and before long, we'd be bumping and grinding again while the kid slept in the corner.

It all came back to the fucking kid. I'd been thanking God for my wife's weirdo life choices when it brought Janine to us. To me. But it was becoming clear to me that the pregnant woman ain't the only one whose hormones get cranked thinking about the little bundle of joy.

Fucking baby.

I found some interesting books, pulled them off the shelves, and staked out a table. I had been wrong about the cat piss screwing with the baby. It was the shit instead. Toxoplasmosis, it was called.

That wouldn't do what I needed, though. It was a longshot and not at all as dangerous as it used to be. Plus, there was no way to really make my wife inhale cat shit if she didn't want to. Not this far along.

The other stuff didn't help either—no soft cheeses? No fish? We didn't eat much of either. Drugs? How would I make her take them? Inject her while she slept? All right, not the worst idea. After all, the goal wasn't to kill Kath. Not at all. It was to kill the baby.

I had to pin it all on a biggie. Cross my fingers and pray that it worked. Bangs and bruises for the wife, and an underdeveloped stillborn for Janine. I shut the books, sat for a few minutes thinking it through, and then decided it would have to do. I was running out of time.

I had to shove my wife down the stairs and make it look like an accident.

◆ ◆ ◆

IT'S HARDER THAN it sounds. I had to make sure there was an honest reason why the top steps were suddenly so slippery. Could be I was trying to fill the tank of the humidifier in the bedroom, but I had a spill.

The handrail, which had always been loose, needed to be looser. Loose enough that a normal grab would pull it clean off.

I set up the scene the night before by dropping the humidifier tank, which shattered into several sharp plastic pieces. The water soaked everything, right up to the bedroom door. Kath was already down for the evening.

She sat right up, as much as she could. "What was that?"

"The humidifier. The damned humidifier bottle. I dropped it, broke it. Shit, I'm sorry baby."

"It really broke? Just from a short drop like that?"

"It's bad. Don't come out here. I'll clean it up. Shit."

"Can you glue it back together?"

"Maybe. I'll see. It'll have to dry overnight."

"We just bought that thing."

And so on while I mopped up the water, which wasn't coming up easily, with four of our towels. I left some water, just in case. Maybe Kath would get the munchies and head down for pickles and ice cream at two a.m. But more likely not. She'd tell me to get her some.

I dumped the wet towels into the bathroom for the night and climbed into bed. Maybe I shouldn't have made such a loud show of it all, because instead of falling right back to sleep, Kath squirmed over to me and rested her head on my chest.

"Thanks for all the help," she said. "I'm sorry about all this. If we didn't need the money, though."

I shrugged. "We don't need it *that* bad, do we? Here I thought we were doing all right."

"Aren't you tired of scraping by each month? Juggling? This will make us both more comfortable, baby. I haven't heard you talk about buying a lake home for a long time. Don't you think if we sock this away for a few years, we can finally do it?"

"Would be nice."

"A place to retire."

An empty spot in my soul, like hunger, welled up and I thought I might cry. Here I'd been thinking that she had abandoned our plans, stuff we had daydreamed about with each other years ago. Sounded more like all along she had been keeping them on the back burner, but easing up the heat as we drew closer.

Very sweet of her.

The problem was that I couldn't imagine that sort of life with her anymore. Not the woman she'd become over this baby bullshit. Maybe after it was all over, I'd get the real Kath back. She's the one who liked to go fishing with me. She even put up with the hockey games. She knew that I liked my steaks charred on the outside but medium well on the inside, but she told everyone I liked mine rare. And she knew how much ice I liked in my tea.

Last time Kath made tea, a handful of weeks ago, it was weak, smelled funny, and was supposed to be served hot.

No thanks.

So forget it. The best way to get my wife back while still retaining some tiny shred of dignity was to kill the parasite living inside her in order to stick it to my lover. But if it went to plan, Kath wouldn't realize that was exactly what happened.

Still, her face on my chest felt wonderful. I'd forgotten how much I liked it.

◆◆◆

I ALWAYS GET up around four in the morning to take a whiz, and I did it this morning too. Only I hadn't been asleep at all. Just lying there, unable to drift off, picturing everything that could go wrong or how it could go so awfully right. I pictured a big gash in Kath's skull, a lifeless gaze, and I stop breathing for a moment. I pictured bent limbs, snapped right in two. I pictured her after a brain hemorrhage. And I started to cry.

I couldn't let her take that fall. No, really, I couldn't.

I eased out of bed and tiptoed across the creaky wooden floor to the door, then out to the bathroom. Still wet in the hall, and colder than I expect. I wiped my feet on the bathroom rug, squinted at myself in the mirror. Puffy-eyed. Blurry. Old.

Jesus, she couldn't take the fall, but I couldn't let her go through with the pregnancy either. Fuck. What the fuck, right? Guilting me with the cabin when this whole stupid business has been about her. Kath, Kath, Kath. The Center of the Universe. The Giving Mother.

Fuck that shit, and fuck Janine and Donald and the goddamned soul-sucking baby.

I grabbed the plunger from beside the toilet and marched back into the bedroom. My eyes had adjusted by then, and I saw clearly Kath's heavy shape, bulging out painfully, skin tightened to the max. A peaceful expression on her face.

I lifted the plunger high over my head with both hands and swung it down hard on her stomach like a sledgehammer.

She sat up like a vampire with a stake in its heart. Eyes and mouth wide-open, never-saw-it-coming O's, her hands playing defense over the womb. She was blinking and frantic—not seeing me yet, but I could see her fine.

I switched to a baseball bat grip and swung again, slamming her fingers so hard that she yanked them back reflexively, giving me another shot at the baby. I give it a go and feel flushed when I connect. Oh yeah. A good triple at least.

"*Mike! Mike! Mike!*"

No idea yet that it was me. Calling out for her rescuer. She should've done that before, back when I had a chance to save her from this stupid idea.

She reached over to my side of the bed, patted up and down, before looking back. I caught it then, the glint of recognition. Her pupils had finally dilated. She knew.

Kath rolled off to my side of the bed and unto the floor, wrapped like a mummy in our sheets. She fought to free her legs.

"What are you doing? Stop it! Please, stop it!"

I didn't answer. Waited. No reason to swing again until I had a better angle.

"Mike, listen, please don't hurt the baby."

Nothing again.

"We can talk about this, can't we?"

I decided to go for her just to shut her up. A good shot to the side of her head. I pulled back, swung, and she ducked. Momentum carried me past and onto the bed. Kath got up and went for the door.

And I thought, *The stairs.*

"Wait, baby, wait a minute!"

"Jesus!"

"Wait!"

I pushed off the bed and lunged for the door just as she was trying to close it back. I grabbed hold of her ankle. She fell down right past the threshold. Kicked at my grip with her free foot, but I dug in my nails while she screamed my name over and over.

Ground the plunger onto the floor and used it to leverage myself up, still holding onto her ankle. By now Astrokitty was down there with her, a shaky little mewl joining the chorus of Kath's teeth-chattering "Ohgodohgodohgodohgod".

I opened the door, stared down at her. She was covering her stomach again as if it was more important than her own life.

I toed one hand off. "Stop that. You're better than that."

"What's wrong with you? You have to stop this now. You have to *stop*."

The plunger was stuck. I gave it a good yank and it plopped free. "This isn't you, Katherine. It's some character or split personality. You need this to find yourself again."

"Please, okay, we can talk about it."

"I don't want to talk. I want it to just…happen. You used to be someone else. As soon as the baby's gone, you will be again."

"Okay, maybe, but it's not the baby's fault. Please. It's not the baby's fault."

A good grip on the plunger now. I unscrewed the rubber bell so that I just had a sturdy rod. Solid. Not going to fuck it up this time.

I stepped over Kath, straddling her. Started to plant my right foot. Kath reached out with both hands and pulled hard, bent my knee forward and set me off balance. I moved my left just enough to redistribute my weight, but I stepped on Astrokitty's tail.

A screech like a hard brake, then some static electricity off the cat, zapping my leg, and I fell forward. Stumbled off Kath, put one foot down beside her head, but then the other hit the water and I was gone.

Two, three slippery steps before the first stair, also wet, and there was no way I was going down the right way. Slammed my shoulder hard, felt my arm crack like a tree limb, then my head, struck hard and long, ringing one loud church bell note. Even though I remember falling the rest of the way, I might as well have been knocked clean out.

◆◆◆

THE REST WAS fragments. Felt like forever. I don't remember Kath coming down to check on me, but she did. I remember Astrokitty tail tickling my nose, but my sneezes were pathetic. I was choking. My breathing sounded like a bad motor. One eye was closed, useless. The other seemed skewed somehow, everything cut at a weird angle and doubled. I couldn't move, or if something on me was moving, I sure as fuck didn't feel it.

Next thing I knew, the three of them are standing over me, the main foyer light a blinding beacon above them, darkening out the faces, but I knew the silhouettes and voices.

"Tried to kill you?" Donald. "I…I don't know what to say. Maybe I thought he was a bit quiet, but not this angry."

I tried to talk. The sounds I thought to say didn't move the muscles in my jaw, my lips, my larynx. The lines had snapped between mind and body. Donald would never hear me say "Asshole" to his face.

Janine stood between him and Kath. She didn't lean close. Peered down from the high heavens. I willed her to tell them the truth about us. I tried sending psychic waves. Tried to express it in my eyes. Nothing. She was a statue.

She said, "This…this is unreal. What are you going to do?"

Kath, the only one crying. The only one feeling any pain about this at all. You bastards. Get to feeling it. *Help me.*

Kath said, "It's just…I don't want, you know. I would hate it if people knew that's what he was. He doesn't deserve it. I know what we did to him was wrong, but still."

Whoa. Hold up. What did she just say?

Donald was poking me all over. Trying to get a reaction, I guess. I felt a few pokes, but the rest, it was like he was poking air. Not one nerve ending alive. He said, "Look, he would've loved that baby. I know it. Yes, it seems mean and all to go through all this just to have us back out, but I promise it would've worked."

Great time to tell me. Really.

Kath said, "I don't know what happened to him. One day he's happy with our life, and the next, he's miserable. I thought another kid would bring him out of it. But the one time I mentioned I *might* be pregnant, he told me to get it vacuumed out before I got too far along. Wow, I'm glad I tested the waters. Can you believe that?"

Janine finally got down on one knee, looked into my eyes. She said, "He's conscious, you know. He knows everything we're saying."

Kath hugged herself and rocked left to right, left to right. "He's....he's really...there's no hope? We can't call an ambulance?"

Janine's lips, the only part of her I could see clearly, curled up into that tiger-like grin I knew so well. She whispered, "You fucking idiot. Tried to kill your own kid."

Then Donald said, "Katherine, let's get you taken care of. We have to get the baby checked out. Let me drive you to the ER."

Really sniffing now. Blubbering, even. "What...what about Mike?"

"Janine will call Nine One One. We can't risk moving him like this. Hurry."

I heard Kath still crying, still protesting as Donald led her out to the driveway and into his car.

♦♦♦

THAT'S HOW WE got here, me paralyzed and broken. Janine in complete control. My head's cranked to the left and resting on the bottom stair. Janine is sitting above me on the third stair, knees wide, one heel on my shoulder. It's hard to see her up there, but I get a good see-thru double version in my periphery. She's smiling.

"Your own kid. But she was so scared of what you would say, she engineered this cool story about how she could be our surrogate, and then in the end, *poof*, we back out, and who's going to raise the kid? You'd really put it up for adoption?" She leans over, her face very large and fish-eyed. "What I'd learned about you, yeah. Maybe you would. You'd go this far to kill it. But Kath believed in you. She really thought you were bluffing."

She was wrong. I hated that baby. I could never love that baby.

"It's a good thing you didn't give a shit about the procedure and lab work and the other stuff. I don't think we could've faked all that."

The cat comes down the stairs, meows softly at Janine, and she pets it.

"Your neck's broken. But you'd already guessed, right? There's one little thread of something left keeping you alive and breathing. But…"

She reaches down, plants her fingers on my temple.

"…One little twist, and I bet it's all over. Good night, dear Mike. Been a pleasure."

I just wanted to grow old like I wanted to. I was tired of being young. Sick of being someone's daddy.

"Before the ambulance gets here, I'm going to give your head that last twist. Just in case. I'm not even going to tell you when. It's more of a surprise that way. But think about this." She tapped my forehead with her middle finger. "Do you really think I'd fuck the guy married to the woman carrying my baby? Are you nuts?"

And now I'm waiting for it. Is she right about it killing me? I don't know. Am I looking forward to it? I don't know. Not like I had much to live for besides more fishing, more fucking, and a lot of hard work. Even more so with a new baby. Not like my insurance would cover much beyond my funeral.

So while we wait, I spin some names through my head. Like a Biblical patriarch, what would I have named my son to reflect how I felt?

Ash, because he burned up my hopes and dreams.

Clay, because he made me filthy in my mind.

Karl, because that was my grandfather's—

Cat's Meow

Mary Logue

It was Bonbon that saved her life. What made it odd was the cat didn't even like Shelley. Bonbon was Tom's cat. He had had it longer than any woman he had ever been with and he probably loved it more. Except for Shelley, he said.

That was all right with Shelley. She wasn't jealous of the cat. She enjoyed coming into a room and seeing the cat curled up in a chair, stretched out on the top of the couch, or snuggled into Tom's laundry basket.

Since the cat moved so little, Shelley thought of it as a piece of statuary and sometimes when Tom wasn't watching she would move the cat around, place it in a patch of light on the floor or hide it under a chair at the dining table.

Once she had put it in the bathtub with a towel and tried to make it look like the cat had pulled it down for comfort off the towel rack. When Tom found it, he had called to her, "Come see what Bonbon has done. What a smart kitty."

Shelley admired the cat and then she and Tom went to bed. That was the favorite part of their relationship for Shelley. She figured that Tom was such a good lover because he had a cat. He knew how to stroke her, pet her. She could swear sometimes she was on the verge of purring.

A few months after they had started dating, Tom had to go out of town on business. Before he left he took Shelley out to a wonderful meal, looked deep into her eyes and said, "Would you please... take care of my cat while I'm gone?"

"Sure," Shelley said.

They discussed it and decided it would be less traumatic for Shelley to move into Tom's house for several days, than for Bonbon to be transplanted to Shelley's. Plus there had been break-ins around the neighborhood and Tom said he would feel better knowing Shelley was there.

The morning he was leaving Tom showed her where the cat food was, how much to give it and then, rather abashedly, revealed that while the cat was eating it liked to hear what a good cat it was.

"What?" said Shelley.

"Just a couple times, tell Bonbon that he's a really good cat."

"No problem." She then drove him to airport and assured him all would be well.

That night Shelley watched TV and Bonbon watched her when he deigned to lift up an eyelid. Shelley liked to watch TV in absolute darkness and when the movie she was watching, "The Birds," was over she walked stocking-footed into the kitchen to feed the cat.

She turned the light on above stove and then went into the pantry to get the cat food with Bonbon right on her heels. As Shelley was filling the heavy crockery cat dish with food, she heard a delicate tinkling noise, almost like a cat walking on a piano keyboard. She cocked her head and listened again as Bonbon swirled around her ankles, eyes glued to the bag in Shelley's hand.

When she heard the noise one more time, she identified it. It was glass breaking and it was coming from the back porch. She peeked out of the pantry in time to see a hand reach through what had once been a window and unlock the dead bolt. Shelley gripped the bag of cat food and dish and sardined herself into the corner of the pantry. She heard the door open and slow heavy footsteps come into the kitchen.

Then things happened fast. Shelley accidentally nudged a pot off a shelf and it made a loud thud when it landed, causing the footsteps to turn toward the pantry. In her panic, Shelley slid down the wall and squished the cat. Bonbon meowed indignantly and took off out of the pantry. There was a curse, a yowl, a kick and finally a booming shot. Shelley held her breath in the loaded silence that followed, then stuck her head out.

A man's broad black-coated back was not even an arm's length away from her. She raised the heavy cat dish and clobbered the guy with it. He spun around like a marionette and stared at her with vacant eyes. Then he crashed to the floor. Kneeling down next to him, she turned the cat food bag upside and stuck it over the guy's head. She tied his feet together with some clothesline she found in the pantry, then dialed 911. She didn't feel she could leave the kitchen so she called and called Bonbon, but he didn't come. Of course he never came when she called so she tried not to be too worried.

After the police came and asked her questions and dragged the guy away, she went in search of the frightened cat. She looked in all his favorite places, and finally as she was about to give up, she found him curled up in Tom's pajamas which were lying in a crumpled pile next to the bed. She gasped when she saw him, but he didn't seem to be in pain. She thought of taking him to the vet, but didn't think there was anything that could be done for him. She petted him and told him several times what a good cat he was and they both went to sleep.

When Tom came back, Shelley tried to prepare him. She told him how brave Bonbon had been, how much she owed him, and then she told him that she thought Bonbon looked very exotic with a clean, round bullet hole in his left ear.

Uninvolved

Lois Greiman

I sat in the waiting room of Sunland Dental, wallowing un-
abashedly in self-pity. My face throbbed like a African war
drum, I'd been unable to masticate English toffee for two
weeks, and I was going to have to pay a too tan, too rich, too
many toothed dentist a mini-fortune to stick his head in my
mouth and ferret out the problem.

"Christina?" The woman who stood in the doorway to the
caverns behind the waiting room was as cute as a puppy. Blond,
bright-eyed and bubbly. Yet another shameless affront to my
simmering sensibilities. "Come with me, please."

I gallumped down the hall after Ms Perky, took the fourth
door on the left and sat down in the lying slut of a chair designed to pretend I would be comfortable there.

"So you've been experiencing some discomfort?" Perky
said.

"Pain," I corrected and noticed the slight bump not quite
hidden by her cheery, pink smock.

"What's that?" she asked.

"I've been in pain," I said.

"Oh." Her little blond ponytail wobbled merrily when she
laughed. "Well that's too bad. Can you tell me what hurts?"

"My head."

She laughed again, jolly as a toddler hip deep in pudding.
"Can you be more specific?"

"Below my eyeballs."

"Is the pain worse in your left side or your right?"

I considered that for a minute but the agony in my cra-
nium seemed to be discombobulating my thinking apparatus.
I don't like to have my thinking apparatus discombobulated.

I am, after all, an intelligent woman. Well educated, bright, and articulate. Dammit. In fact, I'm a licensed psychologist, visiting my solicitations on the greater Los Angeles area. But things haven't been going real smoothly lately. It had started when a rather prestigious client had dropped dead while chasing me around my shrink desk and worsened when one cocky, painfully good-looking officer of the law had accused me of my would-be rapist's murder. "Yes," I said finally. Perky laughed again and patted my shoulder as one might a well-mannered retriever.

"Well, you just sit tight for a minute. Dr. Malborg will make it all better. He'll be in in two shakes."

Dr. Malborg was not in in two shakes. In fact, no one appeared in over four shakes. Voices murmured in the hallway. All of them sounded irritatingly chipper. I closed my eyes and thought about mocha madness ice cream, but the day was already a bust.

"Christina." The woman who appeared finally was just as pretty as Perky, but darker and a couple years older. She was mocha skinned, curvaceous and as sexy as a peanut chocolate parfait. "I'm just popping in to make sure you're comfortable."

"Will Mal be in soon?" I muttered, irritated by the thought of peanuts which I couldn't currently eat and curvaceous women who looked good even in medical smocks.

I wasn't sure, but I thought I saw her eyes narrow the slightest degree before she gave me a dazzling smile. "Are you a friend of Freddy's?"

No. Dr. Mal, a.k.a., Freddy, was merely an irritating friend of an irritating friend named J.D. Solberg. I had met him two years ago while double dating. Freddy, short, with too many teeth and not enough hair, had been just as eye-jabbingly nauseating as Solberg, and had been nuzzled up to his knock 'em dead date like a wood tick on a coon hound. I had disliked him immediately and didn't like him anymore now that I realized he employed nothing but supermodels. But I hadn't been to a dentist since I'd arrived in L.A., and apparently they were in high demand in the land of the ten million dollar smile. So

Solberg had called in a favor for me. But what kind of hygienist called her employee by his first name?

"Have we met?" I asked. "Are you..." I cocked my head, almost forgetting about the pain in my...wherever the hell it was, and trying to remember Mal's unlucky date's name. But, if the truth be told I hadn't been able to see her very well past Mal's groping appendages. "Erika?"

She gave me a zillion watt smile and turned the softball sized diamond on her left hand. "Erika Malborg," she said. "Nearly two years now."

Two years. They must have tied the connubial knot approximately two seconds after I'd met her then. "I think we double dated once," I said.

"Really?" She drew back a little, surprised and happy.

"I was with..." It was hard to admit it. "Solberg."

"I don't think I remember--"

"Short little multi-millionaire," I said. "Laughs like an inebriated donkey."

"Oh, yes, J.D.," she said. "That's right. You're a psychiatrist aren't you?"

"Psychologist."

"Sure. I'm sorry. I'm afraid I don't remember too much about that night." She leaned toward me conspiratorially, disturbingly undisturbed by the bevy of supermodels who gyrated around her husband's business. "A few too many umbrella drinks."

Or too many hits of nitrous oxide. According to Solberg, it was Mal's habit to invite his conquests into his private office for a little happy hour.

"Well, it's very nice to see you again..." She glanced at my chart. "...Christina. Freddy will be with you shortly."

In a second she was gone. I rested my head back against the cushion and wondered grimly why she was so damned happy. If my husband was doing what I highly suspected her husband was doing I wouldn't be quite so--

"Chrissy!" Mal appeared suddenly, too many teeth grinning like a monkey in the florescent lights. "I hear you've got an owey?

I eyed him from my compromised position. He was accompanied by a bleached assistant whose boobs would register somewhere around the middle portion of alphabet. Her top two buttons were open, but maybe that was out of self-defense. There couldn't be many vessels large enough to house them outside of motorcycle helmets and bushel baskets.

"This is Nurse Tiffany," he said.

"Nurse Tiffany?" I echoed. Was he serious?

He grinned, showing a head full of unnaturally pearly whites. "She's new here at Sunland. But I think you'll find that she does a terrific job. Well…" Her cleavage was deep enough to lose small pets in, but he pulled his gaze out with a Herculean effort and rubbed his hands together. "Let's get started. Tiffany, will you help Chrissy lie back, please?"

She fumbled with the knobs for a minute but finally had me in a reclined position. Her boobs were no less impressive from down under. If I were male, the view might have made the use of anesthetics unnecessary. As it was, I was just pissed.

"If you'll open your mouth, I'll do a little visual examination," Mal said, condescended from his superior position of power.

I opened my mouth. Tiffany, The Buxom, hovered over my left shoulder.

"I'll be extremely gentle," he said and jabbed an instrument of torture into my gum.

I jerked.

"Does that hurt?"

On my behalf, I'd like to say that I did not cram his speculum up his nose. Neither did I kill him with a rotating chair. "That's why I'm here." I mumbled the word around seventy-two fingers and a probe.

He nodded, sage as a guru in his white coat. "How about this?" he asked and jabbed again.

"Holy huck!" I screamed.

"Well, we seem to have found the problem already," he said, "but let's just make sure. We don't want to be drilling the wrong tooth do we?"

After another lifetime of him digging around like a drunken miner, he decided that yes indeed, number 18 had indeed been traumatized...unfortunately. I thought I saw him give Boob Job a wink...a filling would be necessary.

Ten minutes later, after a bevy of hot technicians had trailed through my room like bimbos on parade, he sat down beside me once again.

"Well, Chrissy, looks like we're ready to begin. He gave Boobs a nod. She handed him a syringe the size of a watermelon. "Now this won't hurt a bit," he said and proceeded to anesthetize me with what I could only assume was a nail gun.

Thirty minutes later, he was drilling into my mandible with maniacal glee.

"It looks like this cavity goes pretty deep, doesn't it Chrissy?"

I made no attempt to reply...or to kill him. I felt like my jaw was being repaired by a road mender.

Finally he leaned back, still smiling.

"Well, I think that does it."

"Doctor, there's a phone call for you on line one when you get a chance." The voice from the doorway was angel-soft. I rolled my eyes in that direction. This particular employee was small, redheaded, and so pretty it made my eyes water.

"Tell them I'll be right there. The patient comes first, isn't that right, Chrissy?"

I didn't try to speak around the sucker doohickey.

"An excellent job, doctor," purred Tiffany.

"Thank you."

I watched their exchange. She was smoldering. He was smoldered.

Nevertheless, they seemed to be leaning toward each other as if there was a stiff wind blowing at their backs. I stifled my gag reflex, but if they broke into a kiss, I was fully prepared to crack their heads together like sun-ripe melons.

"It's your ex-wife," said Red. Maybe there was just the slightest trace of irritation in her spun sugar tone.

Mal gave Boobs a weak-assed smile. "Tell her I'll be right there."

"Of course," Red said. "But I believe she's in a bit of a rush. Something about getting to the bank with a child support check that is actually two weeks late and--"

He was out of his seat before another word was spoken and crowding her back into the hall. They were hidden behind the wall now, but I could hear their voices quite clearly.

"Surely I've taught you better than to say something like that in front of a client."

"I'm so sorry, doctor," she said, clearly chastised. "My mistake."

"I guess it is. I'd think even you could figure out..." His voice dwindled.

In a moment, I was alone with Boobs. I don't usually like to converse with women whose bra size is higher than my IQ, but I was curious.

"How long have you worked for..." I nodded toward the hall, dragging the sucky doohickey with me.

"Oh, not long. Only a few days. But Freddy's brilliant," she said.

"Glug," I said. The sucker was starting to annoy me.

"Oh," she said and took it out. "I don't think you need that anymore."

"Am I done?"

"Well, I'm not really sure."

"Uh huh." I watched her, squint eyes. "What do you do here exactly?"

"Well...I help out where I'm needed most. Freddy thought I would be good for office moral. Whoops," she said, dropping the doohickey onto my arm. "I'm very good with people."

"Uh-huh." I couldn't feel my left eyeball and gave my cheek a tap to test for sensation. "How long do you have to go to school to become...good with people?"

"Well...I didn't actually finish my formal training. Freddy didn't think it was necessary. He said, with a personality like mine..."

A scream interrupted her soliloquy. She turned toward the door, mouth open, but I was already out of the chair.

Another scream found me. I tottered around a corner and careened toward it. Red was standing in the doorway, hand over her mouth. I squeezed past. Dr. Frederick Malborg was lying on his back, eyes rolled into his skull.

His wife was crouched beside him, two fingers on the supposed pulse at his jaw.

"Is he—"

"Call 911!" she barked and the place burst into action.

Two hours later, I was still sitting in the waiting room. Every door and window had been opened to air out the place. By purest coincidence, my old nemesis, Lieutenant Jack Rivera had arrived. He had questioned and released every other patient in the office.

"So..." He stared at me with his hot-mocha eyes. "What happened?"

I shrugged. "I'm just here for number 18."

He gave me a look.

"My molar," I said.

"Okay." He looked like he didn't believe me. But I didn't take it personally. He would probably look at the pope the same way. "What do you think happened?"

"I think there was a significant nitrous oxide leak into his office and he forgot to refrain from inhaling," I said. I had been listening in on several conversations for the entirety of my visit. Apparently, high doses of laughing gas can cause oxygen depravation, and Dr. Mal's very private office, where he'd entertained so many, had not been well ventilated. He'd dropped like a stone, cracked his head on the corner of his desk and been dead before he'd hit the floor.

"Christ, you have ears like an African elephant," Rivera said.

I didn't respond. Neither did I tell him that Freddy had been late with his child support check, was salivating heavily over his newest assistant or that his current wife was certain to have noticed. I didn't mention Perky's four-month bump, her conspicuously bare ring finger, or the fact that every gorgeous employee seemed far too happy considering old Fred had, by my calculations, been cheating on all of them.

"You going to investigate this?" I asked.

"I've had two assaults and a breaking and entering in the past twelve hours," Rivera said and scanning the room, stood up.

I stood up with him. He motioned toward the door, touching my back in that herding way that men have.

"How bout you?" he asked. "You're a busy body."

I glanced toward the women who huddled together near the water cooler like a herd of uncertain gazelle. One was a widow. One was pregnant. All were responsible.

"My body's busy elsewhere," I said and getting into my undersized Saturn, drove away.

Rage Against the Machines

Terri Persons

As the runner waded through the leaves raked against the curb, she slowed her pace to better savor the scents of the approaching fall. Taking a deep breath, she filled her mouth with the mossy taste of rain and wet foliage. The sprinkle became a downpour and she picked up her speed, her limbs moving with the effortless grace reserved for natural athletes and wild animals.

Glancing to her left, she noticed a sport utility vehicle crawling down the street, moving in the same direction as she was running. The SUV veered next to her and braked. She stopped, ran a hand through her dripping hair and peered through the rain at the boxy hulk. It wasn't familiar, but her girlfriends were always turning up with new cars. She stepped to the front passenger window and it rolled down. Keeping her distance, she peeked inside and didn't recognize the driver. A muscular blond man dressed in khakis and a sweater, he looked to be older than her classmates but younger than her teachers.

He smiled at her and said through the opened window: "Coach sent me to pick you up. Hurry up and get in. Seat's getting wet."

She folded her arms in front of her while the rain pounded her head. "Who're you?"

With a big smile, he leaned across the passenger's seat and popped open the door. "I'm the new trainer."

She didn't move; she hadn't heard anything about a new guy.

"I was hired over the summer."

A clever, cautious girl, she stayed where she stood and waited for more.

The smile didn't leave his face. "Your coach is Bill Svengaard. He's a prick."

That was her coach's name, and he was indeed a prick. She hopped inside and shut the door. "Appreciate the ride."

"I'm a Boy Scout. What can I say?" His hands went to the control panel on the driver's door. Her window rolled up and her door locked with a crack.

"Where's the rest of the team?"

"They're back at school, toweling off."

She rubbed her arms over her soaked sweatshirt. "I suppose I should have turned around when it started…"

"But you're a die hard." He glanced in the rearview mirror, saw the road was clear and steered into the lane. "That's why you're going to take state again this year, young lady."

"I hope."

"Nice newspaper blurb on you over the weekend, by the way."

"Thanks," she said with an embarrassed grin.

"Want me to turn on the seat heater?"

"That would be great."

Leaning forward, he pushed a button on the dashboard. "This thing does everything but make hot cocoa."

She eyed the vehicle's pristine leather interior. "Looks new."

"It's a white loaf of bread, but I like it." He punched on the radio and an alternative rock band blared out of the speakers.

Feeling more relaxed, she bobbed her head to the music. "My favorite song."

"Mine, too." He slowed for a dog dashing across the road. "Looking forward to the season?"

"Not senior year, though."

"It's a snap," he said. "Senior slide."

"I like school," she said, switching from bobbing to swaying. "I'll miss my friends."

"You'll survive." He braked at a stop sign, looked to the right and left, and rolled through the intersection.

Her head snapped to the right. "You missed our turn. You're going the wrong way."

"No I'm not," he said, and accelerated as the SUV cruised onto the freeway ramp.

Her eyes widened. "Where are we going?"

"Don't worry, honey; I've got it all under control."

WHILE SHE WAS driving around the Mall of America ramp looking for parking, the young lady spotted it lurking between two dark mini vans. The white block of metal simultaneously threatened her and seduced her. A rapist trying to be a tender lover. She couldn't say why certain hulks called to her while others stayed silent. Perhaps it was dictated by how the light bounced off the vehicles that day, or maybe it was the way the air moved and smelled. Her mood could be a factor. Her pain. Some days, her limbs ached as if she'd just tumbled out of a moving vehicle for the second time. Regardless, at this moment, a particular beast spoke to her, and she had to listen.

"Coach sent me to pick you up."

"Hurry up and get in. Seat's getting wet."

"I'm the new trainer."

He'd been sly, her abductor, but she'd escaped. Survived. Now it was her turn to be clever, and he wouldn't get away.

She was fully aware the ramp had cameras and made a point of not staring at the Hummer as she passed it. Snapping her head to the right, she searched for a parking spot across the aisle. She found an open space a few cars down and backed into it. With trembling hands, she turned off the ignition and punched off the lights. Her palms were cold and damp, and she wiped them on the thighs of her jeans. Her breathing was quick and shallow, and her head felt light. That familiar falling sensation engulfed her again. Wrapping an arm around her middle, she hoped she wasn't going to vomit.

"I'm a Boy Scout. What can I say?"

"They're back at school, toweling off."

"But you're a die hard. That's why you're going to take state again this year, young lady."

The surrounding cars and concrete lost all color, fading away into uniform grayness. Only one object outside her vehicle remained sharp and bright and clear, and as she concentrated on it, she started to regain her composure.

She couldn't just sit in the car and wait; mall security could notice. She needed to be careful, especially after that mess in St. Paul. Trying to look like any dizzy girl out for a night of shopping, she plucked her purse off the front passenger's seat and took out a brush. She flipped down the driver's visor and glanced in the mirror. She congratulated herself on being smart enough to change her do. Even if a camera caught her, she now bore no resemblance to the girl whose picture was being circulated all over town.

Studying the rear of the SUV through her windshield, she saw it had a Wisconsin plate. The MOA attracted tourists from around the globe, but for many folks in the Twin Cities and western Wisconsin, the massive mall was a utilitarian marketplace. Somewhere to go for shoes, shirts, and socks. She bet the owner of the Hummer came from a town just across the border. Hudson. River Falls. Somerset. She'd wait in her car. When the Hummer's occupants returned, they wouldn't notice her; they'd be too busy juggling packages and car keys. She'd follow them home and make a note of where they lived. Return to their house early in the morning.

"*WANT ME TO turn on the seat heater?*"

"*This thing does everything but make hot cocoa.*"

"*It's a white loaf of bread, but I like it.*"

It didn't matter who was driving the Hummer that night, or who'd be piloting it come morning. In her mind, they were all the same person driving the same vehicle. Each time she took a shot at a white hulk, she could be nailing him.

One car after another turned down her aisle in the mad scramble for parking. She fished out a tube of lipstick and applied a bead to her lips while shooting glances at the white block.

She hoped her quarry wouldn't be too much longer. She couldn't fix her face and hair forever. She stretched out her legs. At least the feeling of being solid was returning to her body. Sometimes when they called to her, she wondered if she was going to float out of herself and drift into the white monsters. Melt into them and become a part of them.

"Don't worry, honey; I've got it all under control."

I'm in control, she thought. I'm the one who is in control, not you.

Looking in her rearview mirror, she saw that a man and woman were coming down the stairs, each carrying a couple of large shopping sacks. They looked to be older than her parents, and not nearly as well-maintained. The couple started down her aisle and stalled, apparently unsure of whether they were in the correct row. The woman pointed down the aisle and the man nodded. Adjusting the bags in their arms, they resumed their shuffling.

Her heart quickened as she watched them. They were a few cars away from the Hummer. Now they were in front of it. The man went to the driver's side of the vehicle and the woman went to the passenger's side. Each opened a back door and tossed their sacks inside. Slammed the doors. The man got behind the wheel and the woman hopped into the front passenger's seat.

She listened for the engine, but there was only silence. They were sitting in the front seat yapping. Struggling to avoid the appearance of staring, she dropped her lipstick back in her purse and pulled out a blush compact. She flipped open the lid and took out the brush. Sucking in her cheeks, she colored the hollows of her face. She was going to look like a whore before these people pulled out of the ramp.

As she glanced down to return the blush to her purse, she heard the sound of the Hummer starting up. "Finally," she breathed.

The vehicle pulled out of the parking spot, passed her car and headed down the aisle toward the exit. She flung her purse on the passenger's seat, turned the key and restarted her own car. Resisting the urge to gun it and get right on their tails, she waited for a Saturn to get between her and the Hummer. Slowly, she steered out of her spot.

She maintained her distance from the Hummer, allowing a banana-colored Corvette to get between her and the Saturn as they all turned down the parking ramp. The Saturn and the sports car turned off. She let other cars get between her and her target, following the Hummer all the way across town on to Interstate 94 east and across the St. Croix River into Wisconsin. The SUV took the first Hudson exit, at the bottom of the bridge. Maintaining a distance but still keeping her eyes on the white Hummer, she followed as it meandered through an older residential area.

The neighborhood didn't meet her needs; the homes were close together and there were no parks or woods to shield her while she set up. "Fuck," she muttered, her hands tightening with frustration over the steering wheel.

Her grip relaxed as the street spilled out onto a road bordered by fields. While she drove, she struggled to find landmarks so she'd be able to find her way back during the daylight hours. It was tough; the country roads were as black as her new dye job.

The Hummer came to a T in the road and she hung back, letting them take a left well ahead of her. When she came to the T, she waited a minute before turning.

Up ahead, the Hummer's brake lights came on again.

"Now what?" she muttered, applying her own brakes.

By the glow of yard lights, she saw them take a left and turn down a long driveway leading to a white farmhouse. She accelerated and rolled past the front of the place, eyeing it while she cruised by. On either side of the property were patches of woodland. "Perfect," she breathed.

She checked the clock on her dashboard. She'd be back here in less than twelve hours. She got to the end of the road and hung a left to loop back to the highway.

MARCUS KEIFFERT rolled onto his side and brought his hand down on the snooze button. He flopped onto his back and pulled the comforter up to his chin. "Ah, shit," he sighed to the ceiling.

When the alarm went off a second time, his wife Gloria jabbed him with her elbow. "Marco."

"I'm up, I'm up." He reached over, shut off the alarm and hiked the comforter up to his nose.

"When're you going to turn on the furnace?" his wife asked, tucking her cold feet under his calves.

"Jeeze, Glor. Get those blocks of ice away from me." He slid out from between the covers and shivered as he padded into the master bath in his underwear. While he emptied his bladder, he continued the furnace discussion that every couple in Wisconsin had every fall. "I was hoping we could make it to November."

"You've gotta be kidding me," she said.

He peeled off his tee shirt and dropped his boxers. Scratching his round belly, he considered stepping on the scale but talked himself out of it. "Let's wait until the weekend at least."

"What's the point?"

"It just seems wrong to turn it on this early." He went over to the shower, reached into the stall and turned on the water. Holding his hand under the spray, he waited for it to get hot enough to use. "I think we need a new water heater."

"Home Depot?" she asked cheerfully.

He liked that his wife enjoyed going to Home Depot. "We should go out to eat tonight. Got out to eat and then go to Home Depot." He stepped into the stall, closed the glass door and shivered as he stood under the tepid spray.

From the other side of the stall door, he heard his wife drop the toilet lid. "We ate out last night," she said.

"Burgers at the mall doesn't count as eating out," he declared.

"What about that chicken left over from Monday?"

"It'll keep." There were always leftovers. Their youngest of six had moved out five years earlier, but she was still cooking for a family of eight.

"You're just trying to get out of eating leftovers," she said, unrolling a wad of toilet paper.

Over a breakfast of coffee and toast, they discussed the other things that needed fixing. "Never seems to end." He chomped on his triangle of toast, working his way to the middle.

She sipped her coffee. "We should get into a new townhouse."

"I don't want to live in town," he said, licking jam off his thumb.

"What about those yellow and white ones outside of town,

with the picket fences around the front yards?"

"This house has been in my family for…"

"It's a farmhouse, Marco. We're not farmers."

He took a sip of coffee and set down his cup. "I might get into farming when I retire. A hobby farm. Llamas."

"How many times have I heard that one?"

"There's money in llamas." He checked his watch. He was the pediatric dentist in a large practice and his first patient of the day—a little guy with lots of cavities—wasn't due for another hour.

She had to get moving, however, since she was the only teacher in a room full of fidgety second graders. She stood up with her cup in her hand. "I don't want to hear anything more about llamas."

"Let's do Italian tonight." He tipped back his cup and emptied it.

She took a final swallow from her cup and set it in the sink. "Let's eat what we've got in the fridge."

"I'll pack up the chicken for lunch."

"Good."

"Take the Volvo. Hummer's low on gas," he said as she headed out of the kitchen. "I'll fill it up on my way in."

"There goes the new townhouse," she said over her shoulder.

He heard the door slam, reached over to snag another charred square and wondered if buying the monster had indeed been a mistake.

◆◆◆

STANDING OUTSIDE his front door, the dentist juggled a set of keys, a briefcase and a greasy paper sack. While he locked up the house, he thought about what he might order that night. Anything with a red sauce.

In the dimness of the smoky dawn, he scrutinized the face of his watch as he went down the sidewalk toward the Hummer parked in his driveway. He had all the time in the world; he'd stop on the way to the clinic and pick up donuts.

As he stood on the driver's side fiddling with his car keys, he dropped his leftovers. The sack split, spilling his lunch all over the gravel. "Crap." He set down his briefcase and bent over the foil-wrapped chicken legs.

From one side of the yard, buried amid the trees and scrub, came the metallic sound of a rifle bolt being pulled back. The instant Dr. Marcus Keiffert stood up with his wife's leftovers in his hands, a sharp clap tore through the country morning.

SQUAD CARS FROM the St. Croix County Sheriff's Department and the Hudson Police Department lined up along both sides of the country road. In the home's driveway were a medical examiner's hearse and a paramedic unit; only the former would be pulling away with a passenger. Television news vans from stations in the Twin Cities and Milwaukee had been forced to park a distance away, but a couple of the reporters and cameramen had finagled their way up to the front of the house. Police tape kept them on the road and out of the yard.

In the driveway, a trio of FBI agents in black jackets stood over a body covered by a tarp.

"Ballistics will have to go to work to confirm," said the tallest man. "But I'm sure we're dealing with the same shooter."

"So this makes six dead," said the shortest one.

"Seven," the middle agent corrected him. "The one shot in St. Paul died this morning."

A fourth agent, a woman, walked up to the three. "Just got a call from Minneapolis PD. A girl swallowed a gun and pulled the trigger. Could be the shooter."

"Shit," sputtered the tall man, burying his hands in his pockets. "Did she leave a note?"

The female agent: "No, but her parents said she was raped by a guy in a white SUV."

"When?" asked the middle agent.

"A year ago last month," woman replied.

"So she spent the last year trying to hunt him down herself?" the short guy asked.

"That's the weird thing," said the woman. "The asshole is dead. Drove his car into a tree before the cops could get him."

Flyover Country

Barbara Collins and Max Allan Collins

Susan Parsus, a thirty-four year old book editor, with long dark hair and round silver glasses, gazed out the little window of the airplane. Below, the brown and green checkerboard blanket of the Midwest extended as far as the eye could see.

Flyover country, she thought. How boring. Thank God, I don't live down there.

Not that New York was so wonderful, she admitted. Lately, the expense and the hassles and crime and just the *smell* of that city had begun to get to her, and started her thinking about moving some place else. But, then, she was in publishing, and publishing *was* New York.

Even Los Angeles—where she'd just come from a book sellers convention—was a big disappointment: even more expensive and over-crowded, the beautiful weather she'd heard so much about covered in smog. Wasn't there *any* place in this country worth living? Cheaply, that is.

"This is your captain speaking," a male voice crackled urgently over the intercom, interrupting Susan's thoughts. "We're having some engine trouble. Flight attendants prepare for emergency landing...."

An immediate murmur spread through the cabin, more noticeably on the right side of the plane, where the passengers—Susan among them—could see thick, black smoke streaming from the engine. As the plane fell sharply, two of the flight attendants—an attractive, young blonde with terror in her eyes, and a balding middle-aged man managing to hold on to his professional demeanor—rushed up and down the isles instructing people to put their safety belts on, tray tables away and seats in an upright position.

In the rear of the cabin, a mother wailed and clutched her baby tighter to her bosom. Others hugged, some sobbing, while many more dug into pockets and purses to scribble a final farewell note to loved ones below.

Fear spread upward from Susan's stomach to her throat like a bad case of heartburn. She tensed and grabbed onto the armrests. Next to her, an older woman with gray hair and orange lipstick (who hadn't been too much of an annoyance on the trip) turned toward her for consolation, but Susan moved away. If this was going to be her last few moments alive, she wasn't about to share them with some complete stranger.

Dear Lord, Susan prayed as the airplane shimmied and shook, *if I make it through this, I promise to be a better person.*

Her thoughts turned to Steven, her fiancé, back in New York. She'd been kind of terrible to him just before she'd left. Arguing about plans for their wedding.

A much better person. I promise, I promise......

As the plane broke through the clouds on its rapid decent, Susan could see they were over some sprawling city. Tall glass buildings sparkled as the brilliant morning sun bounced off them, and everywhere, lush green trees lined clean streets where little toy cars moved up and down them. If she hadn't been so frightened, she might have appreciated this pristine, modern city.

Susan closed her eyes tightly, because the careening silver bullet of a plane seemed much too close to the tops of the trees, and neat little houses. She hoped that in front of them was a runway or highway and not more homes.

A big jolt lifted everyone out of their seats, as wheels touched asphalt—it *was* a runway, she could see out the window—then a smaller jolt followed, and the passengers lurched forward, bracing themselves as the plane braked hard to a stop. A collective sigh of relief disseminated throughout the cabin.

TWENTY MINUTES LATER, Susan walked through the airport terminal on wobbly legs toward a bank of phones, her Louis

Vuitton carry-on (a gift from a former lover) slung over one shoulder. She sat on one of the little round seats, smoothing her black Donna Karan dress (discounted in the district), then dug in her black leather Picasso bag (half-off at Bloomies) for her phone card.

"Steven? It's Susan."

"Where are you?"

"Des Moines fucking Iowa."

"What are you doing there?"

"The plane had engine trouble, and I'm stuck in this God-awful place because I can't get another flight to New York until tomorrow." She moaned. "Oh, *why* did I fly on the cheap? This is *your* fault!"

"My fault?! It was *your* idea to cash in the first class ticket so you could use the extra money for shopping."

"Well, you should've talked me out of it. Every time I do something on the cheap, I get into trouble."

There was silence, then Steven said, "Sometimes trying to save money ends up costing you more."

So they were back to that. The argument before she left.

She said, "I just thought if we got married next Easter we could use the church's flowers. It's being economical. What's wrong with that?"

There was silence again, and when her fiancé spoke, his voice seemed sad. "Some things are more important than saving money."

"Like what?" She couldn't imagine.

He sighed. "Call me when you get in and I'll pick you up."

"Okay," she said, "but don't park the car 'cause it'll cost...."

But he'd already hung up.

Susan picked up her carry-on and walked away from the phones. With the whole day, and night, in front of her, she might was well rent a car.

The line at the Hertz counter was short, and Susan started toward it, then stopped. They'd be the most expensive, she thought. Her eyes traveled down the line of the other car rental companies—Avis, National, Alamo, Budget—and landed on the last. U-Save. That sounded like it wouldn't cost her an arm and a leg.

A fat man in a bright yellow sports coat (why draw attention to himself?) was just stepping away from the counter when Susan came up to it, setting her bag down. Behind the counter, which came almost to Susan's chin, was a forty-ish woman with short, dull brown hair and a plain face. Susan wasn't sure if even lots of make-up would help.

"I want a car until tomorrow afternoon," Susan told the agent, "when I can get the hell out of here. What's that gonna cost me?"

The agent smiled pleasantly. "We have a luxury car for fifty-four dollars, or a mid-size for thirty-four."

"I'll take the thirty-four."

"Would you like collision insurance?"

Susan laughed. "That's just for suckers and I'm not one of them."

"I see," the woman said, her brown eyes seeming to study Susan, the pleasant demeanor continuing. "Please sign here, and here..." She put the contract out on the high counter top.

Susan had to reach up to sign, and there was a plant with broad thorny leaves like a cactus in a terra-cotta pot sitting there that she shoved aside, tipping it over, spilling rich dark soil onto the counter top.

For a brief second an irritated looked flashed over the agent's face, then the professional smile returned, and the woman scooped up the dirt with her hands and put it back in the pot, setting the plant upright again. Susan didn't apologize; the ugly thing shouldn't have been in the way in the first place.

"I'll need to see your driver's license," the woman said.

Susan dug into her purse and handed the agent her card.

The woman looked at the license and commented, "New York City. I've always wanted to go there."

"Yeah," Susan snorted, "it's a riot. Literally."

The agent finished up the paperwork and handed a copy of the contract to Susan. "Just catch our shuttle bus out front," she instructed. "They'll take care of you." Then she added, "Have a nice stay in Iowa."

Susan smiled sweetly. "Is that possible?"

While the smile remained on the agent's face, her eyes grew dark and cold; then suddenly they softened. The woman with the plain face leaned forward and her voice became soft and sympathetic.

"I know how you feel, stranded in a strange place—wanting to get home," the woman said. "Tell you what, I'm going to upgrade your car for nothing—because I want you to have a nice time. And let me give you some advice on where you should go. There's a quaint little village...."

The town of Prosperity, the car rental agent had told Susan, was located fifteen miles south of Des Moines. And there, she had said, the newly refurbished Grand Hotel would cost her a mere fifty dollars (as compared to one hundred in the city).

Susan drove along the highway in a red Mustang convertible. She couldn't believe getting it! She could never drive anything like this in New York. With the top down, the wind blowing her long dark hair around, she felt like a teenager again.

The air was so fresh! Like a cool drink of water. And sweet. Maybe from the green corn growing in the neatly tended fields along the road. She'd never thought of corn as beautiful, but it was: tall and graceful, long slender leaves bending gently in the breeze, and from the top of each stalk, yellow tassels hung like golden strands of hair. Iowa was not at all what she thought it to be, which was flat and boring. The landscape was lovely, with rolling green hills, brilliant wild flowers, and every mile or so a tidy little farm, with its own little garden, and clean clothes flapping on the line....

Susan closed her eyes, breathing in through her nose, remembering how wonderful clothes that had dried outdoors smelled. Back in Poughkeepsie. Where she was raised by her mother who had very little money. After high school, a scholarship to NYU brought her into the city, and a part-time job doing clerical work at a now-defunct paperback house which gave her some monetary help—that and latching onto well-heeled friends.

After graduation, she landed a job at a prestigious New York publishing house working as a copy editor. She had a good eye for detail, and was smart enough to know not to meddle with the author's style and attach herself as a collaborator, like some frustrated, unpublished editors she knew. This was a happy time in her life—Except for still not having much money.

Soon she was promoted to senior editor, and put in the uncomfortable position of deciding the fate of the hundreds of manuscripts that crossed her desk every week. She thought she'd been doing a good job selecting the list, but after a while the publisher called her into his office and told her she was within an inch of losing her job.

"Susan," the older man said, tugging at his course, gray mustache, "we're in the book turning down business, not the book buying business. Get it? Now reduce your list."

After that, she was afraid to buy anything.

Up ahead, the road narrowed to almost one lane, and the tall cornfields gave way to dense forest. A fresh water stream now appeared on the left of the highway and after a curve in the road a weathered wooden covered bridge lead her across the brook, reminding Susan of a best selling novel she'd turned down a few years ago.

About a half mile across the bridge, a large painted sign depicting an exotic plant, welcomed Susan to Prosperity, population 8,000. As she entered the town on a cobblestone street, she slowed the Mustang down. Grand old homes appeared on both sides of the road, and a canopy of ancient maple trees provided shade in the warm summer day.

Here and there, neighbors stood chatting, while young children played—many unattended—in open yards, their bikes and toys scattered along the sidewalk. No one seemed concerned here about theft, or kidnapping or drive-by-shootings.

At the end of the block, Susan saw something that made her laugh out loud as she drove by: a large parcel sat on top of a blue corner mailbox; too big to fit inside, the owner just left it, without a concern that someone might take it.

The turn-of-the-century downtown buildings of Prosperity

were built in a square around a small, immaculate park that had a white wooden bandstand in its center. Here and there, wrought iron park benches sat next to flower gardens of roses, geraniums, petunias and mums. On one of those park benches sat an elderly couple, both gray haired and be-spectacled, enjoying ice cream cones, and each other.

She couldn't remember the last time she saw a happy old couple on the streets of New York; if they weren't scowling, they were in some heated argument.

Susan parked the Mustang in a diagonal spot in front of hardware store, its ancient facade freshly painted, candy-striped awning flapping gently in the breeze. As she started to get out of the car, her foot kicked something on the floorboard by the break. She reached down and picked the item up, a tan leather appointment book that must have been under the seat, sliding forward when she stopped.

Susan opened the appointment book. There was a business card tucked in a plastic see-through pouch on the left. Some woman named Madeline, representing a pharmaceutical company in Dallas. On the right was a calculator with faux-jewel pads, and in the center, in the fold, was a beautiful brown Cross pen. She'd mail it to the poor woman as soon as she could, because Susan knew how upset she herself would be to lose her own appointment book. But then, Susan thought, as she got out of the car, the woman had probably by now replaced it, and besides, *she* could use a new calculator and pen. Which Susan took and put in her purse, tossing the appointment book in a curb-side trash can.

Then she dug in her wallet for some change for the meter.

"Don't got none of them here," a friendly male voice said.

Susan looked up to see a plump man around the age of sixty, with handlebar mustache, wire-framed glasses and mostly bald head. He was wearing a stripped apron (that nearly matched the awning) over a short-sleeved blue shirt and brown pants. The man was sweeping the sidewalk with a big push broom.

"Pardon?" Susan asked.

"Why punish people who come to spend their hard-earned

money by puttin' in meters?" He said with a shrug, and gave the cement walk one last sweep before turning and disappearing into the store.

Susan closed her purse. "I think I'm gonna like it here," she said with a tiny smile.

Then something in the window of the hardware store caught her eye, and she moved toward the glass. The object of her desire in the carefully arranged display window wasn't the blue bottle of perfume called Ode to Venus, or the plant next to it with its large, thorned leaves spread open, nor even the pseudo-gold necklace carefully laid out on a piece of blue velvet....What she was gaping at was an ordinary claw hammer.

"Oh, my Gawd," she whispered, reading the price-tag sticker on its handle, her face nearly pressed up against the glass. "A dollar ninety-nine."

It had been a miserably cold, windy day last February that she had traipsed all over Manhattan to find a claw hammer because she'd loaned *hers* to a neighbor who'd never returned it before he'd left town. And the hammer that she finally did find (a cheaply made foreign one whose plastic handle fell off) cost her eighteen dollars and ninety-nine cents. Eight ninety-nine for the lousy hammer, plus ten bucks in cab fares! Sometimes trying to find the simplest things in New York was almost impossible.

Susan rushed into the hardware store. She crossed the gleaming wooden floor and wound her way through the narrow isles of neatly arranged items toward a large counter in the back behind which the man in the stripped apron stood, filling a glass jar with jelly beans.

"I'd like that hammer in the window," she said.

He looked up from his work. "It's a good one," he told her. "Made right here in the U.S. of A."

He came around the counter and plucked the same hammer from a pegboard on a display nearby. "And you can't beat the price," he added.

"You're tellin' me!" Susan said. "You won't believe what they cost in Manhattan."

Back behind the counter, the man wrote up a receipt on a little pad. "I bet just about everything's expensive there," he said.

"You better believe it."

The man handed a plain brown sack with the hammer inside and gave her an odd smile showing white, perfect teeth. "I hope you enjoy our little town while you're here. We try to make visitors welcome."

Susan smiled back. "Everyone does seem friendly."

She turned to leave, then turned back to asked, "Where is the Grand Hotel?"

"Directly across the square. You can't miss it."

"And a good place to eat?"

"The Venus Diner serves up a great tenderloin."

A tenderloin! She hadn't had one of those since she was a kid on vacation in Oklahoma.

Susan thanked the man and left the store and stood out on the sidewalk by her car in the warm summer sun, wondering which way to go to the diner, when two teen-aged girls walked by her. They giggled as they passed, amused, Susan supposed by her urban clothes. She guessed she did look a little like a witch, all in black, while they wore colorful, crisp, cotton clothes: one, a bright yellow dress with pink flowers; the other, sky blue over-alls with a whiter than white blouse underneath. And sandals! Their toes painted lime and orange. How she envied them. They didn't know that in New York their bright clothing would make them stand out... ripe for an attack, and flimsy little sandals were exchanged for combat boots in order to maneuver the filthy mean streets.

A mother walked by, holding the hand of a small boy—they were in matching nautical outfits—and when the boy saw Susan he pointed. "Mommy, another funeral?"

The mother seemed embarrassed, smiled apologetically, and pulled her son along.

That did it! If it was one thing she hated, it was feeling out of place. She hurried down the street and entered a woman's clothing store she'd spotted when she drove into town, and came out a half hour later in a peach rayon dress and brown sandals.

Her long dark hair was braided loosely down her back and held at the end with a peach floral clasp. She felt euphoric, so feminine, like a college student again. And the best part was she got the whole outfit half-price—and it wasn't even on sale!—because the owner, a nice woman in her forties, wanted Susan to "have a good time," in Prosperity. Boy, was she beginning to love this town!

The Venus Diner, two doors down from the clothing store, was a turn of the century ice cream parlor that had stayed in one family for three generations; Susan read this on the back of the menu as she sat on a stool at the counter, hungrily eating a huge tenderloin with ketchup and pickle, washing it down with a lime phosphate. The owners, Mr. and Mrs. Satariano, a friendly couple in their sixties, ran the establishment together. Right now, Mr. Satariano, a slight man with thinning gray hair and a bulbous nose, was fixing Susan the house specialty: Coffee ice cream topped with gooey marshmallow and Spanish peanuts. He set the dessert down in front of her with a wink. "That's on us," he said.

Susan's mouth dropped open, from both the kind gesture and the sight of the heavenly concoction. "Really?"

"Enjoy yourself."

"How sweet!"

And it was; she eagerly dug into the ice cream, the combination tasting so delicious. In between bites she asked, "Was this place always called the Venus Diner?"

Mrs. Satariano, a tall, still handsome woman, who was washing a glass in a small stainless steel sink behind the counter, answered Susan. "No, the original name was the Candy Kitchen. But we changed it a few years back."

"How come?"

The woman and her husband exchanged glances. Mr. Satariano, wiping the counter around Susan, stopped. "Prosperity wasn't always so prosperous," he explained. "As a matter of fact, seven or eight years ago the town went bankrupt along with half its citizens."

Susan set her spoon down. "My goodness. What happened?"

"A couple bad years for the corn crops. First a flood, then a drought. That's all it took to put everybody under."

"But the town seems to be doing fine, now."

Mr. Satariano nodded. "Thanks to that," he said, gesturing to a thorny plant sitting in a terra-cotta pot by the cash register.

"What *is* it?" Susan asked, intrigued. "I've been seeing that plant in all the shop windows."

Mrs. Satariano smiled proudly, like a pleased grandparent. "It's a Venus flytrap," she pronounced.

Susan leaned forward and looked closer at the plant. This one was about a foot tall, much bigger than the others she'd seen. Out of its center rose a stalk bearing a cluster of tiny white flowers, and around the stalk were leaves about six inches in length. Each of the kidney-shaped leaves lay like a partially opened book and was fringed with long stiff bristles.

"For heavens sake," Susan murmured. "I didn't know the Venus flytrap could grow here. You mean, *that* saved the town?"

Husband and wife nodded together.

"But *how?*"

The screen door of the shop opened with a creak, then banged shut.

Mrs. Satariano looked toward the door and threw up her hands, "Johnny! How is my boy today?"

Susan swiveled on the stool, also looking toward the door, where a young sandy-haired man stood, wearing jeans and a faded blue short-sleeve work shirt. The sun, shinning in behind him, enveloped him like a god. Then he walked out of the light toward the counter, with a shy little smile, his head tilted slightly.

" 'lo Mom...Pop," he said, taking a seat one away from Susan at the counter.

Susan looked from Mrs. Satariano to Mr. Satariano to the

young man, whom she guessed—now that he was closer—to be in his late twenties. She couldn't imagine that they were related, with the Satariano's so dark complexioned (like her) and the young man so fair.

Mr. Satariano, with the rag still in his hands, must have read Susan's thoughts, because he said, "Johnny's not our son, but you might say we think of him as one...ever since his folks died a few years back."

Susan turned toward Johnny. "Oh, I'm so sorry."

For a second sadness flashed over the man's rugged face, then the cheerful but shy manner returned and he said to Susan without looking at her, "That's all right. I'm doing fine...but, of course, Mom and Pop here think I can't tie my own shoes without their help."

Mrs. Satariano set one of the heavy ice cream glasses down on the counter with a loud noise. "Is that so? When have we ever stuck our noses in your business?" she ask with mock anger. "We just give you a little friendly advice on how to run the farm...and other things." She looked at her husband. "Isn't that right, Papa?"

"That's right, Mama," he agreed. "Only a little advice." And he winked at Susan.

"You can see I'm outnumbered," Johnny said, swiveling on his seat so that he faced Susan.

He was handsome—by any woman's standards—but not like a slick male model. While his body was muscular—deltoids and biceps tugged at his chambray shirt—they were muscles obtain from *real* work—not a workout, and his bronze tan came from laboring in the sun, not relaxing in a tanning bed. He was the real thing, not contrived, which made him so much more exciting.

And there was something else that aroused Susan: the scent coming off him; a combination of honest sweat and fresh country air, mingled together, an intoxicating drink, that made Susan both high and dizzy.

"Be careful," he warned Susan, his bedroom brown eyes playful, "or they'll start running your life."

She looked down at her High School Special and felt herself blush (when had she last done that?). The ice cream was a melted puddle...just like her heart.

"Mom...a cherry Coke, please," Johnny said, and slid off the stool. Then to Susan he asked, "Would you like to join me in a booth?"

Now it was she who smiled shyly. "Okay."

"And bring her one, too," he told Mrs. Satariano.

The booth Johnny led her to was against the back wall of the long, narrow room, giving them some privacy. The benches were dark mahogany, as was the lower half of the wall. The upper half was a mirror on which were written menu items in some kind of white paint. Above them, a wooden fan hung from the high tin ceiling, churning slowly, providing a soothing breeze. It was all very quaint and charming.

"You're not from around here, are you?" Johnny asked.

"No. Out east."

"I thought as such." He paused. "From your accent, I mean." Then he added, "Anyhow, I sure would have remembered you." He said this with a drop of his head, and a small one-sided smile.

She studied his face, so open and honest, and thought of all the pick-up lines in sleazy bars from sleazy men she'd ever heard and this approach was so sincere.

Mrs. Satariano appeared with the Cokes and Johnny dug in his front pocket. Susan reached for her purse.

"I'll get mine," she said.

"You will not," Johnny said firmly. "You're my guest here. When I come to New York, you can buy me a Coke."

"Fair enough," she said, then thought wryly, *Johnny in New York.... There'd be a fish out of water, susceptible to all kinds of pitfalls and traps.*

The next hour passed quickly for Susan, as she and Johnny talked about everything under the sun, their conversation punctuated with laughter. She found herself telling him things... personal things...that she'd never told close friends or even her fiancé, Steven. Which reminded her of him. And suddenly, impulsively, her hands went in her lap, beneath the table, as she removed the engagement ring and tucked it in her purse.

She returned her attention to Johnny. What she loved most about him, apart from his good looks, was the way every single thought registered on his face. With him, she would always know *exactly* where she stood. Imagine that advantage! No more evasive looks or cold silences, while she wondered what she'd done or didn't do.

Susan looked at her watch and sighed. "I'm afraid I'm keeping you from your work."

"On the farm, you mean?" Johnny asked. He was leaning back comfortably in the booth, biting on the plastic straw, as if it were a real piece of hay. "Chores are done," he said, "except for the Venus plants, and I do need to water them."

Susan leaned forward in the booth, elbows on the table. "Mrs. Satariano said growing them saved the town's economy," she said. "Tell me about the plants. I want to know all about them."

He straightened, brow furrowed. "Well, there's not much to tell..."

"Are they female?" she asked. "Or male?"

Now he leaned forward, his elbows on the table. "Would you like to see?" His brown eyes were eager, like a cocker spaniel's, hopeful for a treat.

"Sure!" she said.

"Then let's blow this pop stand!" he grinned, and tossed a crumpled dollar bill on the table.

Behind the wheel of the red Mustang, she followed Johnny in his blue Ford truck, through gently rolling green Grant Wood hills. About three miles outside of Prosperity, he turned off the blacktop onto a gravel road.

Even with the car's top down, Susan didn't mind the dust. It seemed so clean and natural! Ashes to ashes, dust to dust. She felt good being this close to nature.

After another mile or so, Johnny's truck slowed down and turned into a short lane that lead to a picturesque farm. To the right sat a white two-story house with green shutters and a large porch with thick white pillars. A porch swing hung by chains from the ceiling swinging gently to and fro in the warm summer breeze. The front door to the house was old and beautifully refinished, with an oval window in etched glass. It lead her to believe that antique furniture might be inside.

Behind the house, to the left, was a big red barn that looked freshly painted. A black wrought iron weather vain of a rooster perched proudly on its roof. The summer sky above was a bright blue, and clouds—like dollops of whipped cream—drifted slowly by. The sun, beginning its decent in the late afternoon, made everything cast long shadows over the farmyard, bringing all its colors to a brilliant hue.

Susan parked her car behind Johnny's truck, in the large driveway which separated the house from a cornfield and got out. Even the grass was picture-postcard perfect: freshly mowed, not an unsightly weed anywhere.

Johnny approached her, with a big grin on his face. "Well, what'd'ya think of the old homestead?"

Susan took a deep breath. "It's so beautiful," she said. "So peaceful." It would be wonderful to live here, she thought.

"The greenhouse is around back," he told her, and led the way.

They stood just inside the screen door of the greenhouse, which was a long, narrow building. Unlike the other structures on the farm, this one was new, with a curved, Plexiglas roof to let the sun come through.

Wooden tables ran the length of the building, with narrow paths in-between. And on those tables were hundreds, maybe thousands, of tiny green plants in black plastic trays.

"You wanted to know about the Dionaea," he said, gesturing to a nearby table. "That's the scientific name of the Venus flytrap."

"But they're so tiny," she said, moving to the table, taking closer look at the little green sprouts.

"That's because this is a brand new crop," Johnny explained. "I start one each month." He gestured again to the plants. "These will be transplanted to the back field, where we're harvesting the crop planted last month."

Susan shook her head. "How on earth did you get the idea to grow them? I thought the Venus Flytrap was some kind of tropical plant."

"No. They're found in the bogs of North Carolina," he told her. "The soil there lacks certain nitrites." He picked up one of the plastic trays holding about a dozen plants and looked at them.

"Seven or eight years ago," he went on, "you wouldn't have recognized this farm. It looked like something during the depression: the land fallow, soil robbed of nutrients that would take years to replace." He was staring now, at the tray in his hands, like it was a crystal ball his was using to look back into the past.

"At that time," he continued, "I was in high school, and we were studying about these plants...And I thought, hey, that was one thing that would grow in the soil."

He looked at Susan. "And it did, with the help of some special plant food. And we made a bundle. Then the whole town—'cause they were in trouble just like us—started to grow the plants, and we sold them all over the world."

Johnny set the tray of little plants down on the table.

"Since then," he continued, "the corn crops have made a comeback, and folks have stopped growing Dionaea—except for me, on the back forty. And everybody helps with the harvest and the proceeds go to better the community."

Susan was so touched by his story, and generosity, that she felt tears forming in her eyes.

Johnny's stomach growled. "Sorry," he said. "Except for that Coke, I haven't had anything since early morning." His face brightened. "Would you join me for dinner? I have some left-over fried chicken and corn from the garden."

She touched his upper arm; his bicep was hard as a rock. "I'd love to," she smiled.

In the cozy kitchen of the farm house, they sat at a round oak table. Before them, lay a feast of fried chicken, sweet corn, and garden vegetables. The meal was simple, but delicious. Just like Johnny.

As they ate, he told her about taking over the farm the summer after graduating from high school, when his parents both died in a freak combine accident. And how hard he worked to keep the place going, fixing it up, little by little, even buying back family heirlooms, piece by piece, that had been sold to an antique dealer when times were hard.

And she told him about growing up poor, and never having any money, and how she hated her job and New York. But that the past hours she'd spent with him were the happiest she been in a long, long while.

To that he replied, "More than anything right now, I want you to be happy."

Later, after the dishes were washed and dried, they went out on the front porch, and sat in the swing, eating vanilla ice cream covered with fresh strawberries, watching the purple-pink sunset, saying very little. And still later, when the fireflies came out, and a chill in the air drove them inside, they sat on a couch in the parlor, in front of a fireplace with a walnut mantle, sipping red wine, watching the flames hypnotically.

And they started to kiss (she wasn't sure who made the first move, which was how it should be) and never before had any man made her feel the way she did.

"I should go," she said after awhile, pulling away. Her face felt hot, flushed. "I need to get a room in town."

"You can if you want to," he said softly, "but the guest room upstairs is free." And he kissed her, and she kissed back, wrapping her arms tightly around him, pushing him back on the couch as the flames danced seductively before them.

Susan woke in the morning in the four poster bed in Johnny's room. The early morning sun streamed in a nearby window and a cool breeze—with just a hint of the warm day to come—softly rustled the white cotton curtains.

She stretched. Never before had she slept so good! The night sounds of the farm was a soothing symphony in her ears each time she woke and went back to sleep. Not to mention Johnny's tender love-making, first on the couch in front of the fire, and later during the night, in the four-poster bed. He hadn't tried to impress her, like other men she'd been with, Steven included. It was obvious he was so completely at ease with the act, that that put her at ease.

Then sometime very early in the morning, he kissed her cheek and told her he had to get up for chores, and she should go back to sleep. Which she did. Perhaps, after they were married, she would get up to help him.

Susan got out of bed and padded across the braided rug to her suitcase that lay on the floor, getting what she needed for the bathroom. Through the open window she could hear Johnny out the in greenhouse, whistling, as he tended to the plants.

A half hour later, she emerged from the bathroom and stopped in front of a hall phone, that sat on a small half-circle table against the wall. Not impulsively, for she'd been thinking during her bath just what she would say, she called Steven's number at their apartment, knowing he'd be at work, and informed him she wasn't coming back, and he should pack her things, which she'd send for later.

Then wearing the same floral dress that she'd bought (she didn't want to scare him with all that black) she skipped down the stairs to the front hallway, and went back to the kitchen. There on the table was a glass of orange juice, and some muffins on a plate and a note saying there was coffee on the counter. Wasn't he thoughtful? She drank the orange juice, took one bite of a muffin, then hurried out the back door to the greenhouse.

When she got there, though, the greenhouse was empty. He was probably off to get something, and would be back soon, she thought. Smiling, she began to walk down one of the narrow paths between the tables. The little green shoots coming out of the black dirt, looked like rolled green dollar bills. Or fifties. That's what he told her they sold for last night.

She stopped, noticing that there was a little metal plaque on the side of the table which held a white card with a name and date. The card seemed to identify the month the seeds were started.

She moved along to the next table which had a similar

plaque. But this one read "Heather, May." The other had been "Jill, April." She continued to the last table, where rows of trays sat empty. Her eyes went to the plaque, its paper whiter, newer than the others. It said, "Susan, July."

Her mouth fell open with delight. Johnny was going to name some plants after her! How romantic. She touched the card and another one, which had been stuck behind it, slid out the bottom of the holder onto the floor. She bent down and picked up the weathered piece of paper, which must have been in there a long, long time because the paper was brown and stained. It seemed to say "Mother" and the date was gone.

The screen door of the greenhouse banging shut made her look up to see Johnny standing in the doorway, in faded jeans and a white t-shirt.

She let the old piece of paper fall from her hands and she hurried toward him.

"Did you sleep well?" he asked.

She was a little out of breath when she reached him. "Oh, yes! And thank you for the breakfast." She pointed to the back of the greenhouse. "I noticed that the last table had a card that said "Susan"...Does that mean those plants will be named after me?"

"Uh-huh."

She squealed and threw her arms around his neck, and kissed him, but he didn't return the kiss. She brought her arms down slowly, and looked at his face, which wore a peculiar expression.

"I want you to know about the others," he said.

Was that all? she thought, and breathed a sigh of relief. She'd thought something was *really* wrong. "It doesn't matter," she said. "I've been no angel."

He shook his head. "But you have a right to know. Just like the others."

She started to say something dismissive, but he continued, looking intently at her. "In April, there was Jill. In May, there was Heather. In June there was Madeline...now you...and that's just this year...."

Madeline? She remembered the appointment book she'd

found in the car...hadn't that woman's name been Madeline?

"....You see it all started seven years ago with Mother."

"Your *mother*..." she said, completely befuddled.

He moved forward, pinning her against the table, his expression now cold, sinister.

"You see," he explained, "the Dionaea can only survive in dry Iowa soil if it's first been given a nutritious start in soil high in nitrates....human nitrates with estrogen."

A chill ran up her spine. Was this why everyone was so nice to her—Johnny included—wanting her to have a good time, as if it was her last day on earth? She tried to escape, but Johnny's strong arms closed around her, and flailing away with her fists was like hitting a stone statue.

"Why me?" she asked, terrified.

His smile was sickening, evil. "U-Save Car Rental sends me their rudest customers...woman so nasty they won't be missed." And his hands went around her throat.

"But I've *changed!*" she managed to rasp.

Johnny shook his head, tightening his grip. "People don't change," he said. "I know because I never could."

And his hands squeezed tighter, like the leaf of the Venus flytrap when a victim haplessly enters its lair.

♦♦♦

THE DIONAEA PLANT sat on a windowsill in an apartment on Seventy-third and Central Park West, warming itself in the late afternoon sun. It didn't even care if some dumb old fly or other idiotic insect came by and landed on one of its many thorned leaves, triggering that leaf to clamp shut, beginning the slow process of digestion....Because earlier in the day that nice woman who lived here alone, fed it the special plant food from Iowa, making it feel big and strong.

It missed the farm. But across the street was a really big park and maybe some day, when it got too big for the little apartment, the nice lady would transplant it over there. There was always some activity going on in the park, although some of it was not very nice.

There was a knock at the front door, and the woman went to answer it. The plant liked the woman, it felt like she was a sister.

"Steven!" the woman said to a tall, dark man who entered. "Thank you so much for the plant. Come and see it."

The man came over and bent his head down toward the plant. It didn't like him. It didn't know why.

"What in the world...?" he asked. "I just told the florist to send something exotic."

"It's a Venus flytrap," the woman said excitedly.

"Wow. I've never seen one." His face came closer and the plant wanted so badly to clamp down on his nose.

"From the Susan series," he read from a little card that lay next to the plant. He made a disgusted sound with his lips.

"What's the matter?" the woman asked.

"That's the name of that bitch who dumped me by leaving a message on the answer machine. I wonder what became of her."

Then they left the apartment—off to eat at some expensive restaurant—and the plant sat alone, basking in the last rays of the late afternoon sun.

Live Bait

Sujata Massey

A photograph stored inside my cell-phone never made it to trial. No one would ever suspect it means anything, but to me it's the world. My old world: Willow Brook, Virginia, in late May. Each time I look at it, I'm sent straight back to that afternoon; high 80s and humid, a Southern summer already started. You can tell because the hedge of azaleas that guards our house have had their day, and the rose garden that Lucy and I planted when we moved in eight years ago is kicking ass.

I've come home from work early, because every Friday night, from May through October, means somebody's having a Friday night garden party. I swing in through the back door, and Lucy looks up from the spinach and strawberry salad she's making.

"You might want to change clothes," she says by way of greeting, and I look down at the polo shirt I wore for Casual Friday and notice a ketchup stain that I must have picked up in our company cafeteria.

Stains of any sort are a faux pas in Willow Brook. Lucy is as well-groomed as ever, wearing the kind of makeup that doesn't look like makeup, and a short, flowery dress that I hadn't seen before: with a waist somewhere around her ribcage, a feature that once were the province of six-year-old girls. Like a kid, Lucy's traded her customary Nikes for pale green pumps with the strangest heel I've seen yet—a rounded ball with a tiny, sharp tip. She sees me looking at them and says, "It's the kitten heel. Audrey Hepburn made it famous."

That means it'll be an Audrey Hepburn convention tonight.

After eight years, I'm still not used to this. Willow Brook

is a distance from where I grew up. In Ely, Minnesota, nobody ever stuck strawberries in their salads, or dropped by each other's yards almost daily, supposedly to discuss lawn growth but really to cadge a G&T. This is what Lucy loved about Willow Brook. She's from South Carolina, and I swear that accent did more to open doors for us here, in Northern Virginia, than anything I ever did. She wanted to live in a place where people still come to your door to borrow a cup of Splenda.

When the Lanahans bought the sprawling neo-Queen Anne next door to us, Lucy went straight over with a coffee-maker and set them up with that, and a basket of blueberry muffins. She invited their kids, Tara and Noel, over to our swing-set to keep busy with our twins for most of the day; the minute the movers were gone she had a bottle of wine open for their parents, Trent and Amy. Watching Lucy light up for the new people reminded me of how she used to light up for me, ten years ago, when we met at an old alumni hockey game in New York. I creamed the opposition that night, but no longer. I don't know if she's just tired, or tired of me; but it seems the only time the lights, the makeup, and high heels go on, are when the neighbors are involved.

That Friday night in June, Jason and Justin couldn't get through the gate to the Lanahans' backyard fast enough, but Lucy made sure each boy carried a six-pack of seltzer. Lucy balanced the salad bowl against her hip, and directed me to dig a couple of bottles of white out of the wine fridge. We were out of cold white wine as usual—Lucy and her friends drink it like water—so I had to go with a Zin. We had a brief argument about whether this was a good choice, because Lucy said it was too hot a wine for the weather. I pointed out that I could chill it, and at that she rolled her eyes but didn't say anything.

The Lanahans need to keep up their yard a little better. From where I stop mowing, and their yard begins, there's an inch of height difference. I snap a picture of our yard, which is perfect since I've done my weekly ten hours' maintenance already, and Lucy says, "Honestly. Can't you give it a rest?"

I slip the phone in my pocket and hand the wine to Trent,

who's just come up. Subtly I mention a sale on riding mowers, but he just says, "Yeah, Buddy." The next thing I know is, he's kissing Lucy on the lips and exclaiming about the salad. That's the way it is in this part of the world; you're expected to kiss all women in the social circle, like it's France or Italy.

"All organic," Lucy says to him, and winks. That's part of the craziness about the Lanahans—they come from California originally, and the first thing they did, garden-wise, was put in a vegetable garden. Amy, Trent's wife, has come out and kissed Lucy, too, and they're talking about grilling rainbow trout that Trent caught that morning. They kiss, but I see Amy staring at Lucy's kitten heels; she's wearing some kind of comfort sandal, and it appears she forgot to shave her legs that morning. She's busy in the mornings, getting the kids up and then herself out the door to Georgetown Medical Center. I've seen her racing the way I do to get out to the Beltway before the traffic comes to its usual morning standstill.

Trent has time to fish any morning of the week because he doesn't work. He claims to be a consultant, but we all know what that means. Weekday mornings as I head toward the Beltway, I see him shooting the other direction, deeper into Virginia, behind the wheel of his Pathfinder with either a canoe or kayak or a mountain bike strapped on, advertising exactly how hard he's going to be working that day. He keeps a sailboat on the Eastern Shore, too. It's a nice life, and I suppose if I were married to one of Washingtonian Magazine's top 5 radiolologists and had a bus take my kids to school at eight and bring them back at five-fifteen, I could have that life myself. I'm about to turn forty, and sometimes, like the line in the Talking Heads song, I feel like I'm watching the days go by, not knowing who I'm living with, why I'm working in pharmaceutical sales, and how I came to live in a house that costs four times its worth, by rural Minnesota standards.

The party swirls with neighbors, most of the wives blond and thin like Lucy, the husbands either in training shape or with the start of a spare tire. I lie somewhere in between all of it, I suppose. And we didn't need to bring the wine. It stands unopened, a lonely red sentry, while Amy pours people South-side cocktails she's premixed and kept in a pitcher. She made the syrup with mint from the garden, she tells me, and I get it; she's trying to prove that she's into gardening, because I've made a few comments about the lawn. I nod and smile and have a second.

The Lanahans' Labrador, Gertie, runs between people's legs, and Jason is suddenly in hysterics, saying the dog stole his cup of Pirate Booty. He wants me to make the Lanahans punish Gertie. Instead, I take him by the hand and head back over to the snack table, where neighbors who are not as enlightened as the Lanahans have contributed bagged chips, pigs-in-a-blanket, and chocolate chip cookies. There is no more Pirate Booty, and I am searching for something similarly salty and junky when a groaning sound catches my ear. I look up and see the Lanahans' garage door descending; the last thing I notice before it closes completely are blue-jeaned guy's legs, and Lucy's slim tanned ones ending in the green kitten heels.

I blink, not quite believing it, nor the fact that the garage door stays down a good thirteen minutes. That's enough time to—well, you know. I don't have to spell it out. Everything that I'd thought about my wife's perfection has suddenly tilted forty-five degrees. When the main door rises Trent emerges, smiling like an idiot, a cooler in his arms. Holding nothing, Lucy follows.

"Having a good time, Babe?" she asks me as Trent looks at me quickly, as if embarrassed, and then rushes on to his wife. There is a fain sheen of sweat on her face, and a long smear of dust across the front of her dress.

"Not as good as you are."

"Oscar-the-Grouch," she says, linking her arm in mine.

"What were you doing in the garage with Trent?" I can't hold myself back from asking it, cannot keep my tone level and casual.

Lucy"s blush is obvious—now that I look at her, her chest in the low cut dress looks flushed, too. Years ago, we used to laugh in bed when we watched that flush rise. "What do you mean, what was I doing in the garage?"

"Just that."

"I—we—the cooler!" she says at last, sounding triumphant to have found an excuse. "He needed another cooler, and I remembered where Amy had put it away, the last time we went to Annapolis with the kids."

He does have the cooler, it's true. But I still don't buy her excuse; her reaction was too odd, and they were in there too long. I turn away, too angry to say anything more.

Lucy goes straight over to Jason, who's now grabbing the front of his pants, apparently in the market for a bathroom escort. She takes him toward the house, passing Trent at the barbecue. Here, she hesitates, says something, and he turns to look at me. So she's warned him. But he's grinning, and lifts his hand, crazy-looking in a giant blue silicone glove,

Keep your paws off my wife, I think to myself, and later that evening, after the kids are down and Lucy's fallen into a deep, Southside slumber, I dig into my wife's email. It turns out she subscribes to a couple of list-serves, one for our church, another for regional child sex predator alerts, and one with organic recipes. I locate a group email sent out from the Willow Brook association to everyone on our cul-de-sac, and while I troll for a likely sounding email address for Trent, all I can find for the Lanahans is "MomAmy."

Persistence pays, and the next evening I am inspired to look through her email trash, and I find a message from "Canoeguy 12," which apparently is in response to something she's sent him.

RE: Big Enough?

It's big enough to satisfy most people, is what I've heard. I've had a lot of fun with it, and you know Amy's opinion. I can take you somewhere else this weekend, if you want to try elsewhere. ;)

Cheers, Trent

What was this nonsense about Amy's opinion, I wonder, as I lie awake in bed that night. I see Trent talking to every woman in the neighborhood but Amy, which makes no sense because except for the comfort sandals, she looks a lot like the others, and Amy's hair is not blond like Lucy's, but a nondescript light brown. Not that Lucy's hair color is real.

But what is real? I thought real was getting married, having kids, and buying a house and planting a garden. But in Willow Grove, the house comes with a swing-set, and the swing-set means play-dates, first between the kids, and then, the grown-ups themselves. How did I get here? And how did a woman who loved me once to the point of distraction became too distracted to love me anymore?

It's Trent, pure and simple. If I could stay at home, canoeing and canoodling while my kids were at school, my wife would notice me again. But if I didn't work, we'd be foreclosed, and as much as Willow Brook can alienate me, sometimes, losing what we planted together disturbs me more.

The school week starts up again. I go to work early, and come home early, but most of my time is spent in the garden. My stomach is twisted with so much grief I can no longer eat the healthy dinners Lucy prepares.

"Honestly, Honey, you're setting a bad example for the kids," Lucy says, as I push quinoa around on my plate. I don't answer. I'm waiting for the charade of a meal to end and for the children and Lucy to go to bed so I can look for email. I'm suspicious because for the upcoming weekend, Lucy casually tells me I can play golf as much as I want, because she's taking the kids and herself for an overnight to her cousin Lolly's house in Fredericksburg.

Lucy hums and smiles, and lets the kids have an extra half-hour of TV in the mornings, even though it's not summer break yet. She wants them occupied so she can check her email, and once when I slip up behind her, I see she's started an email to Canoeguy 12. The moment she senses me there behind her, she hits cancel. She's smart enough to dump her email trash basket now; I've found nothing since that message about Trent, Amy, and their vague plans for going somewhere over the weekend. It must be this weekend, when she is supposedly in Fredericksburg. I imagine her getting the kids off to sleep, then slipping out the door, supposedly on an errand, telling her cousin she has a key and not to wait up. Or maybe cousin Lolly is into swinging, and they're all meeting up with Trent.

It's Trent's fault. Amy deserves some blame too, I suppose, because her working has enabled him to live a life of leisure and the pursuit of pretty neighbors. She doesn't need him. We don't either. And that gives me my idea.

At the last party, Trent was talking about his upcoming plans for a two-day hike in the Appalachian foothills with the Men's Explorer Group. So that Thursday, I tell the office about a dental exam I've forgotten, and am back in Willow Grove at 11 in the morning, when all of them should be gone—Trent to the water, his wife to her group practice, and Lucy to Pilates.

How quiet it is as I enter the cul-de-sac. I see a few moms with strollers, and the mailman smoking as he walks his route, already in the shorts uniform. I ring their doorbell, and look in the backyard to make sure nobody's around, before I open the side door to their garage with my drill, a sanding block and the sawdust I picked up at Home Depot. Inside, it's very hot and dark, but there's a light that I switch on that illuminates the orderly space; Trent's Pathfinder and Amy's Lexus are gone. Two canoes are hanging overhead: one short and well used wooden one, the other a longer fiberglass model in a shiny green, obviously a new toy.

I hadn't known CanoeGuy owned two canoes. Obviously, he would use one of them at a time, so I decide to tackle the new one. I drill a couple of holes underneath the seat. The discs I've cut I sand down further, so that they are smaller than the holes I've made. I fill the holes with sawdust and fit the discs back in. The alteration I make is so slight it's practically invisible, but once the canoe hits water, the sawdust will wash away.

There is always a chance that Trent will be in shallow water when the canoe starts to sink, and he could possibly swim his way to shore. However, he's bragged a lot about taking the canoe into rapids, and the Chesapeake Bay, and so on; and since he often canoes by himself on weekdays, it's not likely there are many guys around to help out when he's in distress.

I'm back to work an hour later, well within the range of time for a dentist visit. That night at dinner, my appetite is finally back.

"You're feeling better," Lucy says. "You're eating again."

I raise an eyebrow, but don't answer. Talking to her is too upsetting, still.

"Hey, I've been thinking. For your birthday, why don't we do something outdoorsy, like have a fishing party? We can all drive out to one of the parks along the Potomac River next Saturday morning. "

I've been fishing since I was younger than the twins, and I have been saying for a while I want to teach them how to do it, right. But it almost hurts, this idea of doing something I've wanted for so long, when everything is lost. But I can't look suspicious. I have to seem as if I'm still connected to everyone. "Sure," I say.

"We've got the fishing equipment in the garage. Let me know if there's anything extra missing, and I'll pick it up beforehand."

"There's worms," Justin says.

"You can pick those up that morning, Honey," Lucy tells him. "There will be stores selling live bait along the way."

"Are you kidding? There's live bait in our yard. He can get it for free," I say.

And so, that's how my birthday starts out. Lucy makes coffee and biscuits and eggs in the morning. The gifts are so meaningless as to make me yawn: a couple of new polo shirts, a book on financial management. My folks have mailed me a book of fishing jokes.

"Of all things," Lucy says suddenly. "I just remembered there's something I need to pick up, on the way to the river. We'll have to go in two cars. Are you OK taking the boys with you?"

"What do you need to pick up?"

"Nothing! I mean, nothing important. I just think if we arrange to meet there at noon it would be best." And then she hands me a map with directions, and an estimated driving time of an hour and twenty minutes. "It's better this way, because I've already loaded your car with the coolers and fishing stuff. All you have to worry about are the boys, and of course—the live bait."

So she's meeting him on my birthday itself. A motel, somewhere along 95 South: a quickie, and then the act of duty, the birthday picnic for her stupid husband. As I dig earthworms in the rose beds, I cut one in half with my spade, and then another.

How beautiful the day is, as I drive south in our Subaru wagon with Justin and Jason in the back. They are lost in their handheld Nintendo games, but my eyes are on the horizon. Sleepy, warm Virginia; it seemed such a better place to live than DC. I remember a bumper sticker from my childhood that made it up to Minnesota; Virginia is for Lovers. How that had spiked my imagination, and perhaps even subliminally driven me there, to the sorority party at UVA where I ultimately met Lucy.

I pull into the parking area Lucy carefully detailed for me; just as she said, there's a shelter there. But she's late. It's noon, and her Honda Fit is not where she'd said it would be. I decide to unpack anyway, but the boys don't want the gloom of the concrete structure; they want to be right next to the water, so I agree and we all carry our things close to the water. I like the idea of Lucy arriving, seeing our car, but no sight of us at the shelter. It will be a bit of work for her to find us.

The waters here are livelier than I expected, with a small series of rapids about 200 feet upriver from us. I explain to the boys that the conditions are excellent for fly-fishing, with trout likely coming downstream to us. I wonder if there's anything in Lucy's car that could be used to start a fire; if we catch something good, it could be grilled for lunch.

Justin catches his first trout, and is ecstatic. Jason has more trouble, and I hold the rod for him, and eventually, there's a tug and a small fish flapping around. I am so busy reeling it in that I don't see what Justin does immediately; the canoe bumping aimlessly toward us, half-submerged, with its front tip pointing skyward.

"Happy," Just said. "Look, the side that's up says the canoe's name is Happy."

I am studying it too, because it's the same deep green of the canoe I saw in Trent's garage. It couldn't be. What were the chances Trent would go canoeing early on the same day and place of our family picnic? Oh, God. Where was Lucy?

The canoe moves haphazardly by, and I can imagine that, around the bend, it's sunk. Happy, I think to myself. I'm not.

"Nobody was in the canoe," Jason says. "Do you think somebody drowned?"

I answer reassuringly, "I don't know how deep it is, but I'm sure the guy with that canoe knows what he's doing."

"Then why's the canoe all empty and upside down?" Justin persists. "Dad, let's get the binoculars out of the fishing basket."

"I don't keep binoculars there."

"Mom put them in. She thought Jason could bird-watch if he couldn't catch a fish."

"Which I did." Jason is indignant.

"Which you did. OK, Jason, you go get those binoculars out and take a look upstream." I stay where I am because I don't want to be put in a position where I might spot Trent. And of course, the kids see nothing. But within half an hour, there is the sound of a siren from the highway. Then another, and one more.

Lucy still hasn't shown up; my calls to her cell are going straight into voice mail, one after the other. The thought comes to me: traffic accident. But is she with Trent?

My stomach is bothering me again, but I must know. I dial the Lanahans' home phone number. Amy answers, saying that Trent is fine; he came home a while ago and is watching TV with the gifts.

"Did you like your gift?" Amy asks.

"I didn't get your gift." I am caught off guard by her question.

"I'm talking about Lucy's big present to you. We've been getting it ready for weeks. I thought you'd be out on it by now."

"I don't understand," I said. "The boys and I are out at Potomac Run Park, waiting for Lucy to meet us for a picnic. She's almost an hour late."

"Well, I guess your little intervention worked, huh?"

"What—what do you mean?" I ask, feeling stupider by the minute.

"Our garage has a security camera, Doug. Did you forget about that?" There is a malicious sound to Amy's voice, a tone I'd heard before, but never directed at me.

"Huh?" It's not playing dumb—I am dumb.

"I can't thank you enough, Doug. Because you know, I have the tape of what happened in the garage during our Friday night party. It wasn't very nice. You sort of took matters into your own hands, didn't you?"

"I didn't mean—but Lucy—what about Lucy?"

"Trent was originally going to help Lucy paddle down the river to surprise you at the park, but I convinced him he was needed here pronto, and you wouldn't like him horning in on your birthday surprise. What a shame there were no life jackets in the canoe—well, I'm sure she'll show up sooner or later."

I hang up without saying goodbye.

It is easy to pack up the car, and just follow the sound of sirens downstream. There's a massive disaster rescue encampment, with ambulances and police cars on land, and rescue workers on rafts and a coast guard boat hitching up the ruined canoe for a tow. On one side of the canoe you can see the words: HAPPY BIRTHDAY DOUG.

A crowd of rubberneckers has assembled in the way people always do, when they sniff death. People are talking about the woman who'd been caught on the underside of the canoe: a petite blonde without a lifejacket. She must not have been a strong swimmer. People like that shouldn't be allowed on the water.

I don't walk over to the ambulance to see who is being loaded up, because of the boys being with me, and the shock they'd suffer.

This is what I have maintained, throughout the trial, but my decision not to go to the ambulance and ask for Lucy has hurt me. More than she ever did.

Dumb Luck

Marilyn Victor

"It's like a furnace in here," Harry complained opening the door of the obsolete trailer. "We can afford to turn on the damn air conditioner once in awhile, ya know."

He shoved Gertie aside and flipped on the switch of the small fan clipped above the tiny kitchenette. For all the good it did. He gave her a considering look, then the dry lines of his face cracked into a leer. "But we can't afford to get you a new ass." Laughing as if he had said something incredibly clever, he swatted her on the butt.

"Buddy," she corrected automatically, moping the sweat from her forehead with a torn handkerchief, "was a mule, not an ass."

What little wall space their eighteen-foot-trailer had, was filled with snapshots of Buddy, the orphaned mule Harry had won in a poker game in Oklahoma. Buddy, trotting along the dusty paths of a carnival. Buddy, giving rides to delighted children. A yellowed front-page news article from the *Denver Post*, featured a photo of the "Daring Duo" diving from a forty-five foot high platform into five feet of ice cold water.

"Doesn't matter." Harry held out his chipped mug for more coffee. "We'll never find another animal to take a dive like old Bud. He was a bullet."

"He hated being pushed off that platform."

"Why do you always say that, Gert?" Harry fixed her with a pained expression. "I never pushed him. Bud was a diving mule. He lived for the thrill of that jump."

He had died for it, too.

Diving acts had been all the rage in those days. Across the country, pretty women in bathing suits perched on the backs of their faithful steeds and plunged into tiny tanks of water below. Not Gertie. She had been all of thirty-eight back then. Too old to attract an audience, in Harry's opinion. She wasn't pretty enough, shapely enough, or smart enough. She could have been Albert Einstein in Marilyn Monroe's body and he would have found something wrong with her. Harry was the star. The strongest, the smartest, the best looking, and tomorrow he'd be the oldest.

He had been all bulging muscles and dimples when Gertie first caught sight of him working the Tilt-A-Whirl at the county fair. To a sixteen-year-old farm girl, he'd been the most gorgeous and brilliant man she had ever met. Shades of black and white had filled the box of her small life up until the day she met Harry. With her parents' farm mortgaged to finance college educations for her brothers, she was expected to do what her mother had done: peel potatoes, clean house, bake pies, and breed sons for some lucky farmer. She couldn't remember her mother doing anything else. Didn't remember the woman ever smiling. Then Harry came along and painted pictures of a nomadic life so brilliant the color had hurt her eyes. When the carnival and Harry packed up to leave, she climbed out of her bedroom window in the middle of the night and went with him.

The door to the camper flew open and Rodney the Rocket barged into the room, his face as red as the sagging leotard he was wearing. "What the hell do you think you're doin'!" Rodney screamed. "You can't paint your damned name on my cannon!"

"You always were a sore loser, Rodney." Harry leaned back in the padded booth that served double duty as kitchen seating and a pallet that didn't deserve to be called a bed.

While a few collectors had offered to buy the old Airstream they had lived in for the past forty years, Harry had turned them all down. He was too cheap to spend money on something new when the old one worked perfectly fine.

"You were cheating!" Rodney accused. "No man gets a royal flush twice in one game."

"I'm lucky." Harry turned to Gertie. "Tell him, Gert. I've

always been lucky, haven't I?"

"Yeah, lucky," she answered listlessly.

His first big act had been jumping a motorcycle over a line of stock cars at a fair in Oklahoma. Still madly in love, she couldn't bear to watch, terrified each time he made the leap that she would soon be playing the part of a tragic young widow. She considered herself lucky that all he'd ever gotten was a broken nose when an angry fan hurled a beer can at him.

When the excitement of the daredevil show wore off, he spent ten years riding a unicycle along a high wire while Gertie watched from below wondering when he was going to fall and break his head open. A poorly healed broken leg ended that act and her chance to play the bereaved widow.

It wasn't long after he got it into his head a Wild West act would make him the headliner he yearned to be. His plan was to have Gertie hold the Ace of Spades between her teeth and he would shoot a hole through the center from thirty feet away. It didn't matter he'd never shot a gun before. All he had to do was aim the pistol and pull the trigger. How hard could it be? By that time in their marriage, Gertie wanted to do the shooting.

Then Buddy came along.

It hadn't been the big time Harry envisioned, but it had at least been comfortable. For fifteen years, the gentle bay mule performed his diving act, traveling from fair to carnival, diving into that little tank of water four times a day, while Harry grew increasingly unreasonable. That golden ring remained just out of his grasp and it was driving him mad. He needed something newer, fresher and Gertie was terrified he was going to sell Buddy the minute her back was turned.

Harry never got the chance. That first dive at the Minnesota State Fair ended the act forever. Harry crawled out of the water tank with a set of cracked ribs. Buddy broke his neck.

"You can't blow yourself out of my cannon!" Rodney leaned across the kitchenette table, nose to nose with Harry.

"It ain't your cannon anymore!" Harry vaulted to his feet, at least a foot taller and half a door broader than Rodney. "Why don't you admit it, bird brain, poker just ain't your game."

"You're going to get yourself killed. There's an art to it. Not just anyone can fire themselves out of a cannon."

Harry waved his hand in dismissal. "I know what I'm doing. Ya think I'm stupid?"

"Give the man his rocket," Gertie said half-heartedly, knowing there was no point in arguing with Harry.

"No!" he grabbed her arm. "This is our big chance, Gert. I ain't givin' it up for anyone."

She knew that all too well. Harry was a man of dreams. What she hadn't known when she had run off with him was just how low the bar of his aspirations had been set.

Harry had only one dream. He wasn't going to be no two-bit carnie all his life like his old man. He was going to be a showman; a headliner at the state fairs. He wanted the best, most daring act anyone had ever seen. "We'll perform for kings, Gert. You just wait and see."

Forty years later, he still held on to that dream.

Disgusted, Gertie pulled her arm free and stalked out into the sweltering heat of Minnesota's August.

As she trudged along the deserted street toward the 4-H building, she imagined she could hear Buddy's hooves clomping along next to her, his warm breath on the back of her neck. Buddy had loved their morning walks together. If the cotton candy vendor was fired up, she'd buy a fresh pink cone of it, sharing feathers of the soft spun sugar with him as they enjoyed the peace and quiet before the fair gates opened and the cake-eaters jammed in. On those mornings, she'd pretend it was a normal day and she had a normal life. She'd imagine the streets of the fair were no different from any other city, and the people here like workers anywhere else getting ready for the day's business.

Her friend Sadie was already bent over the sink of the public restroom, splashing water on her tired face, a thin towel draped around her stooped shoulders. It was quiet in the building, but in an hour or two, the lines to use the facilities would be as long as the lines for the Ferris wheel and the constant noise would be like having a hive of angry bees inside your head.

"You ever worry about the future, Sadie?" Gertie asked staring at her blurred reflection in the tin square that passed for a mirror in the restroom.

She remembered a time when she and Harry had access to the showers in the cattle barns. That was when Harry still had a back end show, capable of drawing crowds from the front gates to get them circulating inside the fairgrounds.

"Standing on concrete all day selling plastic light sabers and stuffed unicorns ain't no work for a woman my age." Sadie raised her hands over her head and bent backwards, the bones popping along her aching back. "You don't think I don't wonder what's going to happen to me when I can't stand no more? I ain't got anything saved for the future. Not like they pay benefits around here."

"You could always rob a bank," Gertie suggested with a half-hearted smile. "Three square meals and a roof over your head, tax free."

Harry had said as much last year when he wanted to buy a bear to wrestle. Gertie could play the damsel in distress, tied to the bars of the cage while Harry rescued her. The crowds would love it, he said. "Like a mule diving off a sixty foot platform, only better."

"Forty-five feet," she'd automatically corrected him.

"Sixty." He glowered at her as if she had lost her mind. "Remember? We raised the platform when we got to Minnesota. We needed something to spiff up the act."

She had gone to her mother's funeral that day, wondering even now why she had bothered. Her family had disowned her when she ran off with Harry. There had been no happy family reunion. No forgiveness. Her mother left the farm and what little she had to Gertie's three brothers, who still refused to speak to her. The oldest, William, Jr., even went as far as to not-so-politely ask her to leave.

When she'd gotten back to the fair, Harry ignored her tears, instead working himself into a rage at their having been relegated to a spot near the back of the fairgrounds on Machinery Hill. But he was going to show them. He and Buddy would fill the bleachers with their daring act.

The scaffolding for the dive looked off to her that day, but she had put it down to the new location. She should have been more vigilant. Buddy trusted her and she let him down. She should have guessed Harry would try something stupid. Should have known he was too full of himself to do any proper testing before he did something as insane as to raise Buddy's diving platform by fifteen feet.

After Buddy's death, Gertie found herself doing what her mother had always done. What she thought she'd never do. She began baking pies. It was oddly therapeutic, and she wondered if that was the reason there had always been fresh baked pies sitting on the windowsill of the farmhouse. Had it kept her mother sane all those years of playing second fiddle to a man, four kids and a pig farm?

"Pies? What do you know about baking a pie?" Harry had scoffed at her. "You can't even make a man a decent sandwich."

On the anniversary of Buddy's death, she had made her two best cherry pies ever. One for Harry and one for the judges. She would have won the blue ribbon, too, if Harry hadn't taken it into his thick head to eat them both.

He'd been lucky Sadie had shown up when she did. Lucky she had known what to do when faced with a purple-faced Harry. He would have died if she hadn't tried that Heimlich maneuver on him.

"You can thank your lucky stars it wasn't one of them judges that choked on that damned thing. You'd be in prison right now," he said shaking a fist at her. "Then you wouldn't have to worry about retirement, would you?"

The judge's pie had been just fine. It had been Harry's pie, the one decorated with a silhouette of Buddy, that held the little ceramic pie weight hiding like a pit in one of the cherries. If luck had sided with her that day, Harry would have been dead and she would have been playing the merry widow and living out of their trailer somewhere in Phoenix with the rest of the snowbirds.

By the time Gertie had finished washing up, Harry and Rodney had moved their argument to the small allotted corner of Machinery Hill where the amazing Rodney the Rocket was supposed to perform his daring feat of bravery by being shot out of a cannon.

"You can't use a teddy bear to test the damned thing," Rodney protested, hopping around as if the beaten grass had turned to hot coals.

Gertie tried to grab the stuffed animal out of Harry's hand. "Where did you find that? That's Buddy's!"

He dodged away from her and with an evil grin, dropped it into the end of the brightly painted cannon.

"It was time you got over that stupid old mule," Harry told her with a snarl. "You mourn over him like he was a kid."

She had never had any children. Harry wanted to wait until they were better situated, until they had hit that big time that never came. Buddy may have been a mule, but in a lot of ways he had been like a big kid, carrying that stuffed animal in his teeth like a child clutching a security blanket. She couldn't get him to settle down at night without it.

On those nights when Harry had been particularly rough on her, Gertie would crawl into Buddy's stall and try to sleep in a pile of straw pushed into the corner. Buddy would lower his head and nuzzle her with his soft nose, licking at the salty tears that streaked her face. If that didn't cheer her up, he'd drop that smelly old stuffed toy in her lap, more than willing to share the comfort of it with her. After Buddy's death, she hid the toy under her pillow, afraid Harry would call her a baby if he knew she had kept it. It still smelled of mule and straw and brought as much comfort to her as she could find these days.

Now it exploded out of the end of the cannon, flew sixty-five feet into the air, and bounced off the safety net, landing on the roof of the nearby Pet Center.

"See, it works perfectly," Harry announced with a satisfied nod.

"Maybe if we're lucky, you'll end up on the roof next to it!" Rodney shouted as he stomped off.

"Gert is going to be my trigger lady. She won't let anything happen to me."

Gertie tore her eyes away from the Pet Center's roof. "Me?" He'd never trusted her with anything to do with his acts before.

"Sure, why not? All you gotta do is push a button. How hard could it be?"

Harder than he thought.

Gertie had listened to Rodney bellyaching enough to know it only took a minor adjustment in the aim of the cannon to make a huge change in the trajectory of the person being shot out of it. If Harry refused to go up on the roof of the Pet Center to get Buddy's stuffed animal down, she was going to send him up there to get it.

Only a handful of people came to watch, most of them more interested in finding shelter from the late summer rain than watching some old fart getting shot out of a cannon.

"You're going to kill yourself," she warned, as Harry prepared to squeeze into the mouth of the cannon. While he didn't look bad for sixty-eight, no weight lifting in the world would make those knobby old knees and bowed legs look good in red spandex.

"Harry's lucky," Sadie said, standing beside her. "Haven't you always said, Harry is lucky."

Gertie turned on the pre-recorded drum roll and watched the uninterested faces on the people in the bleachers. Some talked on cell phones, others looked skyward as if they could determine when the all day drizzle would finally let up.

She poised her finger over the trigger button, closed her eyes. "Bud, this one's for you," she whispered, then pressed the button.

For a moment, there was silence and she cursed under her breath, thinking Harry had gotten lucky yet again. Then there was an explosion and a fume of smoke as Harry soared over the heads of the small crowd, past the net and over the roof of the Pet Center.

"That'll be five dollars," Gertie said, taking money from a sticky-handed little kid while trying to keep surveillance on a teenage boy who was spending too much time appraising a stuffed unicorn his girlfriend was whining over.

Instead of landing on the Pet Center's roof, Harry had landed right smack on top of their Airstream. The vintage trailer was beyond repair. Even if it hadn't been completely totaled, she didn't have the money to fix it. The life insurance policy Harry had gotten such a good deal on barely covered the cheap metal box she buried the old bastard in and naturally, he had been too cheap to insure the trailer. There would be no blissful retirement in Phoenix, or anywhere else.

When she went to the police and confessed her crime, they had treated her like a misguided child, confused and bereft. There would be no jail cell, no three square meals a day or free roof over her head compliments of Minnesota's taxpayers either.

Sadie shot her a sympathetic look. "Standing on concrete all day, selling plastic toys to the kiddies is no work for women our age."

Neither was sharing a Super 8 hotel room with a woman who chain-smoked and put her teeth in a jar each night.

Once again, Harry had been the lucky one.

I Seen That

S. J. Rozan

Hey, Frank, my man. Yeah, a Bud. No, you can't interest me in a freakin' microbrew. I still can't believe you even carry that yuppie crap. Yeah, well, just because the neighborhood's changing, that don't mean this joint's gotta change! I swear to God, it was better before, when a working man could come in for a drink without getting that look. Oh, you know what look, Frankie. Like I'm gonna give 'em cooties. They give me that look, pal. I seen that.

What? Oh, damn, yeah, that girl. I seen that, on the news. Reporters sure do love blood, huh? And that story had plenty blood. On the walls, the freakin' white carpet, that huge back window. She crawled around a lot after he sliced her, before she bled out. Ten, fifteen minutes. I don't know, channel five or something. You didn't see that?

But Jeez, Frankie, you'd think she was the first girl got whacked by some psycho she picked up, way they covered it. No, I know they got no idea who it was, but, I mean, it musta been some hook-up, what else? You seen her in here. More money than God, and she's flashing her headlights at tattooed freaks. No, for real, Frankie, that girl was *rich*. Well, look where she lived. What? Oh, yeah, right, she invited me in for a drink. Screw you, Frankie. Bitch probably drank microbrews anyway. Yeah, okay, I tried to get friendly once or twice, when she first come in here. But she gave me that look.

So how do I know what? Where she lived? Jesus, Frankie, she had a floor in the McGill building! See, me, I'm across the alley from there, I'm over on 1st. Eighteen years, all I seen is Spanish girls and sewing machines. One day, bang! The girls are gone, sewing machines in the Dumpster. In six months they got five apartments there. That's what I'm telling you, Frank, whole floors! Made the whole back wall into windows, like the front! That girl, she had the third floor. Right across from me.

Frankie boy, I never knew how big that building was. I could see the river, right through her living room! Well, what do you think? She didn't want people looking, she should've got curtains. You remember the ferry had that fire? I seen that. She watched from her window. I watched too. Watched it with her.

Yeah, I'll have another. Anyhow, that's how I know about her liking the rough stuff. Like one time, get this. After work, I'm having a beer—yeah, a freakin' Bud!—and I seen her walk into her place with some guy. A little smooching, then suddenly I'm watching him rip her clothes, punch her face. He throws her on the rug, she tries to get up, he pushes her down, and I'm on the phone, 911. I mean, damn, you know, Frankie?

Yeah, you'd think so, but listen what happened! I seen the red cop lights, heard the sirens. A minute later the action on the rug stops dead. He rolls off, she grabs her coat, goes to the door. There's two cops, lots of handwaving. They come in, talk to the guy—nah, by then he's got his pants on—and they leave. When they're gone she grabs the guy, and she runs her hands all over him, tries to get started again! Damn, Frankie, she was into it! But he must've lost his, uh, interest. He left. And then, Frankie, then, she walks over, this bitch walks over to the back window, and flips me off! No. No way she knew it was me. I didn't tell 911 what apartment I was, and my lights were off. They musta told her one of her neighbors called it in. She was flipping off the whole building.

And giving us that look.

Well, after that, forget it. She's into handcuffs, guys smacking her around—not my problem, Frankie boy.

Hey! Another Bud, okay?

Some of those tattooed freaks, I got to say, they messed her up pretty bad. But whatever floats your boat, right?

This skinny one, though, he was a change. Mostly she liked 'em built. But he was mean, like she liked. He could knock her around as good as a big guy could. Still, when he picked up that kitchen knife, I was surprised.

What? No, I didn't say that. I said, She musta been surprised. Surprised as hell, Frankie. Finds herself bleeding, crawling around, trying to reach the phone. And lying on the carpet, staring out that big back window, for a long time.

Not that look, though. Not that freakin' look no more.

Hey, another Bud.

No, I don't freakin' think I've had enough! Oh, cut the crap, Frankie! What the hell do you mean, you're out? You got plenty in the cooler.

Just now, when you went to get one of those freakin' microbrews.

I seen that.

About the Contributors

Photo: Roger Carey

C. J. BOX is the author of ten novels including the award-winning Joe Pickett series. His most recent titles, *Blue Heaven, Blood Trail,* and *Three Weeks To Say Goodbye,* were New York Times Best Sellers. His first novel, *Open Season,* was named a New York Times Notable Book. Box is a past winner of the Anthony, Prix Calibre 38 (France), Macavity, Gumshoe, and Barry Awards, an Edgar Award, and was an *L.A. Times* Book Prize finalist. His novels have been translated into 21 languages. *Blue Heaven* was optioned for film and has been nominated for an Edgar Award for Best Novel of 2008.

Box lives with his family outside of Cheyenne, Wyoming. His next Pickett novel, *Below Zero,* will be released in June.

KEN BRUEN was a finalist for the Edgar, Barry, and Macavity Awards, and the Private Eye Writers of America presented him with the Shamus Award for the Best Novel of 2003 for *The Guards,* the book that introduced Jack Taylor. He lives in Galway, Ireland.

Photo: Steve Woit

GARY R. BUSH is the co-editor of Once Upon A Crime Anthology. He writes for the children's, YA, and adult markets. His writing credits include: A children's novel, *Lost In Space, The Flight of Apollo 13* (Stone Arch Books); "If They Harm Us," in *Twin Cities Noir* (Akashic Books); "The Last Reel," in *Flesh &*

Blood: Guilty As Sin (Mysterious Press); "Two Pastrami Sand-wiches" and "The Price of Justice," in *MXB Magazine*; "Down Highway 61," in *Fedora II* (Wildside Press); and "Deep Doo-Doo" in *Small Crimes* (Wildside Press).

Co-editing this anthology was a labor of love. Gary lives in Minneapolis with his wife Stacey and their Kerry Blue Terrier, Homer. He is currently doing research for a young adult novel about Barbary Pirates.

 Brooklyn born and bred, REED FAR-REL COLEMAN is the former Execu-tive Vice President of Mystery Writers of America. He has published ten nov-els in three series including two under his pen name Tony Spinosa. His elev-enth novel, *Tower*, co-authored by noted Irish crime writer Ken Bruen, is sched-uled for release in September 09. Reed is a two time recipient of the Shamus Award and has won the Barry and Anthony Awards as well. He has been twice nominated for the Edgar Award. He was the editor of the short story anthology *Hardboiled Brooklyn*. His short fiction and essays have appeared in *The Darker Mask, Brooklyn Noir 3, Damn Near Dead, Wall Street Noir* and several other publications. Reed is an adjunct lecturer in creative writ-ing at Hofstra University. He lives with his wife and family on Long Island.

BARBARA COLLINS is one of the most respected short story writers in the mystery field, with appearances in more than a dozen top anthologies, including *Murder Most Delicious, Women on the Edge, Deadly Housewives* and the bestselling Cat Crimes series. She was the co-editor of (and a contributor to) the bestselling anthology *Lethal Ladies*, and her stories were selected for inclusion in the first three volumes of *The Year's 25 Finest Crime and Mystery Stories*.

Two acclaimed hardcover collections of her work have been

published—*Too Many Tomcats* and (with her husband) *Murder – His and Hers*. She and her husband, Max, have written the novels *Regeneration* and *Bombshell* together, and their Trash and Treasures mystery series is published under the joint by-line, Barbara Allan, the most recent entry being *Antiques Flee Market*.

MAX ALLAN COLLINS has been hailed as "the Renaissance man of mystery fiction." He has earned an unprecedented fifteen Private Eye Writers of America Shamus nominations for his historical thrillers, winning twice for his Nathan Heller novels, *True Detective* (1983) and *Stolen Away* (1991), and received the Eye, the Private Eye Writers of America's Lifetime Achievement Award. His other credits include film criticism, short fiction, songwriting, trading-card sets, and movie/TV tie-in novels, including *Air Force One*, *In the Line of Fire*, and the New York Times-bestsellers *Saving Private Ryan* and *American Gangster*. His graphic novel *Road to Perdition* is the basis of the Academy Award-winning Tom Hanks film. Max's many comics credits include the "Dick Tracy" syndicated strip (1977–1993); his own "Ms. Tree"; "Batman"; and "CSI: Crime Scene Investigation," based on the hit TV series, for which he has also written video games and an internationally-bestselling series of novels. An acclaimed and award-winning indie filmmaker in his native Muscatine, Iowa, Max recently adapted his Edgar-nominated play *Eliot Ness: An Untouchable Life* into a film.

TROY COOK has worked on more than 80 feature films, writing and directing his first at age 24. Shooting films in exotic locations led to brushes with the Russian Mafia, money launderers, and murderers. After surviving an attempted coup, riots, and violent demonstrations,

he's decided it's safer to write novels.

His award-winning debut, *47 Rules of Highly Effective Bank Robbers*, received eight nominations including the Anthony, Book of the Year, the Macavity, and the Lefty Award. His second novel, *The One Minute Assassin* (Sept 2007), was immediately picked by the Independent Mystery Booksellers Association, as a Killer Book and was featured in *Publishers Weekly* as a Fall Indie Surprise. Visit www.troycook.net for more information.

PAT DENNIS is the author of *Hotdish To Die For*, a collection of six culinary mystery short stories and 18 hotdish recipes. Her fiction and humor has been published in National Public Radio's *Minnesota Monthly*, *Woman's World*, The Minnesota Crime Wave's two anthologies, *Resort to Murder* and *The Silence of the Loons*. She is the Creative Director  of Penury Press, a publisher of fine mysteries and mirth. Penury Press titles include *Who Died In Here? Hotdish Haiku*, and *Stand-Up and Die*.

Pat is also a stand-up comedian, specializing in special events and women's organizations. Her 1,000 performances include comedy clubs, special events, Fortune 500 companies, women's expos and national television. She is ten years older, and twenty pounds heavier, than any photo of her she allows to be printed.

CHRIS EVERHEART is co-editor of the anthology *Once Upon a Crime*, author of action/adventure and thriller books for young readers and stories for adults. He is a contributor to the anthology *Twin Cities Noir* by Akashic Books. His short story "Flicker" will appear in the International Thriller Writers Association's young adult anthology scheduled for publication October, 2010, by Dutton/Penguin. Chris is a native of Minneapolis, Minnesota, where he studied fine art, and has worked in film and advertising. He lives in Tennessee with his wife, Pat.

MAUREEN FISCHER spent fifteen years as an award-winning advertising copywriter. Her journalistic career includes stints with United Press International and magazine reporting. Her articles have appeared in more than a hundred publications—from Inc. to Advertising Age to the Chicago Sun-Times. She now runs her own public relations firm, MaureenInk Communications.

"Pinked Off" is her first foray into short fiction. She recently completed a medical thriller and has embarked on her next book titled, *Adversity*. Maureen lives in Eden Prairie, Minnesota, with her husband and two sons, and periodically redecorates her house without the help of an interior designer. Her living room is pink.

USA Today bestselling author ANNE FRASIER's nineteen novels have spanned the genres of mystery, science fiction, horror, and romance. *Garden of Darkness* (2007), continues a dark tale of a spooky Wisconsin town started in *Pale Immortal* (2006). In *Before I Wake* (2005), a secret government medical experiment goes wrong. *Play Dead* (2004) plays out amid the voodoo scene in Savannah, Georgia. *Sleep Tight*, a traditional police procedural, is set in Minneapolis. Her work has been recognized with the RITA and Daphne du Maurier awards for romantic suspense. Anne is a member of Sisters in Crime, Mystery Writers of America, and Crimespace.

LOIS GREIMAN is the author of more than 25 novels consisting of mystery, children's fiction, paranormal, and romantic comedy. She's the winner of numberous awards and lives on a small farm in Minnesota with her family, some of whom are human.

PETE HAUTMAN has written sixteen novels for adults and teens, as well as many nonfiction books for younger readers. Awards include three Minnesota Book Awards for *Mrs. Million* (2000), *Sweetblood* (2004), and *Godless* (2005). *Godless* also won the 2004 National Book Award for Young People's Literature. His poker-themed crime novels *Drawing Dead* and *The Mortal Nuts* were selected as *New York Times Book Review* Notable Books.

Hautman lives with novelist and poet Mary Logue in Golden Valley, Minnesota, and Stockholm, Wisconsin. They are currently collaborating on The Bloodwater Mysteries, a series for middle grade readers. The first book in that series, *Snatched*, has been nominated for an Edgar Alan Poe Award.

LIBBY FISCHER HELLMANN's 5th suspense novel, *Easy Innocence* (Bleak House Books) is a spin-off of her award-winning Ellie Foreman series. Libby also edited the acclaimed anthology *Chicago Blues*. Originally from Washington DC, She has lived in Chicago for 30 years and finds the contrast between the beautiful and the profane in

that city a crime writer's paradise. Libby is the former President of Sisters in Crime, and Midwest Chapter President of MWA. Her next work, the sequel to *Easy Innocence*, tentatively called *Double Cross*, will be released in October, 2009.

A reformed newspaper reporter and ad man, DAVID HOUSEWRIGHT earned the 1996 Edgar Award for Best First Novel from the Mystery Writers of American as well as a Shamus nomination from the Private Eyes Writers of America for *Penance*. His second novel, *Practice To Deceive*, won a 1998 Minnesota Book Award. *Tin City* was nominated for the same prize in 2006. Other novels include *Dearly Departed*, *A Hard Ticket Home*, *Pretty Girl Gone*, *Dead Boyfriends*, *Madman on a Drum* and *Jelly's Gold*. Housewright has taught writing courses for the University of Minnesota and the Loft Literary Center. He lives in Roseville, MN.

WILLIAM KENT KRUEGER is the author of the best-selling Cork O'Connor mystery series set in the great Northwoods of Minnesota. His work has received a number of awards including four Minnesota Book Awards, the Anthony Award for Best First Novel, and back-to-back Anthony Awards for

Photo: Tony Nelson

Best Novel in 2005 and 2006. Kicked out of Stanford University for fomenting revolution, he logged timber, worked construction, and researched human development before becoming a full-time mystery author. His work has been optioned by Hollywood and translated into more than a dozen languages. He does all his creative writing in a coffee shop in St. Paul, Minnesota.

LORI L. LAKE is the creator of the "Gun" series, which is a trilogy consisting of romance/police procedurals *Gun Shy* and *Under The Gun* and the adventure/thriller *Have Gun We'll Travel*. Lori has published three other novels, two books

of short stories, and edited two story anthologies. She teaches fiction writing courses independently in Sacramento and at The Loft Literary Center in Minneapolis. Lori is currently shopping around a mainstream mystery series set in the Twin Cities. For more information, see her website at *www.lorillake.com.*

Award-winning poet and mystery writer MARY LOGUE was born and raised in Minnesota. Her most recent books are *Snatched*, a middle-grade mystery she wrote with Pete Hautman (which was nominated for an Edgar Award); *Poison Heart*, her seventh crime novel; and *Meticulous Attachment*,

her third book of poems. *Meticulous Attachment* was awarded honorable mention by the Midwest Booksellers Association in 2006 and *Dark Coulee* won a Minnesota Book Award in 2000. She has also published a young adult novel, *Dancing with an Alien*, with HarperCollins. Her non-fiction books include a biography of her grandmother, *Halfway Home*, and a book on Minnesota courthouses, both published by the Minnesota Historical Society Press. She has been an editor at *The Village Voice*, Simon & Schuster, Graywolf Press, Mid-List Press, and The Creative Company. She has taught for many years at the Loft Literary Center in Minneapolis and at Hamline University in St. Paul. She lives with writer Pete Hautman in Minnesota and Wisconsin.

SUJATA MASSEY is author of the ten-book Rei Shimura mystery series, which includes *The Salaryman's Wife*, an Agatha Award winner for best first mystery, and *The Flower Master*, which won the Macavity Award for Best Traditional Mystery. She is a graduate of the Johns Hopkins University in Baltimore, MD, and spent many years working as a reporter at the

Baltimore Evening Sun. She currently lives in Minneapolis with her family, and is at work on a historical suspense novel set in India.

TERRI PERSONS was a newspaper reporter for the *St. Paul Pioneer Press* for twenty-five years before leaving journalism to write fiction. Her most recent book, a murder mystery called *Blind Spot*, was published by Doubleday in 2007. She lives in Minnesota with her husband and two sons.

Photo: David Persons

Photo: Sergio Carrera

GARY PHILLIPS has written stories about rugged people doing rugged things in several mediums. He practices the fine arts of the grift, the grab and the dust-off in various mediums. His current work includes short stories "The Kim Novak Effect" in *Las Vegas Noir*, "Swift Boats for Jesus" in *Politics Noir* (an anthology he also edited) and "What Shall We Call You?" in the *Darker Mask* (a collection he co-edited with Chris Chambers). *Los Angeles Noir*, which includes one of his stories, recently won the Southern California Independent Booksellers Association award for best mystery. Two of his graphic novels, *Cowboys* and *South Central Rhapsody*, will be published soon. He's got a crime graphic novel coming out from Vertigo/DC Comics, and produces *Citizen Kang*, an online, serialized political novella at *www.thenation.com*.

S.J. ROZAN, the author of ten crime novels, is a life-long New Yorker. Her novels and short stories have won the Edgar, Shamus, Anthony, Nero, and Macavity awards. SJ is a former Mystery Writers of America National Board

Photo: Steven Blier

member, a current Sisters in Crime National Board member, and ex-President of the Private Eye Writers of America. She's at work on a new Lydia Chin/Bill Smith novel, *The Shanghai Moon*.

ANTHONY NEIL SMITH is the author of *Hogdoggin'*, *Yellow Medicine*, *The Drummer*, and *Psychosomatic*. Originally from the Mississippi Gulf Coast, he is now the Director of the Creative Writing Program at Southwest Minnesota State University. When he's  not cursing the icy wind, he edits the noir ezine *Plots with Guns* (www.plotswithguns.com). You can visit his "Virtual Dive Bar" at anthonyneilsmith.typepad.com.

 MICHAEL STANLEY is the writing team of Michael Sears and Stanley Trollip. Both were born in South Africa and are retired professors who have worked in academia and business. Michael is a mathematician, specializing in geological remote sensing. He lives in Johannesburg. Stan is an educational psychologist, specializing in the application of computers to teaching and learning, and a pilot. He splits his time between Minneapolis and Knysna, a small town on the South African coast.

They have been on a number of flying safaris to Botswana and Zimbabwe, and it was on one of these trips that the idea surfaced for their first novel, *A Carrion Death*, which was published by HarperCollins in 2008. Their second novel, *The Second Death of Goodluck Tinubu*, came out in June, 2009.

MARILYN VICTOR, a native Minnesotan, shares her home with a senior Bichon Frise and a revolving menagerie of homeless pets she fosters for a local animal rescue organization. An animal lover since she could walk, writing a mystery novel set at a big city zoo was a natural. Co-authored with friend Michael Allen Mallory, *Death Roll* features the first  zookeeper sleuth, Snake Jones. Marilyn is currently president of the Minneapolis/St. Paul chapter of Sisters in Crime. In her spare time she beads jewelry and is not sure which will overrun the house first: the pets or the bead collection.

Photo: Patti Neil